The BLACK Stallion's

Blood Bay Colt

Jimmy Creech was old and tired. After fifty years of harness racing at county fairs, he was being crowded out by the newcomers who had made the sport a business at the large, modern racetracks.

His only hope lay in the blood bay colt, second son of the Black Stallion, and his young driver, Tom Messenger. Only they could put Jimmy Creech on top again, with the fastest two-year-old in America.

Here is another exciting racing story by Walter Farley, author of the popular *Black Stallion* series.

Books by
WALTER FARLEY

The Black Stallion
The Black Stallion Returns
Son of the Black Stallion
The Island Stallion
The Black Stallion and Satan
The Black Stallion's Blood Bay Colt
The Island Stallion's Fury
The Black Stallion's Filly
The Black Stallion Revolts
The Black Stallion's Sulky Colt
The Island Stallion Races
The Black Stallion's Courage
The Black Stallion Mystery
The Black Stallion and Flame
The Black Stallion Challenged!
The Black Stallion's Ghost
The Black Stallion and the Girl
The Horse-Tamer
Man o' War

*All titles available in both paperback
and hardcover editions*

The Black Stallion's

Blood Bay Colt

formerly titled *The Blood Bay Colt*

by WALTER FARLEY

RANDOM HOUSE 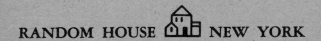 NEW YORK

Formerly titled *The Blood Bay Colt*

Library of Congress Cataloging in Publication Data

Farley, Walter
The black stallion's blood bay colt
New York, Random House [1950]
1. Title   PZ10.3.F22Bn   50-9584 [67x3]
ISBN: 0-394-80606-9 (trade hardcover)
       0-394-90606-3 (library binding)
       0-394-83915-3 (trade paperback)

For Frank Lutz, Dave Ford and George Milhimes,
who remembered the way it was

Contents

The Black Stallion's

Stallion's

Blood Bay Colt

The Queen

1

Although the early June morning was unusually cool and the sky overcast, the boy's body perspired freely beneath his thin sweater. For this morning, as on every Saturday morning, he had walked the five miles from his home to the training track just outside the town limits of Coronet, Pennsylvania. And now he stood beneath a tall elm tree, his eyes upon the drab gray sheds before him. Grim-faced, he walked toward them, his gaze never leaving the sheds—not even for the horses, who trotted about the half-mile track to his left. He heard neither the rhythmic beat of hoofs over hard-packed clay nor the clucking of the drivers to their colts as they sat in their two-wheeled training carts. And this was very unusual for Tom Messenger.

He walked down the road until he came to the last shed in the row, and there he hesitated, his long, thin face grave with concern, his arms hanging loosely beside his big-boned but gaunt frame. It was many moments before he moved to the closed door of the shed, his steps noticeably shorter and slower.

Looking through the window, he saw the two old men working over Symbol. Jimmy Creech stood before the horse's big black head. As always, Jimmy's muffler was wrapped snugly about his scrawny neck, and his cap was pulled far down over his ears. The tip of Jimmy's prominent nose held the only color in his pale face. George Snedecker stooped to the other side of the horse, his hands feeling about Symbol's hoofs.

Slowly the boy slid the door open, and he heard George Snedecker say, "Pains in my legs again this morning, Jimmy. Makes a man wish he were dead, that's what it does."

"We ain't so young any more," Jimmy Creech grumbled; then he saw the boy standing in the doorway. He nodded to him but said nothing, and turned back to Symbol.

With great effort George rose to a standing position. "'Morning, Tom," he said. The chaw of tobacco in his mouth was passed from one side to the other as his gaze shifted uneasily between the boy and Jimmy Creech; then he took a cloth from the pocket of his overalls and brushed it over Symbol's neck. He said with attempted lightness, "No need to work over Symbol, heh, Jimmy? He'll stir up enough wind to wipe him clean."

Jimmy Creech looked sullenly into George's grinning, tobacco-stained mouth. "Sure," he said. "Let's get the stuff on him now."

The boy stood there while they slid the light racing harness on Symbol and tightened the leather about the shafts of the training cart. Jimmy Creech had taken hold of the long reins when the boy said, "You're really going to sell *her*, Jimmy? You haven't changed your mind since last Saturday?" His voice was low and heavy with concern.

Jimmy Creech turned to George, motioning him to open

the shed doors. "I'm selling her," he said quickly, without looking at the boy. "This morning . . . the guy's coming this morning, just as I told you last Saturday."

"But Jimmy—" The boy was close beside Jimmy Creech now, his hands on the man's arm, his words coming fast. "Her colt may be everything you ever hoped to own. You figured it that way. You said—"

Jimmy Creech had slid into the cart seat. "I know what I said, what I figured," he interrupted, turning away. "You don't have to tell me, Tom."

"Then why do you want to sell the Queen at this late stage of the game?" the boy asked with sudden anger. "She'll have her foal in another three weeks. Why don't you do as we planned?"

Jimmy Creech drew his muffler tighter about his neck, and his eyes were upon Symbol's black haunches as he said bitterly, "I figured out one night that it was a pretty late stage in the game for me, too. I figured up how old I was and I got sixty-two. I figured that it's no time for me to be looking ahead a couple of years, and I'd have to wait that long before I could race this colt of the Queen's. So I figured two years is much too long for me to wait. That's the score, Tom. I'm sorry."

"But, Jimmy. You're being silly. You're not old. You're—"

But Jimmy Creech was taking Symbol from the shed.

The boy watched Jimmy until he had driven Symbol around the corner of the shed; then he turned to George, now seated heavily in his chair beside the door. "What's gotten into Jimmy?" the boy asked. "Why's he talking like that?"

"He ain't been feeling good again," George said. "And

sixty-two's not so young any more; like Jimmy says. Age is like that, Tom. For years you go along thinking you're a young bunny, then one morning you wake up and it's hit you right smack in every bone and muscle in your body. Like it did with me some years ago. And like it's doing to Jimmy now. And when that happens you find you don't start figuring too far ahead any longer." George leaned back in his chair. "Yep, I know what Jimmy means when he says he don't want to wait two years for the Queen's colt to come along."

Shaking his head, the boy said, "But all winter long Jimmy felt good. I know he did. He'd talk about this foal of the Queen's for hours at a time, telling me the colt was going to be the one he'd always wanted. You heard him, George. And you know our plans. He was going to send the Queen up to my uncle's farm, where she was going to have her foal. And I was going to take care of them both this summer while you and Jimmy were at the fair tracks racing Symbol. It was just the setup he wanted for them. Uncle Wilmer has plenty of pasture, everything the Queen and her foal could want during the summer. I don't understand why—"

"You got to be older to understand, Tom," George said slowly. "And Jimmy started changing last summer at the races. He started feeling old then, but he never admitted it. But I saw he was more careful in his driving, never taking any chances of a spill. And before that they never came any nervier, any better than Jimmy Creech. He became very critical of the driving of other men, too. And he got crabby and, I thought, a little bitter. It was old age creeping up, but Jimmy didn't know it. He's stuck to harness racing for near forty years because he loves the sport and the horses. And that's what made him great. But it's different with him now. It's like he's sore because he's suddenly discovered he's getting old and he wants to take it out on everybody."

George paused and took off his soiled cap, exposing his bald head to the rays of the sun that had broken through the overcast sky. "When you came along this last winter," he went on, "and Jimmy took such a liking to you, I thought maybe he was coming out of it. He liked the interest you took in the horses, although you didn't know a trot from a pace at the time. But you asked a lot of questions, and Jimmy liked that. He enjoyed talking to you and you were a good listener. Maybe he saw himself as a kid in you. I don't know. But he lived in Coronet, too, when he was about your age, an' he used to come out here on Saturdays, just hanging around, same as you do."

George stopped again, chewing his tobacco thoughtfully. "I heard Jimmy talk about sending the Queen to your uncle's farm when you told him you were going to be there for the summer. I knew then how much Jimmy liked you or he wouldn't be trusting you with the Queen like that. An' I liked the way you had perked Jimmy up and I thought everything was going to be all right again. But week before last Jimmy had a couple of bad nights. I guess he must have been really sick, because he showed up here looking pretty awful. I guess I knew then that this was the beginning of the end for Jimmy Creech, professional reinsman.

"A few days later this guy from Hanover Farms comes around looking for broodmares and he sees the Queen. And he asks Jimmy how about selling her. He'd asked Jimmy that same question for the last three years, but Jimmy never even listened to him. But this time it was different. I hear Jimmy say quick-like, 'Sure, if you give me my price.' And that wasn't like Jimmy. Not in the 'most fifty years I've known him has he ever put a price on any horse he loves—and he sure loves the Queen. He lost mighty few races with the Queen."

"If he really loved her he wouldn't sell her," the boy said bitterly. "Why's he doing it, George?"

"He's asked a good stiff price, Tom. And with the money he can buy another horse to race this summer—maybe even two or three more."

"He's got Symbol to race," the boy said quickly.

"Symbol is too old jus' like Jimmy and me," George muttered. "He oughtn't to be racing any more. Jimmy picked him up at the sales a couple of years ago. He was the only horse Jimmy could afford to buy. Jimmy doesn't have much money any more. He's just hanging on . . . that's all Jimmy's doin'." The old man paused to spit tobacco juice in the pail which he used as a spittoon. "So I guess Jimmy wants enough money to buy a good racehorse now. It's like he wasn't figuring on having many more years and he wants to do this one up big."

"I still don't understand," the boy said.

"I do," George returned slowly. "I guess I understand pretty well how Jimmy Creech feels."

The boy shifted uneasily upon his feet, his eyes leaving George for the semi-darkness of the shed's interior. Finally he walked inside, coming to a stop directly beneath the bared light bulb just within the door. He twisted the bulb almost savagely, extinguishing the light; then, turning, he slid the shed doors wide open, allowing the sun to penetrate the gloom. "It's like a morgue in here," he shouted angrily to George Snedecker. "It's almost summer. Remember?"

"Sure," George mumbled. "It's almost summer."

The boy walked into the tack room, his eyes gleaming, his steps hurried. He took a quick look at the worn harness, then went to the two windows, opening them wide. Leaving the room, he hurried down the shed, passing the empty box stalls. When he came to the door at the opposite end he pushed heavily against it until, creaking, it too slid open, and the morning light flooded the shed.

For a moment the boy stood in the doorway, staring at the track before him. Two trotters swept by, the wheels of their training carts gleaming in the sun. Then Jimmy Creech went by with Symbol, and tears welled in the boy's eyes at the sight of Jimmy's thin huddled figure in the seat. "Why don't you take off that muffler and that silly cap, Jimmy?" he muttered angrily. "Why don't you look up at the sun? Let it get at you, Jimmy. That's what you need."

Then abruptly, Tom turned and walked toward a box stall on his left. Opening the door, he went inside, and his eyes and voice were soft as he said, "Hello, Beautiful."

The heavy-bellied bay mare came to him, shoving her soft muzzle against his chest. And as his hand followed the white blaze that ran from her forehead to her nostrils, she sought the pockets of his sweater for what she knew would be there. He let her pull the carrot from his pocket, then took it from her again, breaking it into small pieces and feeding them to her one at a time. "And chew them well, Queen," he said. "You have to be careful about everything you eat and everything you do now. It won't be so very long before your foal comes."

Then the boy stopped talking and looked at the docile head before him. He raised his hand to touch her again, hesitated, then threw his arms about her neck, burying his head in her long black mane.

When Jimmy Creech brought Symbol back from his workout, he found Tom in the Queen's stall. For several minutes he stared at Tom's turned back without the boy's knowing it, then moved on.

George Snedecker had the cooling blanket on Symbol and was walking him alongside the shed when Jimmy joined him.

"Tom's taking it pretty hard," Jimmy said quietly.

George nodded but continued walking Symbol.

Jimmy fell in beside him. "I never should have let him hang around so much," Jimmy said. "That's what I get for taking an interest in the kid."

George looked at him but still said nothing.

"Have you seen that guy from Hanover Farms yet?" Jimmy asked. "He said he'd be around at eight o'clock."

"I saw his car up the row. He might be in one of the other sheds." George paused. "Why don't you go up and see? Let's sell the mare if we're going to," he added sullenly.

Jimmy looked at him. "What's ailing you?"

George Snedecker made no reply.

"Has the kid got to you, too?" Jimmy asked bitterly. "I suppose you think I'm a heel too. Whose mare is she, anyway? And who has to foot the bills around here?"

"Your mare. You foot the bills," George said brusquely.

They walked for a while before Jimmy spoke again. "That's what I get for playing nursemaid to a kid. I should have sent him on his way when he first came around."

"But you didn't," George said quietly, turning Symbol around. "You let him stay and you talked horse to him by the hour. You wanted it that way. For some reason you wanted it that way."

Jimmy Creech said nothing, but George heard his footsteps and knew he was following him.

"Find that guy from Butler and sell the mare," George said again. "They don't get a chance every day to buy a broodmare like the Queen. An' like you said, she's yours. I don't care what you do with her. I only work for you. And what do you care how the kid feels? He's nothing but one of the hundreds running around towns like Coronet. He'll forget all about the Queen in a week. Maybe he'll forget all about horses, too—forget everything you ever told him. He's nothing but a skinny, overgrown high-school kid who ought to be running around with fellows his own age anyway, instead of hanging out with us old fogies."

The footsteps behind him had stopped, but Jimmy's tense voice came easily to George. "He'll never forget the Queen—or horses. It's in him deep, just as it was in me."

The footsteps came again, but this time they were retreating and George knew that Jimmy Creech had gone to find the buyer from Hanover Farms.

George was still walking Symbol when he saw Jimmy Creech returning. Jimmy's head was burrowed deep in his brown muffler, but his skinny legs moved quickly over the road. George stopped walking Symbol.

"Shall I get the mare out?" George asked when Jimmy was within hearing distance. "Does he want to take her now?"

Jimmy raised his thin face, and the only thing about him

that seemed alive were his hazel eyes flecked with tiny pin-points of brown. "No," he said. "He didn't buy her." His gaze dropped as he added. "He wouldn't give me my price."

"Uh-huh," George said.

Jimmy looked up at him. "He tried to talk me down, but I wouldn't have any of it."

"Sure," George returned, smiling. "Sure, Jimmy."

Their gazes met and held.

"That's the story," Jimmy said.

"That's *your* story," George replied. He motioned with his head in the direction of the shed. "Go in and tell Tom. He'll be anxious to hear it."

Jimmy moved away. "Yes, I'd better," he said, "because he'll be taking care of the Queen this summer—"

"And the foal," George interrupted, laughing. "Don't forget to tell him what to do when the foal comes."

George watched Jimmy until he had disappeared inside the shed; then he turned to the sun, shining brightly now in a cloudless sky. "Summer," he said. "Good old summer. What it can do to a man! The sun and the kid. What a com-bination! Maybe it's not the end of Jimmy Creech, profes-sional reinsman, after all. Maybe not by a long shot." And humming, George continued walking Symbol.

The Foal to Come

2

Ten days later Tom Messenger stood anxiously at a fork in the road, awaiting the Queen. He had been there for many hours, watching the heavy traffic come over the hill, most of it speeding by to his left on its way to Philadelphia. To his right was the blacktop road which led through rolling fields beyond to the sanctuary of his uncle's farm, where the Queen would have quiet and peace to bring her foal into the world.

Very often Tom would glance at the clock on the gas station behind him. It was well after three o'clock. If Jimmy had shipped the Queen at dawn, as he had planned to do, the truck should have arrived an hour ago. It would be an open truck, a two-and-a-half ton truck, Jimmy had said. He couldn't miss it, for the Queen would be standing right there for him to see. She would have been on the road nine hours by now. Would it have hurt her any? In her condition, he meant. The Queen was due to foal sometime next week. Jimmy had said the trip wouldn't hurt her. He'd said he had shipped many mares only a few days before they foaled, and it had never bothered them. Tom hoped Jimmy was right. He hoped desperately that Jimmy was right. He didn't want anything to happen to the Queen—or the Queen's foal to come.

The boy's eyes remained on the traffic coming over the hill. He wouldn't look at the clock again, he decided. It didn't make any difference how late the Queen got here, just so long as she got here. That it was late was so much the better. It meant that Jimmy had hired a good driver, one who was going slowly, taking it easy for the Queen's sake. *So there's no rush,* Tom thought. *I've got all the time in the world. Just take it easy with the Queen, Mr. Driver, and I'll be here whenever you come.*

While Tom waited patiently, he let himself think of what it would mean to care for the Queen all by himself. There would be just the Queen and himself this week, but maybe next week there would be three. He'd always dreamed of something like this happening to him. And Jimmy Creech had made it possible.

"I know the Queen will be in good hands, Tom," Jimmy had said. "I know how much you love her, and that's more important than anything else at this point. Just take good care of her, as I know you will, and nature will do the rest."

Jimmy had made it sound so easy. But then Jimmy had seen a countless number of foals born, while this would be Tom's first experience. As he thought about it, Tom felt a little queasy. What if something went wrong? Jimmy had said it wouldn't be necessary to get a veterinary unless complications set in. Nine chances out of ten everything would be all right, Jimmy had said. But then, Tom figured, there was one chance in ten something *would* go wrong, and it was this lone possibility that caused the palms of his hands to sweat while he waited for the Queen.

He saw the open truck as it came over the hill. He made out the Queen's blanketed body as the truck drew closer. Her haunches faced the front of the truck. Jimmy had put her in backwards to keep the wind from her face.

Tom moved quickly to the middle of the fork, one arm raised, his heart pounding. The truck pulled out of the long line of cars and headed for the blacktop road, slowing as it neared him.

Tom's eyes were upon the Queen. He saw that her hooded head was down low, her body slumped. "Is she all right?" he asked anxiously of the driver.

"A long haul, but I took it easy," the man said. "Where do we go from here? I've got to get back tonight," he added impatiently.

"Just a few more miles," the boy said. "Follow this road. I'll ride in back."

Quickly Tom climbed over the rail of the truck. It lurched forward and Tom steadied the mare. She raised her hooded head, recognizing him; then her nose went to his pocket. Smiling, he produced a carrot and fed it to her.

"Soon you'll be home," he said. "Just a little farther and then you'll be able to take it nice and easy."

The road wound with the foothills, going ever upward in the direction of a low range of heavily wooded mountains. Tom looked toward them, for in the valley at their base was his uncle's farm and a home for the Queen.

The driver called back to him through the cab window, handing him a long envelope. Tom held the letter in front of him, shielding it from the wind. It was, of course, from Jimmy Creech.

R.D.2
Coronet, Pa.
June 17

Dear Tom,

I've shipped the Queen the best I know how, and she should arrive okay. Feed her light on grain this week, about three quarts in three feedings. Add a little bran each time. Let her have all the grass she wants; it's the best thing for her now. And don't forget to exercise her daily, working her on the longe same as we did here. It'll make it easier when her time comes to have the foal. This week I'd leave her in the pasture every night the weather is good; but next week you'd better bring her in nights. And you'd better watch her closely then. As I said, there won't be much to do when her time comes, but it's better to keep a close watch over her.

George and I are starting off the season at the Carlisle Fair next week, but you can reach us by writing to me c/o the race secretary at the track. Write as soon as the Queen's had her foal. I'm hoping it's a colt, but George says he's hoping for a filly (he always was partial to girls!). Either way it should be a good one. And Tom, I've got full confidence in you. Use your own judgment if anything comes up. You've got a good head and, most important, the right feeling for horses, and that always pays off in the end.

There are just a few routine things I want to tell you to do when the foal comes. Be sure to wipe him dry if the mare doesn't take care of that. Pay special attention to his nostrils, wiping them clean so he can breathe good. It'll be important to a little fellow like him. And next thing you do is see to it that the foal nurses as soon as possible. The mare's milk right after she's given birth is the most beneficial of all, and it's important he should get it right away. You help him, if he needs any help. After that you can pretty well relax. Feed the mare light the first two days, giving her a hot bran mash right after she's foaled. That's four quarts of bran and a handful of salt; pour enough boiling water over it to wet it good, then put a sack over the pail and let it steam until it's cool enough for the mare to eat.

Handle the little fellow from the moment he's born. That way he'll just accept your being around, and it'll make things easier for me later, when I go to break and train him.

I guess that's about all for now. As soon as I hear from you that the foal has been born, I'll write more on what you should do. The money I gave you should be enough to buy all the grain you'll need in addition to paying your uncle whatever he may want for keeping the mare there, but if anything comes up and you need more, let me know.

Your friend,
Jimmy Creech

P.S. It might be best to have a vet lined up just in case anything goes wrong. As I said, use your own judgment in anything like that.

The boy reread the letter several times before folding it and putting it away. There were an awful lot of things to remember, he thought. And they came so easily to Jimmy Creech.

Tom turned to the Queen. "But I'm going to watch you every minute, and I'm going to have a veterinary there when your foal comes. I'm not going to take any chance trying to get a veterinary *after* complications set in. Jimmy says to use my own judgment, and that's just what I'm going to do."

The truck had reached the valley, and Tom directed the driver up a side road. They had gone only a short distance when Tom told the man to stop before a dirt lane entering the woods on the left.

"I'll lead her up from here," the boy said. "It's a bad road and bumpy. It wouldn't do her any good to ride it."

"Just as you say," the driver returned. "Guess this is as good a spot as any we'll find." Putting the truck in reverse, he backed up to the low embankment on the side of the road.

The Queen's ears pitched forward as the back gate of the truck was let down.

"Steady, girl," Tom said, holding her by the halter.

The driver walked up the backdrop. "Steeper than I thought it would be," he said. "You'd better take her down. I got her here. She's your responsibility from now on. If she breaks a leg, I want no part of it."

Tom looked at him. "Yes," he said slowly. "She's my responsibility now, all right." Then he turned to the job ahead of him.

The Queen hesitated as Tom led her to the backdrop. Patiently Tom waited, talking to her all the time. It wasn't too steep or he wouldn't be taking her down. The Queen could get down all right. He brought her forward until her forefeet were on the board; then he stopped again, talking to her. His grip tightened about the halter, steadying her. "Now, Queen," he said softly.

The mare followed him down, her haunches tucked beneath her. But as she neared the end of the backdrop she let herself go and jumped down to the embankment. Seeking the grass, she thrust her head down, pulling away from Tom. He let her alone, knowing she was all right now. But he took the lead rope from his pocket and snapped the clip to the mare's halter.

"I'll be getting along now," the driver said.

"How about the blanket and the hood?" Tom asked.

"Jimmy said to keep them here with you. I'll be coming back for her in September. We can use them on the return trip." The driver walked to the cab of the truck. "So long," he said.

"So long."

Tom allowed the Queen to graze until long after the truck had disappeared down the road. Finally, taking her by the halter, he said, "Let's go, girl."

She walked quickly beside him as he led her up the lane, and Tom carefully avoided the sharp rocks for he knew the mare was shoeless. And when his eyes left the road ahead, they would turn always to the Queen. He was alone with her now. She was his responsibility, just as the driver had said. Jimmy Creech wasn't around; neither was George. It frightened him a little, having all this responsibility. Yet it was what he had wanted. He had wanted to take care of the Queen all by himself. He had wanted to help bring her foal into the world. And even though he was a little frightened just now, things would work out all right. He felt sure they would. Jimmy said he had good judgment, and Jimmy should know.

The Queen shied nervously around a branch lying in the lane. Tom held her, talking all the while. She was easy to handle. They didn't come any gentler than the Queen. Here he was, walking beside the Queen. All anyone had to do was to look in any book on harness racing and he'd find the Queen's name there. "Volo Queen," that's the way the record books had it; "a dark bay mare by Victor Volo established new track record for two-year-old fillies at the Reading Fair track.

The Queen hadn't held the record very long before it was broken by a score of others. Jimmy said the Queen had showed potential greatness that day at Reading, and he had expected her to get better and better. But she hadn't. The Queen had never become the great racer Jimmy had thought she would. Close to it, but not quite.

Tom turned to the mare. "Maybe," he said softly, "you left that for your colt. Maybe you decided that if only one of you were to be great, you wanted him to be the one."

And he really could be great, Tom thought, he really could. For there just wasn't any mare with better bloodlines than the Queen. She had been bred to the Black, the fastest horse in the world. Yes, he knew the Black was a runner while this colt to come would race at a trot. But Jimmy Creech had said that this wasn't important, for the Black's pedigree showed a preponderance of Arabian blood and such blood was the source of all racing stock in the world today, trotters as well as runners. Jimmy believed that it was necessary to breed back to the Arabian horse whenever possible in order to renew and strengthen the strain. And he had done just this with the Queen. Jimmy's eyes had become two glowing balls of fire as he discussed the potentialities with Tom.

"I gave this mating of the Queen to the Black a lot of thought, Tom. I figured that in the Queen I had 'most everything that any breeder would want to have in a broodmare. She has a gentle disposition and is easy to handle, as

you know. She never gets upset about a thing, either on the
track or in her stall. Her action is smooth and beautiful to
watch. She has the speed . . ." and then Jimmy Creech had
hesitated, "even though all of it never did come out of her.
If the Queen lacks one thing, Tom, it's gameness and the
drive and will to win. She never extended herself and that's
why she never became a champion." Jimmy Creech had
paused before going on. "And that's why I bred her to the
Black. I've never seen any horse—runner, trotter or pacer—
with the fire and the intense desire to win that he has. I'm
hoping he'll pass that on to the Queen's foal. If he does,
we'll have a colt which'll be hard to beat."

A short distance farther on, the woods gave way to cleared
fields. To the right lay a long, rambling chicken house in
front of which there was a brook that crossed the lane and
went winding far into the rolling pasture land.

The boy stopped when they reached the brook. "Look,
Queen," he said, "your new home." Directly ahead of them,
and built on the gradual slope of a hill, was a stone barn
with its red roof gleaming in the sun. Before it was a fenced
barnyard and below a spacious green lawn leading to a stone
house.

The short, stocky figure of an elderly man appeared at one
of the stall doors of the barn. Closing the door behind him,
he walked across the paddock, his left arm thrust behind him
as he bent over slightly.

Tom Messenger waved to him. He knew it was useless to
call to Uncle Wilmer, for one had to be very close and almost shouting before his uncle could hear anything. He was
almost stone deaf.

His uncle waited while Tom led the mare into the paddock. Tom saw Uncle Wilmer's narrow lids open slightly,

disclosing more of his keen gray eyes.

"Wait'll I get her blanket off," the boy shouted proudly. "Just wait until you see her."

The man nodded but said nothing. He held the Queen while Tom removed the hood and blanket.

Finally the boy stepped back, his eyes shining. "How do you like her, Uncle Wilmer?"

But his uncle only said brusquely, "Give her some water, Tom. Give her some water. She's thirsty."

The light left the boy's eyes as he led the Queen to the trough. "I was going to give her water," he said, knowing his uncle couldn't hear him. "I only thought you might like to take a look at her."

When the Queen had finished drinking, she turned to the grass. Tom unsnapped the lead rope and closed the paddock gate.

His uncle stood quietly beside the mare as she grazed, his battered hat sitting ridiculously high on the top of his egg-shaped head. Finally he said, "She's purty big for a fast one. The best ones are smaller. Like the ones Harvey Moorheart's got over at Amityville."

The boy's face flushed. "She's only fifteen hands," he shouted angrily. "That's not big."

"She looks more like a workhorse. I'll bet she'd be good in front of a plow, all right." The flickering specks of light in his eyes went unnoticed by the boy.

Tom started to say something but stopped.

"You oughta go over and see Harvey Moorheart's horses," his uncle was saying. "He's got one, a sorrel gelding, that raced once't at the Allentown Fair. Did purty well, Harvey says."

"The Queen's got a record of two-o-seven for the mile. There are no horses like her around here," Tom said proudly.

"What's that?" his uncle asked, cupping an ear.

"Nothing, Uncle Wilmer. Nothing."

Tom heard his aunt Emma calling, and he turned to look at her as she stood in the doorway of the small house. She was tall and thin, and her gray hair was parted in the center and drawn back to a knot in the back.

"Tom!" she called. "Tell your uncle to bring some wood for the stove. I've been shouting to him for the past fifteen minutes. And come to supper yourself. Everything is ready."

"But Aunt Emma, the Queen's here!" Tom shouted. "Come and look at her." But his aunt had disappeared within the house.

I guess I can't expect them to understand, he thought. *Living on a farm, as they do, they've always taken animals for granted. Neither of them can get excited about having a horse around. Even one like the Queen. They'd never understand if I tried to tell them how valuable she is—or how I feel about her.*

"She's not going to foal for more'n a month," his uncle said.

"She's going to have it sometime next week or soon after," Tom said as loudly as he could.

His uncle walked around the mare. "I had mares around here for fifty years up until last summer," he said. "I know when a mare is goin' to foal, all right."

The boy bit his lower lip. "She's going to have it—" He stopped, then shouted, "We've got to get some wood. Supper is ready."

His uncle heard him, for he followed Tom to the wood-shed. They picked up some wood and went across the recently cut lawn to the house. Entering the large kitchen, they placed the wood in the bin beside the stove. Aunt Emma was setting the table when Tom walked up to her.

"Aunt Emma," he inquired anxiously, "is there a veterinary in town? A good one, I mean."

Her blue eyes looked as cold as the steel about the rim of her glasses as she said, "A veterinary, Tom? What do you want with a veterinary?"

The boy shifted uneasily upon his feet. "I want him for the Queen."

"She sick?"

"No, but her foal comes next week."

"Glory, Tom! You don't need a veterinary. Why, we never had a veterinary for any of the animals when their young 'uns were born. We'd 'a' been in the poorhouse long before this if we had. Save your money, Tom. There's no need for you to be callin' a veterinary unless something goes wrong."

Tom's gaze was steady. "That's just it, Aunt Emma. I don't want to wait until something goes wrong. I want to make sure everything goes right."

"There's nothing to having a foal, Tom." His aunt went over to the stove. "Now you go wash up. I'm putting the food on the table this minute." She turned around, looking for her husband, and not finding him went to the door. "Wilmer!" she shouted. "WILMER! Tom, please go find that man for me." Her eyes were on the boy again. "And stop worrying about your mare, Tom. You'd think she was the first mare in the world to have a foal. There's nothing to it, I tell you, nothing."

Tom left the kitchen. "And nothing's going to stop me from getting a veterinary," he mumbled. "Nothing. I've got to be sure everything goes right for the Queen's sake."

Troubled Days

3

Early Monday afternoon of the following week Tom Messenger stood quietly in the veterinarian's office and listened to Doctor Pendergast explain why it was impossible for him to be at the Queen's side when she gave birth to her foal.

The doctor's low-pitched voice droned on while Tom held his gaze, hoping for some hesitancy that would mean a chance the doctor might change his mind. He saw the sympathy and the kindness in the man's earnest eyes, but what he was saying was the same as what the two other veterinarians in town had said.

"Mares, more so than any other of our domestic animals, are very irregular in the length of time they carry their young. The average time for a mare is around eleven months, but I've known some to go as long as twelve months before having their foals. You understand, then, why it would be impossible for me to stand by, waiting." The doctor smiled kindly before continuing. "But of course you should keep your mare under close observation all the time, as I'm certain you're doing."

"I know she'll have it this week," Tom said, his words coming hard.

The doctor smiled again. "Perhaps you're right. Perhaps she will have her foal this week," he said softly. "But it's just as impossible for me to stay close beside your mare for a week as it would be to stay there a month." He patted Tom on the shoulder. "There's really not much to worry about, young man. Why, I've known mares to have their foals while at work in the field. And I've known some of them to go back to work immediately afterward!"

"But this isn't a workhorse," Tom said, a little angry. "She's a very valuable horse, Doctor. I can't take a chance on something going wrong."

The veterinarian walked back to his desk. "I'm sorry," he said, handing his card to Tom, "but the best I can do is to come as soon as possible after the birth, if you need me. And the chances are that you won't."

"If I paid you for the whole week would you come now?" Tom asked hesitantly.

Picking up some papers from his desk, the doctor replied brusquely. "It's not the money. It wouldn't be fair to all the farmers who really need me. If you want me after the foal is born, call and I'll get there as soon as I can. If I happen to be out, just leave the message with my wife."

The veterinarian had picked up his telephone, and Tom knew that this was the end of their conversation. He was walking toward the door when the doctor called to him, his voice soft once more. "See that your mare gets enough exercise, and keep your eye on her at night. They usually have them at night, at the most unreasonable hours. And if you're so sure it'll be this week—"

"I'm sure," Tom said. "Quite sure."

He had the door open when the veterinarian called again. "Leave everything to nature. And don't worry. Don't worry at all."

It was three miles from town to the farm, and all the way back Tom kept thinking, *"Don't worry," everyone tells me. "There's nothing to it." Even Jimmy said there's nothing to it. But how can I help worrying when there's so much at stake? Perhaps I'm not made for this type of thing. Everyone else is so casual about it. A few weeks ago, back at Coronet, maybe I was casual, too. But it's different now that the mare's time is so close at hand and she's my responsibility. That's it, she's my responsibility. I wouldn't want anything to happen to the Queen or to her foal. And now I'm alone. It's up to me. It's what I wanted. But I'm wondering whether I can shoulder all this responsibility. I guess that's why I wanted to have a veterinary around. I didn't want to go it alone. I lack confidence in myself. I might as well admit it.*

But there's Uncle Wilmer, Tom thought eagerly. *He'll be around. I've got him to turn to. He doesn't understand a horse as finely bred as the Queen, but he's had workhorses and cows that have given birth here at the farm, and he'll know what to do.*

Tom's pace quickened as he reached the lane. Having thought it all out, having decided to put his faith in Uncle Wilmer should have made him feel better, but it didn't. He knew that somehow he had let himself down, and let Jimmy Creech down, too. He lacked confidence in himself. He was groping for someone's hand. First it had been the veterinary's and now his uncle's. It wasn't the way he had thought it would be or planned—or the way Jimmy had planned. Jimmy had placed the Queen in his hands, not in those of Uncle Wilmer.

Upon reaching the farm, he saw the Queen grazing in the

pasture. He called to her and she raised her head, the white blaze standing out vividly against her dark-brown face. She whinnied, then went back to her grazing.

Tom went to the barn and picked up a longe line. Carrying it, he went back to the pasture. He had reached the gate when his uncle appeared at the door of the chicken house. Tom waved to him but said nothing. His uncle called to him.

Tom waited while Uncle Wilmer came toward him, walking in his slow, loping way with one hand, as usual, bent behind his back.

"What you goin' to do?"

Tom raised the line. Uncle Wilmer knew perfectly well what he was going to do, yet every day since the Queen had arrived he'd asked that same question when Tom had gone into the field. The boy turned away, knowing that his uncle would follow him, watching as he always did while Tom worked the Queen on the longe.

Tom went up to the mare and snapped the line to her halter; then he backed away until the line was extended its full length. Uncle Wilmer was standing a few feet behind him. "You'll have to get farther back," Tom shouted. Ever day he had told his uncle the same thing.

The Queen stopped grazing when Tom shook the line. And at the first sound of his clucking, she moved into a trot, slowly encircling the boy.

Tom pivoted with her, his eyes never leaving the mare's heavy, cumbersome body. He kept her at a slow trot for a long time before letting her come to a stop. Then he went to her, unclipping the line. The Queen moved away.

"If I was working my land again, I'd see that she got

plenty of exercise, all right." The words were spoken by
Uncle Wilmer, who was standing directly behind Tom.

Tom neither turned around nor said anything.

A shout came from the woods at the far end of the
meadow, and Tom recognized the voice of Mrs. Yoder, who
lived on the lower road.

"Telephone!" Mrs. Yoder was calling. "Emma or Wilmer
is wanted on the phone!"

His Uncle was saying something about using the Queen
to pull a cultivator when Tom turned to him. "Phone!" he
shouted, pointing to Mrs. Yoder.

But his uncle continued talking about what he'd do if he
was working the farm again and the Queen belonged to
him.

Aunt Emma appeared in front of the wash hanging in the
yard. She'd heard Mrs. Yoder, for she was coming through
the back gate.

Tom watched his aunt as she hurriedly made her way
through the pasture's knee-deep grass. When she was parallel
with Tom and Uncle Wilmer she turned a withering glance
upon her husband. "Good for nothing!" she shouted. "I've
got to do everything!"

Uncle Wilmer moved sheepishly and it wasn't until his
wife was some distance away that he regained his composure.
"You oughtn't to have taken the shoes off the mare," he
told Tom defiantly.

Tom looked curiously at him. Jimmy Creech had removed
the mare's shoes because running around on the soft ground
without them was the best thing for her feet. Tom was certain that his uncle realized this, too. Then why did he say the
Queen shouldn't be running around shoeless?

Tom fastened his gaze on the tall, bustling woman who had now joined Mrs. Yoder at the far end of the pasture, and thought he knew the answer. Aunt Emma did a good job of bullying her husband, so Uncle Wilmer, in turn, enjoyed the opportunity of taking it out on someone else—and right now it was Tom Messenger. The boy smiled until he realized his uncle's eyes were upon him, then his lips closed tight.

They stood there for a while, watching the Queen while she grazed. But Tom noticed that frequently his uncle's gaze would leave the mare for the lower meadow and the path over which Aunt Emma would return.

"She won't have it fer a month's time," his uncle said. "You better listen to me. You leave that mare out nights. No use to bring her in, usin' good straw to bed her down."

Not wanting to shout or to argue with his uncle, Tom simply shook his head.

"She's your mare," Uncle Wilmer said after a few seconds of silence. "You do with her as you like. You oughtn't to be giving her grain now. Grass is good enough for her. Grain costs money. Grass don't. You oughtn't—"

His uncle had stopped talking with the reappearance of Aunt Emma in the lower meadow. Tom watched her as she came toward them, her long legs moving effortlessly over the ground. She was still a good distance away when she shouted, "Tillie's sick again. She wants us for the night."

The man turned to Tom. "What she say?" he asked.

"Aunt Tillie is sick. She says you're going into town for the night."

His uncle lowered his eyes. "Tillie's always sick when she wants company. That's the way Tillie is, all right."

Tom nodded sympathetically. He had met Aunt Tillie

once. It had been three years ago, the last time he had spent the summer here at the farm. Aunt Tillie had taken sick then, too, and they had gone in for the night. He had watched Aunt Tillie and Aunt Emma play rummy until he had fallen asleep on the couch. Aunt Tillie was old and unmarried, and every few months she wanted company. When she did, she got sick and called Aunt Emma.

His aunt stood before them now. "We're going in right away," she said. "You two get ready."

She was moving past them when Tom said, "I'd better stay here, Aunt Emma. I've got to watch the mare."

"Your aunt Tillie's sick," Aunt Emma said with finality. "You come."

"I can't do anything for Aunt Tillie," the boy returned quietly. "I might be able to do something for the Queen. Surely you understand, Aunt Emma."

"Wilmer told you the mare won't foal for a long time yet," she said.

"But I think she will," Tom returned slowly. He couldn't have said anything else. He swept a glance at his uncle, but the man's eyes were turned away.

"We'll be back the first thing in the morning," his aunt was saying, "My land, Tom, you can be away from your mare that long when your aunt Tillie is sick."

"I couldn't . . . I've got to stay here. Please, Aunt Emma, you just have to understand." But then he added diplomatically, "I'll feed the chickens and the pigs, too. You won't have anything to worry about back here then."

Their eyes met and it was several seconds before the woman spoke again. "You get ready," she bellowed to Uncle Wilmer. "If some people think more of horses than they do of their own kin—" She moved away from them.

The man looked at the boy in wonder and admiration; then he followed his wife toward the house.

Tom's aunt and uncle had long since departed for town when he finished his supper. As he sat in the deep leather chair before the kitchen table, he watched the last rays of the setting sun rest upon the wooded mountains. The Queen had been fed and bedded down in her roomy box stall for the night. There was nothing to do now but wait—wait for morning, hoping the Queen wouldn't have her foal tonight while he was alone.

He thought of his bringing the Queen into the barn for the night. Uncle Wilmer wouldn't like it; he'd said it was a waste of straw. And telling Aunt Emma that he thought the Queen would have her foal this week in spite of what Uncle Wilmer had said wasn't going to help matters, either. Not at all.

Restlessly Tom rose from his chair and carried the dishes to the sink. As he washed them he found himself thinking, *I hope I'm wrong. At least, I hope it won't be tonight. I'd like to have Uncle Wilmer around just in case something goes wrong. I'm afraid. Not for myself, but for the Queen. If anything happened to her through my ignorance or carelessness . . .*

Tom finished the dishes and put them away in the corner cupboard; then he went to the stove and banked the fire before returning to the chair and looking out the window again. It was almost dark now.

Jimmy Creech told me what to do, he thought. *He said he had full confidence in me. And Jimmy wouldn't put his faith in just anybody. He must believe it, so I've got to believe it, too. I've got to have confidence in myself. George Snedecker said I wouldn't have any trouble, either. . . . That's exactly what he wrote in the letter I got from him yesterday.*

Tom reached for the letter lying upon the mantle just above the kitchen table. He read it again.

Carlisle Fair
June 21

Dear Tom,

 Jimmy is off with some of his old pals who are racing here, so I got a chance to write, like I was going to do all week.

 I wanted to tell you how well Jimmy is doing, because I know you been worrying about him, like I been doing. We don't have to worry no more. At least that's the way it looks right now. Old Jimmy is driving like he used to drive. He's almost picking up Symbol and carrying him! That's the kind of driving Jimmy is doing here. He ain't won no races yet, but he's gotten two seconds and three thirds, so he's paying expenses all right. But most important to you and me is that he's in very good spirits, acting young and happy-like, and getting a big kick out of driving. That's more like the Jimmy Creech I used to know.

 I wanted to tell you that I think you did it to him. You and the Queen. And don't you think for one minute that that man from Hanover Farms didn't meet Jimmy's price for the Queen. Jimmy just didn't sell her. He couldn't when he saw how you felt about her. Jimmy feels the same way about the Queen as you do, but when he got sick he forgot, I guess. You made him remember. Now he's looking forward to the Queen's foal like a papa expecting a baby. And it's done him a world of good.

 Like I said before, you did it. You and the Queen. So we're waiting to hear from you. And we know that our Queen couldn't

*be in better hands than yours. You just watch her, Tom. That's
all you have to do. You won't have any trouble, and being good to
her and loving her as you do is the best thing in the world for her
at this time.*

*It's getting late, so I got to quit now. We got a big day ahead
of us tomorrow.*

*Your friend,
George Snedecker*

After folding the letter, Tom put it back in the envelope.
If loving the Queen and watching her would take care of
everything, as George wrote, then he had nothing to worry
about. He went eagerly to the door and across the lawn. Perhaps he didn't need Uncle Wilmer at all. Perhaps he could
do it all by himself, just as he'd planned.

Upon reaching the paddock in front of the barn, he saw
the Queen's head thrust over the half-door of the box stall.
She whinnied and he went to her. He stroked her nose, then
opened the door and went inside. He tried to get far enough
away from the Queen to look at her body, but she kept
moving closer to him, nuzzling his pocket for carrots. Finally he gave up trying to keep away from her and she
pushed her nose into his pocket.

As she stood quietly beside him he thought, maybe Uncle
Wilmer is right. Maybe she won't have her foal for a long
time. She's so calm, and not a bit nervous. I don't believe
she'd be acting this way if her foal were due very soon.

But that night, when Tom went to bed in his room above
the kitchen, he set the clock's alarm for midnight. He would
look at the Queen at that time just to make sure she was all
right. And at two o'clock and four and six, he'd do the same

thing. Jimmy Creech had said she would have her foal this week, so he must look at the Queen every few hours. From tonight until she had her foal, whether it was to be this week or a month from now, he would keep this schedule that he had set for himself.

The alarm at midnight awakened Tom from a sound sleep. Sluggishly he reached for the clock, groping until he found it in the darkness. Turning off the alarm, he lay back again, his eyes closed. Then, quickly, he opened them again and turned on the light. He reached for his overalls, pulling them over his pajamas; then he made his way down the stairs, picking up the flashlight as he went out the door.

It was a moonless night and the air was cool. He walked over to the barn, the light flashing ahead of him. As he reached the door of the stall he saw the Queen's head, her eyes blinking in the light of his flash. He turned the beam away, talking to her. Leaning over the half-door, he flashed the light around the straw, then back to the Queen. Everything was all right, he decided. He had probably awakened her. He'd go back and let her get some sleep. But he stood there a few minutes longer, stroking her, before he left.

At two o'clock and at four the alarm went off, and each time Tom found the Queen comfortable and regretted that he had awakened her again. Perhaps he was doing more harm than good, visiting her so often during the night. He didn't know. But he couldn't take any chances.

No alarm awakened him at five o'clock, for he had set it for six. He looked at the clock to make sure of the time, then his head fell back on the pillow. But he found he could not close his eyes. He remembered very well that he had been dreaming. It had been more of a nightmare than a dream. He had lost Jimmy Creech's letter, and the Queen was having her foal. He couldn't remember what to do. He had run, looking for Uncle Wilmer, but Uncle Wilmer had refused to come because he said the mare couldn't have her foal for another month. So he had run to town to get a veterinary, but none of them could come. They were too busy and appointments must be made a year in advance, they'd told him. He'd been running through the woods, shouting for help, when he had awakened.

And now he couldn't get back to sleep again.

The sky outside his window to the east was a somber gray, and the sun wouldn't be up for another hour. Tom tried keeping his eyes closed, but it was of no use. He sat up in bed and turned on the light. Perhaps if he just took another look at Jimmy Creech's letter telling him what to do when the foal came, he'd be able to get to sleep again. Just one look to make sure he hadn't lost it.

The letter was in the top drawer of his bureau, and he sat down on the side of his bed and read it again. Everything was there. He knew exactly what to do, without the aid of Uncle Wilmer, without a veterinary. He had it down pat now.

He put the letter away, thinking, *Even if I'd lost the letter, I'd remember Jimmy's instructions. I've read it over enough times to know them by heart. Wipe the foal dry—that's the first thing I do. Make sure his nostrils are clear, so he can breathe well. Then make sure he nurses right away. He'll need all the nourishment he can get at that time. And feed the mare very light the first two days, giving her a hot bran mash right after she's had the foal. There's really not so much to remember. I can do it.*

Tom let his head fall back on the pillow, figuring he could

sleep until six o'clock. But sleep didn't come, nor was he able to keep his eyes closed. Instead he found himself gazing out the window to the west, toward the barn. It wasn't like him not to be able to sleep. Usually he could fall asleep at the drop of a hat. There must be something wrong with him; perhaps getting up so often during the night was responsible for it; perhaps—

Tom felt the pounding of his heart, the swift surge of blood within his veins. He was out of bed and pulling on his overalls. He plummeted down the stairs, rushing out into the gray light of early morning. As he ran across the lawn, his gaze never left the stall door. *But the Queen's head couldn't be seen.*

He flung himself through the rails of the paddock fence and ran to the stall door. The light was dim, but he had no trouble seeing inside. And Tom's body slumped hard against the door at the sight of the foal lying in the straw beside the Queen.

Wipe the Foal Dry!

4

The Queen, her dark coat wet and matted with straw and manure, turned to Tom, and he saw the wildness in her eyes. He stepped back from the door, frightened, as she came swiftly to him.

He didn't know how long he stood there, just staring at her disheveled head, trying to remember what he should do. But nothing came. His mind was a blank. He was dazed, bewildered.

He found himself running along the corridor that led to the rear of the Queen's stall. He heard himself saying, "It's here. It's here." He repeated it over and over again, all the while knowing there were things to do, things to remember.

He stood before the grain box, his hands plunged into the oats. The mare whinnied and, quickly, he turned to her. She was watching his every nove.

Feed her lightly the first two days.

His mind was working better now. He wasn't calm yet, but things were starting to come. Jimmy had said— What else had Jimmy said?

Bran mash. Give the mare a bran mash right after she's foaled.
His eyes left the mare for the pail beside him. Picking it
up, he went over to a sack of bran. The pail was half-filled
when he set it down and turned again to the mare.

It would take time to prepare the mash. He needed hot
water and salt. He'd have to get the stove going.

But the foal. What about the foal? The foal should come
first.

He walked to where he could get a better view of the stall,
and the mare followed him. He could see the foal now, and
his eyes became as liquid as those of the Queen as he
watched.

The small, dark bundle in the corner of the stall moved.
With great effort, the foal raised its heavy head from the
straw, only to let it fall back again. Its long legs, half-buried
in the bedding, were straight and rigid. Slight ribs showed
plainly beneath the wet coat, and there was a slow but regular expansion and contraction of the tiny body as the foal
took the first breaths of life into its lungs.

Filly or colt? Tom did not know or care. Nothing mattered but that the foal was alive.

*Wipe the foal dry, if the mare doesn't take care of that. Wipe his
nostrils clean, so he can breathe good.*
He was thinking now. He was remembering Jimmy's instructions. But there was still the frantic pounding of his
heart, the uncertainty, the lack of coordination between
mind and body.

Close to the wall there was a narrow entrance to the box
stall from the rear. Tom went to it, one hand reaching for
the clean handkerchief in the pocket of his overalls.

The Queen moved with him. And when he set a foot inside the stall, she bared her teeth and came between him and her foal.

Frightened, Tom withdrew his foot. There was nothing docile about his Queen now. She was a protective mother, fearful that he meant harm to her first foal. And she wouldn't let him near it.

No one, not even Jimmy Creech, had told him that this might happen.

He heard the rustling in the straw behind the Queen. The foal must be trying to get to its feet. Tom's fist closed tightly about the handkerchief he held in his hand.

And as he continued standing there, he suddenly realized that his heart was no longer pounding, that his mind was clearing of the dazedness and bewilderment that had be-clouded it. There were no instructions to follow now, nothing to remember. He had but one thing to do, to get to the foal. He was on his own.

When Tom moved finally, he went to the grain box again. And there was a resoluteness to his face and step that hadn't been there before.

The Queen had followed to the other side of the stall, her head thrust over her manger, waiting.

Tom came back to her, his lips moving, his voice soft. But the Queen had eyes only for the container of mixed oats and bran he carried in his hand. He dumped the contents of the tin into her box and stole a glance in the direction of the foal that was struggling to its feet.

Tom moved quickly toward the narrow entrance to the stall, then stopped abruptly and hurried back to the grain box. Quickly he filled his pockets with bran and went back to the entrance to the stall again.

The mare was eating ravenously and paid no attention to him as he stepped inside. Tom's eyes widened as he watched the foal.

It was on its feet, wobbling unsteadily on long, thin legs. Its head seemed much too large for so small a body.

The foal's gaze was upon him, and as Tom looked into the soft, seeking, bewildered eyes, he knew that nothing in the world would ever equal this moment for him. He wanted to love, to cherish, to protect this foal.

He sprang forward as the foal's legs gave way and it fell heavily to the straw. He had reached it, had touched the wet, limp body, when the mare came at him with bared teeth and ears flat against her head.

Quickly he rose from his stooped position beside the foal. The mare stopped before his raised hand, blinking and uncertain. Tom brought his hand down softly on the Queen's muzzle.

"I wouldn't hurt your foal. You know that. I want to help." As Tom continued talking to the mare, he fed her the bran from his pocket.

The foal had risen to its trembling legs again and was looking at them. Tom's eyes devoured it. Its legs were straight. It wasn't deformed. It was—yes, it was a colt! *Jimmy Creech had wanted a colt.*

Stilt-legged, the foal moved toward them, shuffling, pushing his feet through the straw. He had gone only a short distance when the straw became entwined about his legs, causing him to fall. He lay still for a few minutes, then struggled to his feet again.

Tom was beside him now. The Queen shoved her head down, seeking the bran the boy had been feeding her. Tom's eyes took in the foal's wet, sticky coat; then, taking a handful of bran from his pocket, he sprinkled it over the colt.

The Queen turned to her foal and began licking the bran off him.

Smiling, Tom said, "Lick him dry, Queen. That's your job as well as mine."

As he steadied the wobbling body with one hand, Tom reached for his handkerchief and then wiped the foal's face, beginning with his nostrils.

The small colt stood still amidst all this attention, yet his soft muzzle moved searchingly about Tom's face and chest.

"You're hungry," Tom said softly. "There's your mom."

He pushed the foal gently to the side of the mare, helping him to find his mother. While the colt nursed, Tom fed the Queen from his hand.

"You're supposed to be having a bran mash, Queen," he said to the mare, "and in a little while you'll have it. I don't know whether I'm doing the right thing or not. Things just happened this way. But the worst is over now. Everything is going to work out all right. I know it is. And you have a beautiful colt. Just as beautiful as we knew he'd be."

When Tom left the stall a few minutes later, the sun was just coming up. It was a wonderful, wonderful morning, and he knew what he had to do in the hours to come. It was as if he'd always known.

In the kitchen, he set the pail of bran on the floor, got the stove going and put the kettle up. Soon it was steaming. Lifting it carefully, he carried it over to the pail.

Wet it good, then put a sack over the pail and let it steam until it's cool enough for the mare to eat.

He poured the water over the bran. There was something

else. *Salt*. Yes, that was it, a handful of salt.

After adding the salt, Tom gazed about the room until he saw his aunt's dishtowels folded neatly on the shelf above the sink. Quickly he went over and, removing one, placed it over the pail.

He was leaving the kitchen, carrying the pail of steaming mash, when he stopped and looked again at the dishtowels piled high on the shelf.

They were soft, very soft. He would find nothing better to use on the foal's soft body.

He hesitated but a moment, then removed another towel from the pile and hurried out the door.

Arriving at the barn, he set the pail down once more and went inside.

The Queen was licking the last bit of bran off the foal. She looked at him, and again there were fear and uncertainty in her eyes.

But he belonged here. She had to accept it. And knowing this, Tom walked straight ahead to the foal and placed his hands upon the soft and still trembling body. The liquid, luminous eyes were turned on him. There was neither fear nor timidity in the foal's gaze, only wonder.

The mare snorted as Tom drew the towel across the foal's back. The boy spoke to the Queen without turning around, for he was concentrating on the teetering body before him. He brought the cloth gently down over the velvet-soft, furry coat and the thin legs.

The foal stood very still, as though grateful for Tom's steadying hands.

When he had finished, Tom stepped back and watched while the colt nursed again. The mare looked at Tom, the fear gone from her eyes. She had learned he would do no harm to her foal.

Tom left the stall but returned very soon, carrying the pail of mash. He held it for the mare and hungrily she shoved her muzzle into the mash.

Tom looked out at the paddock and the bright sun rising over the eastern hills. He would put the mare and foal outside, he decided. No one had said they shouldn't go out, and it would be much better for the colt. The sun would dry him well, and there would be no straw to become entwined about his slim legs, causing him to fall.

When the mare had finished the mash Tom left the stall, leaving the door open behind him. The Queen followed him quickly into the bright sun, then stopped, turned abruptly and neighed.

From the semi-darkness of the stall the foal emerged, standing just within the doorway, his large eyes blinking in the light of day.

The Queen neighed again, then dropped her head to graze.

Tom moved back to the door as the foal shuffled his way forward with rigid legs. Suddenly the foal stopped, teetering precariously. And Tom remembered the slight step in the doorway which the foal's forefeet must have encountered.

He stooped beside the foal, steadying him, while his hand went to the small hoof. "You'll have to lift it," he said, smiling. "Everyone lifts them."

Slowly, cautiously, the foal picked up his feet and moved out into the sun. He stood there, still trembling and unsure of himself. He moved his head seldom, having learned that the heaviness of it could easily offset his balance. But his eyes were wide and incredulous at the world before him. With forelegs spread far apart to steady his weaving body, he watched the chickens crossing the paddock. He watched the mare. He watched Tom. And all the time his eyes blinked rapidly in the light of his first day.

Tom sat down on the side of the water trough, his elbows upon his knees and his long, angular face resting heavily between the palms of his hands. Never once did his intent gaze leave the foal. He watched the stilt legs move carefully upon tiny, fawnlike hoofs. He watched the bushy stump of a tail swish ridiculously from side to side, slowly at first, then ever faster like the swift movement of an automobile's windshield wiper. It was as though the colt had just discovered his tail. There were so many things for him to discover, and Tom sat there watching, content to do only that.

It was difficult to explain the emotions he felt within him, nor did he try. He knew only that something beautiful and fine and wonderful was happening. Never once did he think of the years ahead, when this colt would race. Neither did he ask himself, "Will he be a champion?" Nor did he think of Jimmy Creech or George Snedecker or anyone else, even the Queen. His mind, his eyes, his whole being were concentrated on the foal who stood on trembling legs before him—the foal who was looking at life for the first time. It was enough that Tom was there, sharing the experience with him.

An hour passed and Tom still sat there without moving. He watched as much of the unsteadiness left the colt's legs and the first confident steps were taken. He saw him lose his balance repeatedly and fall to the ground. But the colt always struggled to his feet to try once more. And when he strayed too far away from his mother, the Queen would neigh a shrill reprimand, then go back to her grazing. The foal would watch her as she cropped the grass; then he too would lower his head cautiously until his short neck could stretch no more.

But finally the colt grew weary of activity and carefully lowered himself to the grass, stretching out in the sun.

It was only then that Tom moved away from the water trough. Quietly he walked over to the foal and knelt beside him. The large eyes were closed, the breathing regular. The colt was asleep.

For several minutes Tom kept looking at him; then he got to his feet and walked toward the barn. There was work to be done, for the stall had to be thoroughly cleaned. This would be a good time to do it, now that the foal was asleep. *I won't miss anything if I hurry,* Tom thought.

Half an hour later, when he had finished his work, Tom sat down once more on the side of the water trough. The foal still slept in the sun.

For some time Tom sat there as before, just watching the colt, but then the sound of a car caused him to turn his head in the direction of the lane. And even though the trees concealed the approaching vehicle, he knew from the sputtering of the motor and the rattling of the loose body that it could be no other car but his uncle's.

The Queen turned toward the lane, her head alert. And the foal, too, aroused by the noise of the car, struggled to his feet and stood close beside his mother.

The car moved out of the woods and, crossing the brook with undiminished speed, drew up before the paddock fence.

Tom rose to greet his uncle and aunt.

"So it came," Aunt Emma said quietly. And then she turned to her husband, who was leaning heavily upon the fence. "It came after all you said!" she shouted to him.

The man's gaze never left the foal, and if he heard his wife's sharp criticism he ignored it, for all he said in his slowest drawl was, "It's all right."

"It's a colt," Tom said, his eyes shining. "Jimmy Creech wanted a colt."

Aunt Emma nodded while Uncle Wilmer asked, "What'd you say?"

"He said it's a colt!" the woman shouted.

"I know that, all right," Uncle Wilmer said.

The colt encircled the mare, then swept beneath her belly and came up to gaze at the three onlookers with his large, curious eyes.

Aunt Emma, glancing around, saw the wet dishtowels hanging on the fence. She recognized the green border stitching and her eyes lost their warmth as she bustled her way toward the towels. Sweeping them off the fence, she waved them vigorously in the air. "Thomas!" she bellowed. "What have you been doing with my new Miracle dishtowels!"

"I–I dried th-the foal with them," Tom stammered. "They're soft," he added feebly.

They looked at each other for several seconds while Uncle Wilmer's gaze shifted uneasily from one to the other.

"I had to have something soft," Tom said again. "I'm going to give them a good washing."

Aunt Emma looked at the foal, then at the boy. She lowered her eyes as she said, "Well, see that you do, Tom." And her voice was amazingly soft for Aunt Emma.

Uncle Wilmer had had his head cocked, listening, but he hadn't caught the woman's words. He turned to her questioningly, but she swept by, ignoring him.

When Aunt Emma reached the gate, she stopped. "Wilmer!" she shouted. "You come along. I got work for you!"

Grudgingly, Uncle Wilmer moved away from the fence after one more look at the foal. "It's a good one, all right," he said mostly to himself. And only when he was about to follow Aunt Emma did he turn to the boy to say, "Don't suppose you fed the chickens, did you, Tom?"

The boy's gaze left the foal for Uncle Wilmer. "I forgot them. I'm sorry. I'll do it now."

His uncle walked toward the gate and, without turning his head around, said, "It's all right. I'll feed them. You stay with him."

So Tom stayed with his colt. And he decided he was going to stay there all day, if he could. He didn't want to miss a thing. He'd even write Jimmy from here. He would say, "Dear Jimmy, he came this morning. A colt, just like you wanted. And I think he's the most beautiful, most wonderful colt there ever was. . . ."

Hard Hands

5

Very often during the following week, Aunt Emma suggested bluntly to Tom that he might as well sleep in the barn for all she saw of him. "Land sakes!" she told him. "Next thing we know you'll be eating oats!"

And, more often than not, whenever the word *oats* was mentioned, Uncle Wilmer would turn to Tom, shake his head sadly, and say, "You're wastin' good money, Boy. The mare don't need oats now. Grass is plenty good enough for her. Grass makes milk for the colt."

And Tom would always reply, "She needs both, Uncle Wilmer. Jimmy Creech says she does."

" 'Jimmy Creech says this'! 'Jimmy Creech says that'!" Uncle Wilmer would bellow, stalking from the room.

But his uncle's tantrums did not bother Tom any more than did his aunt's sarcastic remarks about his living in the barn. For Tom's world now centered there and he accepted it. Hour after hour, day after day, he watched the colt.

He saw the sharp ribs seemingly disappear overnight and

the chunky body fill out before his eyes. No longer did the colt shuffle along on uncertain legs. After his second day he was trotting about the paddock, falling only when he took too fast a turn.

And Tom watched him with wondering eyes, marveling at the rapid growth and agility of one who only a few days ago had been so helpless.

By the end of the first week, the paddock was almost too small for the frolicking colt, and Tom knew that the time had come to put him and the Queen in the pasture. He had waited for the colt to gain full confidence in his long legs before putting him to the task of coping with the pasture's hilly and uneven terrain. He had another reason, too, for having kept the Queen and her colt in the paddock. Here he could get to the colt more easily than he'd be able to do in the acres of pastureland. Winning the colt's confidence and handling him often was his most important job now. And it was a job he loved doing.

Tom would enter the paddock, slowly approaching the colt. And the colt would watch him with curious and still uncertain eyes. For the colt now knew who his mother was, and he kept close to her, using her big body as his protection against the world.

Always Tom would stop a few feet away from the mare. He would then stoop down, and sometimes even sit on the ground, for he had learned that the smaller he made himself the more confidence it gave the colt.

The Queen would come to him, looking for the carrots in his pockets, and the colt would follow. While feeding the mare, Tom would remain very still, never making a move to touch the colt until the small head was thrust down to him and the soft muzzle searched curiously about his clothes. Tom would let him nibble his fingers and felt only the slightest edges of the colt's teeth, which were finding their way through tender gums. Very often then, the colt would encircle him, pulling at his clothes, while Tom ran his hand gently over the furry body and down the long slim legs to tiny hoofs.

Uncle Wilmer watched Tom's handling of the colt with great curiosity and apparent concern. "Y'oughtn't to make so much of him," he would say. "You'll get more out of him if you show him who's boss right away, while you can still handle him. No sense in makin' up to him like you do. Git in there and hold him, if you want to brush him. You let him do what he wants and he'll kick the teeth out of you before long. He's gettin' stronger every day, an' if you don't act now, it ain't goin' to be so easy later on."

Tom had listened, knowing his uncle meant well, but he wanted the colt to come to him of his own accord. He couldn't have done it any other way. But he knew, too, there was much to what his uncle was telling him. He knew he had to be more careful now, for the colt was throwing his hind legs around more often and with more force. The hoofs, while still small, could do some injury if well directed.

So as Tom sat on the ground with the colt encircling him, he was more cautious, more alert than he had been the first few days, and he was on guard against the slightest movement of the hindquarters toward him.

Jimmy Creech had said to handle the colt as much as possible, but he hadn't told him how to go about it. Until he heard from Jimmy, he would go ahead as he was doing, regardless of his uncle's advice, even though Tom knew it was being given in his own best interest.

Jimmy Creech's next letter came with the late afternoon mail during the middle of the colt's second week. Eagerly Tom took it from the mailbox in the upper road. But before opening the letter, he turned to look at the barn set far below him. Across the waving fields of tall grass he could see a corner of the paddock, and there, sprawled in the sun, lay the colt.

He opened the envelope and began reading Jimmy's large handwriting.

> Clearfield Fair
> July 10

Dear Tom,

I couldn't have asked for anything more than a colt, and I'm so glad everything worked out okay. I sure understand how you must have felt, and George says he does, too.

I only got your letter today because George and I are now at the Clearfield Fair, and your letter was forwarded back home before reaching us here.

Now I'm going to tell you what to do until we all get back to Coronet. It's not much you have to do, Tom, but it's very important. I can't tell you how important it is.

First thing you have to do is to win the confidence of the colt. Make sure he learns he has nothing to fear from you. Handle him all you can. Get him used to having your hands running all over him and picking up his feet. The more used to it he gets the easier it's going to be later for all of us.

I want you to get a halter. A soft web one is best if you can get it. Put it on him now, so he can get used to it. It'll also make it easier for you in catching him when he's in pasture. I want you to start leading him around in a few weeks, first behind the mare, and later away from the mare. You'll need help, so maybe your uncle will give you a hand. But I want you to be leading the colt, remember that.

He might give you a little trouble at first, Tom. He might not like being led about and not being allowed to go his own way. You got to be patient with him. I know you will be, and that's why I turned over the mare and now the colt to you. Most men, and that includes myself, don't have the patience we had when we were your age. That's why I believe the colt will do better in your hands than mine or anyone I know. You'll have to work slow, teaching him one thing at a time. When you first try to lead him, let him go his own way, if he has a mind to. Don't fight him. Just go along with him, until before long you'll find that you're guiding him and he's going along with you. But it may take days or weeks, Tom, and that's what I mean when I say you got to have patience.

I don't mean that you shouldn't have a firm hand with the colt. He's got to learn obedience and he has to learn it early in life or else he'll be a rebel later. And when he gets to be over a thousand pounds it's a terrible job trying to make him unlearn any bad habits he picked up as a youngster. I'm simply saying that you can teach him obedience by winning his confidence and having him learn willingly just as easily as anyone can do it by force. And the results are a million times better! I've seen too many people try to knock obedience into a colt by giving him the rough treatment. They say it's faster, and they're right. But what they forget is that they usually break the colt's spirit, too. And when that's done you've killed what may have been a fine horse.

I didn't mean to go on for so long, Tom, but I did and I'm glad I did. Do what you can with the colt, and if you can bring him back to Coronet in September knowing how to be led and having full confidence in you, I'll be a very happy man.

Just one other thing, and that is I want you to give the colt *all the oats he wants as soon as he starts stealing any from the mare and shows an interest in grain. Crushed oats are better than whole oats, for remember he'll only have milk teeth in a couple of weeks and he won't be able to do a good job of masticating his food.*

George and I did pretty well at the Carlisle and Indiana County fairs, because Symbol is showing some speed. I'm hoping for even better results here at Clearfield. We'll be here a week, then on to the Bedford Fair. Write to me c/o race secretary at either place.

George and I send our very best to you, and we'd sure like a photograph of the colt when you get one.

Your friend,
Jimmy Creech

Tom reread the letter before starting down the hill toward the barn.

I've been doing the right thing then, he thought happily. *I've been trying to win the colt's confidence just as Jimmy has told me to do.*

When Tom reached the paddock, he found his uncle leaning on the fence. The colt was racing about, while the mare watched him. The Queen suddenly whirled, following the colt about the paddock. Together they ran, sending large divots of earth flying in all directions.

"They ought to be out in the pasture, all right," Uncle Wilmer said.

"I'm putting them out tomorrow morning," Tom shouted, as the colt flung his hind legs high behind him, imitating his mother.

Uncle Wilmer nodded approvingly, then said, "You shoulda done it days ago."

Tom said nothing until the mare and colt had stopped running; then, turning to his uncle, he asked, "Where can I buy a halter in town?"

"Heh?" his uncle asked, moving closer to Tom.

Tom repeated his question in a louder voice.

"What you want it for?" Uncle Wilmer asked.

Tom gestured in the direction of the colt.

"Don't need a halter yet," the man said. "Y'won't need one for a couple months at least."

Tom raised the envelope he held in his hand. "Jimmy Creech wrote—" he began.

Uncle Wilmer shook his head so severely that the battered hat toppled from his head. Bending down to pick it up, he muttered, "Jimmy Creech. All I hear from you is Jimmy Creech."

Tom said nothing, and his uncle turned to look at the horses.

Shrugging his shoulders, Uncle Wilmer continued, "If it was my colt instead of Jimmy Creech's, I'd—" He paused and, shaking his head again, added, "But it ain't. I got a pony halter you can use. It'll fit him. You won't find anything better in town."

Tom waited while his uncle went into the barn and came out again, carrying the halter.

There was an unusual gleam in Uncle Wilmer's eyes as he tossed the halter to Tom, saying, "You go ahead, then."

Tom felt the leather and found it soft. Jimmy had said a web halter, if he could get one, but certainly this would do until he was able to find a web halter. *But,* he decided, *I'd better punch a couple more holes so I can make it smaller; the colt's head isn't very big.* Turning to his uncle, he asked him for his jackknife and Uncle Wilmer produced it from his pocket.

"I'll do it," Uncle Wilmer said. "You just hold the strap up against the fence here."

The man made several attempts to locate the strap before the point of his knife sunk into the leather. "Eyesight ain't what it used to be," he muttered. "I remember the day when out huntin' I could pick off a rabbit over two hundred yards—" His voice descended to the depths of his chest, and Tom turned to look at the colt.

There was a flurry of flashing legs as the colt once again dashed about the paddock, while his mother remained still, grazing, with only an occasional look at him. Taking too sharp a corner, the colt stumbled and went down hard. He lay still for a few seconds, then raised his head, looking dazed and a little surprised by his sudden collapse. He pulled his forelegs up and then just sat there, still looking about him. Finally he uttered a short snicker, his hind legs came up, and once more he was on his way, madly encircling the paddock, pausing only occasionally to rear upon his hind legs and paw the air with his forehoofs like a boxer feinting a blow.

"There it be," Uncle Wilmer said, finishing his job.

Taking the small halter, Tom climbed through the bars of the paddock fence.

The colt stopped playing and stood still when he saw him.

Tom moved forward, calling to the colt. He had gone only a few yards when he stopped, hoping the colt would come to him.

The forelegs were spread far apart, the big and fuzzy eyes upon him. There was a moment's hesitation, then the colt was moving slowly toward him.

For a few minutes Tom remained still, only talking to the colt; then, slowly, he raised the halter.

There was a quick, sudden movement as the colt pulled back, startled by the leather that had touched him. Twirling, he ran to his mother and hid behind her.

Tom heard his uncle's deep chuckle, then, "Grab him, Tom. You ain't goin' to get it on him that way."

Tom walked slowly toward the mare. He touched Jimmy Creech's letter in his pocket. Jimmy had said, "You got to be patient with him. You got to work slow."

The Queen raised her head to look at him. She pushed her muzzle into his hand, and finding nothing to eat turned back to her grazing. The colt was on the other side of her, and Tom walked around, only to have the colt move quickly beneath his mother's whisking tail and away from him.

Tom waited a few minutes before following him. The colt knew something was going to be done to him and he was going to avoid it if he could. Tom held out a handful of crushed oats. But the colt ignored the feed, sweeping beneath the mare's belly to reach the other side of her.

The Queen saw the feed and reached for it. Tom let her have it, hoping the colt too would show an interest and come to him. But he didn't. He remained behind his mother, hidden from Tom's sight.

Several more times Tom cautiously attempted to approach him, and only once did the colt stand still long enough for Tom to put a hand on him. He was able to run his hand up and down the short neck, but as soon as he moved the halter toward the head the colt drew back, frightened and rearing.

"You're goin' to make a balker of him sure as anything,"

Uncle Wilmer called. "You let him get away from you now and you're goin' to have trouble with him, all right. Like I been tellin' you, you got to show him who's boss. You got to show him now."

Close to an hour went by with Tom making futile attempts to reach the colt. The sky glowed with the brilliant red of sunset. Tom moved with the colt, hoping to get the halter on him.

Uncle Wilmer still leaned upon the paddock fence, shaking his head repeatedly, shouting his criticisms.

And his uncle's words rang in Tom's ears even when the man was quiet. "You're lettin' him get away with it. I never seen the like of it. You're goin' to make him an outlaw, all right, if you don't show him who's boss right now. You got to teach him to do what you want. You got to have a firm hand."

As the minutes passed, Tom's eyes became more grave. Was his uncle right? he wondered. Was he letting the colt get away with too much? Jimmy Creech had said that he must have patience, but he had also said, "I don't mean you shouldn't have a firm hand with the colt. He's got to learn obedience and he has to learn it early."

Wasn't his uncle saying exactly that? Perhaps he was doing more harm than good by letting the colt get away from him. Perhaps the colt should be held, even against his will, while the halter was put on. He'd find the halter wouldn't hurt him. He'd get used to it and everything would be all right.

Tom waited until the colt's interest was diverted from him to the Queen, then he went forward, quietly walking up to the foal as he nursed. He placed a hand on the fuzzy coat, and the colt was too absorbed in his feeding to pay any attention to him. Tom ran his hands over the small body, waiting.

When the colt had finished he turned to Tom, but made no effort to get away. The boy knew that only his raising of the halter would cause the colt to run. His arm was around the colt, his body pressed close to him. All he had to do was to hold him still for a minute while he got the halter on him. His grip tightened about the muscular body. He thought he'd be able to hold him now. As he continued talking to the colt, he raised the halter.

A startled look came into the colt's eyes at sight of it. He felt the arm about his body. He pulled back, dragging Tom with him. Then he half-reared, twisting and turning as he came down.

Tom felt his grip on the writhing body slipping, and realized he couldn't hold him. Rather than fight the colt any longer, he let him go.

"Now y'did it!" his uncle yelled, coming into the paddock. "Y'tried to hold him an' he broke away from you! He'll never forget it if you don't teach him better."

Uncle Wilmer swept past Tom, still shouting. And before the boy had any inkling of what his uncle intended doing, the man had the colt hard up against the Queen's side.

The colt tried to get away, but Uncle Wilmer moved quickly, his long arms encircling the colt's chest and haunches. Then there was a sudden twist, and the man heaved the colt off his feet and threw him to the ground, holding him still with his hands and knees.

Tom was standing over his uncle, shouting and trying to pull him away from the colt, but the man paid no attention to him.

"Give me that halter," Uncle Wilmer growled, snatching it from the boy. "I'll teach him who's boss," he muttered as he slipped the halter over the small head. "I'll teach him, all right."

Uncle Wilmer and the colt were on their feet at almost the same time. The colt, now wearing the halter, ran quickly behind his mother.

Uncle Wilmer was leaving the paddock. Aunt Emma was calling to him and Tom to come to supper. The skies were darkening fast, and it would be night in a matter of minutes.

Tom stood there, dazed by the quick turn of events. He shouldn't have let Uncle Wilmer. But how could he have stopped him? The halter was on. Uncle Wilmer's way had been swift, firm and hard, yet he hadn't hurt the colt. The job had been done quickly, easily. But he had done it by force.

"I've seen too many people try to knock obedience into a colt by giving him the rough treatment," Jimmy Creech had written. "They say it's faster, and they're right. But what they forget is that it usually breaks the colt's spirit, too. And when that's done you've killed what may have been a fine horse."

Tom thought of Jimmy's words as he moved to where he could see the colt. He found him standing close beside the mare, yet bending down, trying to reach the grass to graze. The colt was more intent upon his effort to stretch his short neck as far as possible than he was upon the halter about his head.

Again Aunt Emma called Tom to come to supper, and her voice was more demanding now.

Tom led the Queen into the box stall and the colt followed close behind. After feeding the mare, Tom stopped beside the colt, who was beginning to show an interest in the Queen's oats. It was dark inside the stall and Tom could only see the outline of the small body. The boy attempted to place a hand on the colt, but he moved away quickly from him.

"I couldn't stop Uncle Wilmer this time," Tom said. "But it won't happen again. I promise you that."

Tom knew that his uncle had only done what he thought best. Tom realized too that he himself had made a mistake in attempting to hold the colt. He should have had more patience. He should have spent days, if necessary, trying to coax the colt into letting him put the halter on his head. And if that had failed, he could have asked Uncle Wilmer simply to hold the colt still while he put it on. But Uncle Wilmer had thrown the colt hard to the ground. It shouldn't have been done that way. It wouldn't happen again. Some way, Tom decided, he'd have to make it plain to Uncle Wilmer that he wanted no further help from him.

Tom managed to get his hand on the colt's body, but as he reached for his head the colt swerved away from him, moving behind the Queen. Concerned and worried, Tom left the stall.

Setback!

6

Early the following morning, Tom came downstairs to the kitchen to find his aunt and uncle already there.

"Good morning, Tom," his aunt greeted him cheerfully. But her eyes were searching as they met his, and he knew that his uncle had told her what had happened the day before.

Uncle Wilmer stood by the door, ready to go out. He didn't look at the boy as he repeated his wife's greeting. He shifted uneasily upon his feet, obviously waiting for Tom to join him.

"You got a while till breakfast," Aunt Emma was saying. "I'm making pancakes this morning."

"You comin'?" his uncle asked.

Nodding, Tom followed him out the door, stopping only to douse his head in the water trough outside. He was wiping his face on the roller towel when Uncle Wilmer said, "It's a mighty nice morning, all right."

The sky above held all of summer's brilliant blue and the

fields, heavy with valley dew, sparkled in the sun's first rays. But Tom turned quickly from all this to the red-roofed barn and the stall door over which the Queen peered. She neighed loudly at sight of them.

They walked across the lawn, Tom following his uncle. He wondered if it was necessary to tell him how he felt about the throwing of the colt. Certainly his uncle must know. It was apparent by his unusual silence of the evening before and even now. Uncle Wilmer's use of force had been instinctive, for he'd always done it that way.

They were nearing the gate when Tom touched his uncle's arm. "It *is* a grand day," he said, smiling, when his uncle turned to look at him.

"Heh?" Uncle Wilmer's eyes were puzzled and a little troubled as they met Tom's.

"A nice day!" Tom shouted.

Uncle Wilmer nodded his head vigorously. "I already said that," he replied. But there was a lightness to his eyes that hadn't been there before, and when they went through the gate he put his hand on Tom's shoulder.

Uncle Wilmer was heading for the chicken house, but before leaving Tom he said, without turning to him, "I oughtn't to have done what I did yesterday. It's your colt and you do with him the way you think you ought . . ." He was still talking as he moved away from Tom.

For a moment, Tom watched his uncle while the man walked toward the chicken house, his arm slung behind his back, his body bent forward. Tom realized the effort it had taken for his uncle to apologize. He knew too that his uncle meant it, and that there wouldn't be a repeat performance of what had happened yesterday. It had turned out the way he had hoped it would.

Eagerly, Tom ran to the Queen. She neighed repeatedly as he stroked her head; she struck her forehoof against the door in her anxiety to be let out. The colt was hidden behind the mare, and Tom couldn't see him.

He opened the door and stepped back, allowing the Queen to come outside. The colt followed closely behind her and when Tom saw him, the boy's face suddenly became pale, then distorted in pain and anguish. The colt's nose was swollen far out of proportion to the small head. The nose band, much too tight, had cut into tender skin!

Sick at heart and furious with himself, Tom ran toward the colt who, frightened, avoided him. Unthinking, Tom made desperate efforts to grab the colt, but all to no avail. He knew he had to get the halter off immediately, so he kept running, trying to chase the colt into a corner of the paddock where he could get his hands upon him. But always there would be the quick twisting and turning of the slim legs and the colt would be away.

Finally Tom's eyes lit on the open door of the box stall and then on the Queen. He ran inside the barn and to the grain box. Taking a container of oats, he poured it into the Queen's manger, calling loudly and banging the empty container against the side of the box.

The Queen came through the door and moved quickly to her feed. Behind her followed the colt, staying close to his mother.

Tom went into the stall again and closed the door. Without hesitation he approached the colt, who now stood between the mare and the side of the stall. Tom moved quickly, pushing the mare to one side to get to the colt. He had to get the tight halter off now. For the colt's own good, he couldn't afford to be patient.

The colt moved to the front of the mare, then to the other side of her, and Tom followed. He went around the Queen again before he was able to get the colt in a corner of the stall. He had his hands at last on the small, writhing body. The colt's eyes were white with fury and fright, and his fore-legs struck out as Tom pinned him against the side of the stall.

Tom reached for the halter and the colt fought with such frenzy that only the boy's desperation gave him the strength to hold the heaving body. He had hold of the buckle; he pulled; the strap loosened. Tom tore the halter off the colt's head and flung it down on the straw; then, sickened by the sight before him, he stepped back and away from the colt.

He watched him go to the mare and, trembling, snuggle close to her. He saw the blood come to the open welt, slowly at first, then even faster, until rivulets of blood ran down the small nose.

Weakly, Tom leaned against the wall. Why had he let this happen? And then his face flamed in anger. He didn't de-serve Jimmy's confidence! He knew nothing about caring for horses! He was stupid! A fool! Anyone should have seen that the nose band was too tight. Anyone!

"Burn the halter. Burn it."

It was his uncle's voice, and Tom turned to find him standing by the door. How long he'd been there he didn't know . . . or care.

Tom didn't meet his uncle's eyes. He just stood there un-seeing. But a few minutes later, the door opened and his uncle entered the stall. It was only when he was going past Tom that the boy angrily turned him. "Keep away from him!" he shouted. "You've done—" He stopped when he saw the whiteness of his uncle's face. Tom's gaze fell. What good would it do to take it out on his uncle? Sure, he could say it was his uncle's poor eyesight that was responsible for his putting the halter on so tight. But *he* was more to blame. It was *his* colt. He should have made sure the halter fit correctly. He couldn't say it was the darkness of the stall that was responsible for his not noticing the tight nose band. He had no excuse. He should have made certain last night. It was too late now.

"I was just goin' to get the halter," his uncle was saying "I'm goin' to burn it, if you won't." He had the halter and was leaving the stall, when he stopped in front of Tom. His sad eyes sought those of the boy. "I'd let it bleed good, Tom. Bleedin' will help," he said in a low voice.

Tom nodded, but didn't raise his eyes.

It was only when Tom heard his aunt calling him that he left the stall. He didn't feel like eating, but it would be better if he went to breakfast. Aunt Emma would ask a lot of questions if he didn't, and he didn't want to talk about it. He would let the welt bleed a while; it would help to cleanse the cut and reduce the swelling. After breakfast he would do what he could for the colt. He would do it his own way. He wouldn't ask any help from Uncle Wilmer. Tom had a lot to make up for, and it would take time—much longer than if this hadn't happened.

All through breakfast Aunt Emma knew there was something wrong, but she didn't ask what it was. Nor did Tom or Uncle Wilmer volunteer any information. They ate in silence, Tom toying with his pancakes. And for the first time since he had arrived at the farm, Aunt Emma didn't urge him to eat more.

He left before his uncle and aunt had finished their breakfast. And if his aunt wondered why he had poured hot water into the porcelain washbowl and carried it with him, she did not ask.

When he reached the barn, Tom went into the end stall, which had been used for the tack room. He went to the chest and, removing a small bottle of disinfectant, poured a few drops into the hot water. Next, he tore a piece of gauze from a roll and folded it carefully; then he left the room.

The Queen moved toward him when he entered the box stall. But his eyes were for the colt, standing close beside her. The bleeding had stopped and the swelling was beginning to go down a bit. The Queen pushed her nose toward the bowl Tom carried. He put it high on the window sill, where she could not get at it; then he went to the rear of the stall and pitched some hay into the Queen's rack. It would be best if she ate while he took care of the colt.

He went inside the stall again and soaked the gauze in the disinfectant solution. Then, holding the gauze behind him, he extended his other hand toward the colt, still half-hidden behind the mare. In the palm of his hand were some crushed oats. He knelt down beside the mare, his hand thrust beneath her belly toward where he could see the slim legs of the colt.

He was content to wait, and wait he did. Many minutes passed while the mare continued eating and the cloth dried in Tom's hand, yet the colt made no move nor did he attempt to eat the feed offered him.

Tom looked up to find his uncle standing in the doorway.

"I could hold him for you," Uncle Wilmer said slowly. "That way you could do it easier an' faster—" He stopped abruptly, looking toward the floor. "You'd better do it your way," he added finally.

A short time later, Uncle Wilmer left while Tom still sat on the straw beside the mare, waiting for the colt to show an interest in the oats he was offering him.

He didn't know how long he had been there when he felt the colt's breath on his fingers; then, seconds later, the soft muzzle touched his hand. He held it still and steady as the colt ate the feed, and when it was gone Tom reached for more in his pocket. He wet the gauze again, hopeful that he would be able to get close to the colt this time.

Now he moved to the front of the mare and the colt stood before him. He began talking to him softly as he once more offered him the oats. There was a moment's hesitation on the part of the colt. Big-eyed and not quite certain, he watched Tom. Finally his muzzle reached for the feed.

Tom continued talking to him as he ate, but his eyes were upon the welt, now blood-caked. After a while his hand went to the small head. The colt drew back, but not before Tom's hand had come to rest upon his nose. Gently the boy held the gauze there as the colt backed away until his rump met the wall. The colt was a little frightened, but he wasn't fighting him. Tom took the gauze away and offered him the feed again. The colt came closer to it. Cautiously Tom dabbed at the cut, cleansing it well, while the colt licked the oats from his hand.

Much later, he left the stall again to go to the chest in the tack room. He found the bottle of methylene blue, and soaked a clean piece of gauze with it. When he returned to the stall, the colt was moving restlessly about. But as Tom entered, the colt hurried behind the mare once more.

Tom went forward, his hand finding more feed in his pocket. It would take time to paint the methylene blue on the cut, but it would take longer still, days and perhaps weeks, before he won the colt's full confidence again. And what would happen the next time he attempted to put a halter on the colt? It would take a long time for the cut to heal properly, and only then would he know. Meanwhile, during the weeks ahead the colt would grow in body and strength. If it was difficult holding him now, what would it be like a month from now?

Tom knelt down a few feet from the colt, offering him the crushed oats. And as he waited for the colt to come to it, he thought of the letter he must write today to Jimmy Creech. He would have to say, "A terrible thing happened today, Jimmy, and I'm so ashamed because I know how much you trusted me to look after our colt. . . ."

Light Hands

7

It took a full month for the colt's nose to heal. And during that time Tom's days were the busiest he had ever known. With anxious eyes he watched the hard scab form over the cut. He looked at it frequently for any signs of infection beneath. But none appeared and finally the scab fell off, giving way to new skin. For a long while Tom wondered if the colt would carry a large scar to remind him of his neglect; but then the soft brown fuzz appeared, and Tom knew his sole reminder would be that which he carried within himself. His only hope was that the colt wouldn't remember, and Tom's hours with him were spent in helping him to forget.

During the day, he was away from the colt only to attend to the chores his uncle and aunt had assigned to him. There were a thousand and more chickens about the farm, and Tom helped his uncle feed them and collect their eggs to be crated and sent to town. But when his work was done, he would follow the colt about the pasture, watching him roam inquisitively to the far corners of this new great and endless world that stretched before him. Only when the colt showed an interest in his presence and came to him would Tom run his hands over the furry brown coat and down the long legs. And in time the colt's visits became more frequent, for he knew he would find crushed oats in the boy's hand and there was always, too, the soft brush that felt so good on his body.

As Tom groomed him daily he noted the definite physical characteristics that were becoming more prominent in the colt. His eyes were clear and bold; his head was fine and delicate; and there were the straight knees and broad hocks, the shoulders which would be high and clean, and the chest with its good depth.

What Tom saw pleased him greatly, and he knew that Jimmy Creech would find many other fine qualities that would give evidence of the speed and stamina within this colt. For Tom was certain he would have the speed Jimmy sought; it was evident in his love of running about the pasture, urging the Queen to join him in his mad dashes across the green fields. Speed showed early in youngsters like him, and it was there plainly for Tom to see.

The colt's gait even now was long, low and sweeping. And when he ran, he usually carried his ears flat against his head, yet there was no viciousness in his nature.

Tom never tired of watching him, whether the colt was speeding about on lightning hoofs or emulating his mother by eating grass, which he now found much to his liking. He grazed with forelegs spread far apart and slightly bent to enable him to reach the ground.

Tom had heard from Jimmy Creech soon after he had written to him about the tight halter. "It's too bad it happened," Jimmy wrote, "but what's done is done, and cuts heal fast in youngsters like him. So I'm not worrying about that none. What bothers me more, Tom, is your uncle's throwing the colt. You say he won't do it again, and you must make sure he don't. You'd better have it out with him if he tries any more rough treatment. I won't stand for it, and I'm telling you not to, either. You wouldn't throw a year-old baby around to get him to do what you want, and the same thing goes for a colt. The use of force has no place in his training. Your uncle may not know it, but yanking a colt around or throwing him before he knows what is expected of him is liable to cause some slight injury to his spine or legs that will become worse in time and end up in the breakdown of a good racehorse. And, just as important, rough treatment can kill his will to win and his spirit. I'd just as soon have him dead as that.

"So you don't have to worry none about the cut on his nose, Tom. He'll pick up a lot more cuts before he's through. What you got to be concerned about, though, is your uncle. I know he means well, like you say, but I hope he won't take matters in his own hands again. You got to make sure he doesn't or I'll have to take the colt away from him. . . ."

But Uncle Wilmer never again attempted to handle the colt the way he thought best. And while he watched Tom and the colt very often, he offered neither advice nor criticism. Instead, he would lean upon the pasture fence as he did now, following the boy and colt with his eyes as they played together in the field. And he would wonder and be a little bewildered by the sight before him.

Breathing heavily, Tom stood about fifty feet away from the colt. He had been running with him for the past half-hour and was tired. He was ready to stop playing but the colt wasn't.

Long-legged and high-headed, the colt stood watching Tom and waiting. He waited for all of five minutes before moving, then he turned to look at the Queen, who was grazing, and back at the boy. Suddenly his ears swept back flat against his head, and he ran toward Tom. Five yards away, he swerved with the agility of a broken field runner and plunged past. Before coming to a stop, he flung his hind legs high in the air with reckless abandon.

Calling to him, Tom ran down the slight slope, passed the mare and, jumping the brook, set out across the fields. Behind him he heard the rhythmic beat of hoofs; then the colt sped by him swiftly, running a hundred yards or more ahead before coming to a stop and turning to face Tom.

But the boy was on his way again, running in another direction. With a snort, the colt went after him.

Uncle Wilmer watched until he saw Tom come to a halt and sit down upon the grass. The colt stopped too, but after a few moments he walked slowly over to the boy and shoved his nose into Tom's chest.

Shrugging his shoulders, Uncle Wilmer left the fence and walked toward the house. His face was twisted in thought. He was trying to understand Tom's strange way of training this colt. *No,* he decided, *it's Jimmy Creech's way. Jimmy Creech, whoever he is. Tom's doin' what Jimmy tells him to do. And why shouldn't he? It's Jimmy Creech's colt, ain't it? What do I care what he does? But I wouldn't do it that way.*

Reaching the gate, Uncle Wilmer opened it and went across the lawn.

"But some of these racing fellers make good money at it,"

he muttered. "You got to admit they ought to know what they're doin', all right."

Entering the house, Uncle Wilmer decided to dismiss the subject from his mind altogether. It made no difference to him how Tom handled the colt. None at all.

But it was less than an hour later when Uncle Wilmer returned to the pasture fence. He had tried to stay away and had made every effort to convince himself that he wasn't at all interested in what Tom was doing with the colt, but he hadn't succeeded. Although he had buried his head in the poultry section of the latest issue of the *Farm Journal,* he couldn't help hearing the occasional shouts by Tom and the high-pitched neighs of the colt. So finally he had put down his paper and left the house to return to the pasture.

He found Tom standing close to the fence, holding in his hand the new web halter he had bought a couple of days ago while in town.

"You goin' to put it on him now?" Uncle Wilmer asked.

Nodding, Tom lifted one foot to a rail of the fence and tightened the laces of the light sneakers he wore.

"You ought to wear heavier shoes," Uncle Wilmer said with concern. "He might step on your foot. He ain't so small any more." He glanced at the colt, who was grazing a short distance away from them.

"I can get around faster in these," Tom said.

"Heh?" Uncle Wilmer asked, cupping an ear.

"Faster!" Tom shouted, pointing to his sneakers.

Uncle Wilmer shook his head in wonder, and it was only when the boy turned to the colt that he asked, "You want any help?"

Tom turned to him, surprised not by the offer of assistance from his uncle, but by the note of eagerness in his voice. He tried to meet Uncle Wilmer's gaze, but the man would have none of it, for he had moved toward the chicken house.

"I can use your help a little later," Tom called to him.

Without turning, Uncle Wilmer said, "You call me, then. I got work to do."

Reaching the chicken house, Uncle Wilmer looked carefully over his shoulder until he could see Tom without being observed. He waited many minutes before turning completely around; then he sat down on the steps, well knowing that Tom would be too busy with the colt to notice him sitting there.

His eyes were grave with concern as he saw Tom go to the colt and kneel before him. After a while, he saw Tom raise the halter.

"He's goin' to have trouble," Uncle Wilmer mumbled. "He shoulda let me hold him. I could still do it, all right."

But Tom didn't raise the halter directly to the colt's head. Instead, Uncle Wilmer saw him run the halter over the colt's body as he handled him. After a long while, Tom moved the halter to the front of the colt, and Uncle Wilmer saw the colt reach for it, attempting to pull it from the boy's hand.

For all of a half-hour, Tom made no attempt to put the halter over the colt's head. Uncle Wilmer's interest in the proceedings had given way to restlessness and several times he thought of leaving and would rise to his feet. But always he would sit down again.

"What's he puttin' it off fer?" he asked himself aloud. "It ain't goin' to be no different no matter how long he waits.

He's goin' to need me to hold the colt in the end, all right."

His attention was diverted by the chickens that were clucking in their mad scramble to get inside to roost. The sky was darkening. It was getting late. He should be collecting the eggs instead of sitting here. He looked back at the pasture, and saw that Tom had placed the halter on the colt's ear. It dangled beside the small head until the colt shook it off. Uncle Wilmer shook his head sadly. What was Tom trying to do anyway? Why was he wasting all this time?

Finally Uncle Wilmer rose to his feet and started to enter the chicken house. Then he stopped and turned around. He'd better wait, for Tom would be needing him.

For many minutes he stood there. Suddenly his eyes narrowed and he looked with new interest at what was going on in the pasture. Tom held the halter in both hands now; he had moved even closer to the colt. He was going to put on the halter!

Uncle Wilmer waited for what he knew must happen. The colt would pull back, rear and twist away from Tom before the boy could buckle the strap about his head. Uncle Wilmer moved from the doorway, ready to go to Tom's assistance.

Tom had the colt's nose through the nose band; he was going to place the strap behind the pricked ears. Uncle Wilmer knew the boy would have trouble now, so he moved quickly toward the pasture fence. But he came to an abrupt stop, his eyes widening.

The strap was not buckled yet, but the colt stood quietly. The boy held the halter strap over the small head. He used his other hand to lift the buckle to the strap. The colt snorted as Tom fastened the buckle, but the boy stroked the furry neck. The halter was on and there had been no fight, no resistance by the colt.

Tom tested the halter with his hand. The nose band was loose, so there would be no recurrence of what had happened before. And the head strap, while not tight, was snug enough to prevent the colt from getting it over his head.

Tom rose from his kneeling position, and saw his uncle standing by the fence. The man's face was puzzled and Tom smiled as he walked toward him.

"Y'did it," Uncle Wilmer said when the boy reached him. "An' I didn't think you could."

"He knew it wouldn't hurt him," Tom said eagerly. "He just wants to know what you expect of him, that's all . . . that and to know you wouldn't do anything to hurt him." Tom had reached for the lead rope hanging on the fence, and was holding it in his hands when he finished talking.

"You ain't goin' to try leading him yet, are you?" Uncle Wilmer asked.

Tom moved toward the colt. "No," he said, "I won't try try leading him—not yet. He'll be leading me now."

The colt was beside the Queen, but moved away from her when he saw Tom approaching.

Tom waited for the colt to come to him, then ran his hands behind the small ears, finding spots he knew the colt enjoyed having rubbed. But at the same time he clipped the lead rope to the ring of the halter.

It was some time before the colt decided to return to his mother and moved away from Tom. But the boy walked with him, the rope swinging between them.

The colt's walk changed into a trot, but the rope remained

loose, for Tom's pace too had quickened. Reaching the Queen, the colt walked around her, still followed by Tom. The colt encircled his mother several times, eying curiously the rope stretched between him and the boy. Finally he stopped, standing close beside the Queen, and Tom waited, talking to him.

After a while, the colt moved away from the Queen again and Tom followed, still holding the lead rope. There were sudden spurts of speed as the colt trotted about, but always Tom managed to stay near enough so the rope never became taut. He didn't want to control the colt's movements now, for Jimmy Creech had written, "When you first try to lead him, let him go his own way, if he has a mind to. Don't fight him, just go along with him, until before long you'll find that you're guiding him and he's going along with you. You got to have patience."

Tom thought of Jimmy's words over and over again while he followed the colt to the left and to the right, back to the mare and away from her. Fortunately the colt neither ran his fastest nor strayed too far away from the Queen, and Tom was able to stay with him. Jimmy Creech was right when he said, "You got to have patience," but he should have said too, "You got to be fast." And Tom was thankful he was wearing his light sneakers.

The colt had returned to the mare to nurse when Tom first became conscious of the darkening sky. It was time to take them in from the pasture. He turned to the gate hoping to find his uncle there, and he was not disappointed.

He waited until the colt had finished nursing, then unclipped the rope from the halter, and led the Queen to the gate.

"You could help me now, Uncle Wilmer," he shouted. "I'd like you to lead the mare to the barn while I take the colt."

Nodding, Uncle Wilmer opened the gate while Tom held the Queen. The boy released her when his uncle had hold of her halter, and then turned to the colt. He snapped the rope on to the ring of the colt's halter.

Uncle Wilmer led the mare through the gate and walked toward the barn. The colt followed quickly in the shadow of his mother, while Tom walked beside him. On the way, Uncle Wilmer turned several times to look at them. And always there would be a wondering, almost incredulous light in his gray eyes when he saw the colt walking quietly beside Tom, and making no effort to break away.

The Fair

8

For a long while that night, Tom lay in bed reading a voluminous book entitled *The American Trotter*. He read again of the horses which had etched their names among the immortals of harness racing, the great sires and dams, and the stories of famous races. And he thought of the colt now sleeping beside the Queen, and wondered if some day he, too, would be recorded among the famed.

Finally he put the book to one side and reached for the copies of *Hoof Beats,* a racing magazine, which Jimmy Creech had been sending him. He found the June and July issues, but the copy for August was missing. He remembered having read it while in the kitchen the day before. He had probably left it there.

The radio was playing softly below and the kitchen lights were still on. Someone must be there, although he had heard no voices for some time.

Getting out of bed, Tom went down the stairs. His aunt wasn't there, but Uncle Wilmer sat reading in the big leather chair. He hadn't heard Tom.

Without moving, the boy stood in the doorway, his eyes on the August issue of *Hoof Beats,* which his uncle was reading so intently. Smiling, Tom was about to go back upstairs when his uncle raised his head. Seeing the boy, he quickly put *Hoof Beats* to one side and picked up his *Farm Journal.*

Tom was going up the stairs when his uncle called to him. "You can have it. It don't interest me none. I was jus' lookin' at the pictures." He buried his head in the *Farm Journal* and looked up again only as Tom's footsteps began ascending the stairs. "Your aunt will be throwin' it out, all right, if you leave it here," he shouted after the boy.

Tom continued up the stairs and climbed into bed once more. He put out his light and lay in the darkness. But it was a long time before he went to sleep, for the light from the kitchen came through the cracks in the floor of his room. Occasionally too, he heard his uncle turning pages, and the sound was not that of the light newsprint upon which the *Farm Journal* was printed, but the slick heavy-coated stock of *Hoof Beats.*

During the remaining weeks of August, Uncle Wilmer's interest in harness racing grew and his knowledge of the sport along with it. For Tom never failed to leave an issue of *Hoof Beats* in the kitchen, and in time he kept his book, *The American Trotter,* on the kitchen shelf. And although his uncle never admitted reading them, he made remarks that could be attributed only to them. But he spoke with the casualness that implied he had always known that "They'll have to go some to beat Greyhound's record for the mile of one fifty-five and a quarter. Greyhound is a big horse, Tom. You know that, don't you? Big all right—he stands sixteen hands one and a quarter inches at the withers."

Tom recalled his uncle's saying, the day the Queen arrived at the farm, that "the best ones are small"; but he hadn't reminded him. He didn't want to do anything to discourage Uncle Wilmer's new interest in harness racing. For not only did he enjoy talking to his uncle of records and bloodlines, but he needed his help while teaching the colt his first lessons.

It wasn't much that Uncle Wilmer had to do, but it was important. His job was to lead the mare about the paddock while Tom followed with the colt. The first few days, Uncle Wilmer had consented only grudgingly to help Tom, claiming he had "more important things to do than lead an old mare around in circles." But when Tom guided the colt first to the left of the Queen, then to the right of her, Uncle Wilmer stopped complaining and watched the boy with puzzled but interested eyes.

They spent several hours each day in the paddock while Tom taught the colt to respond obediently to the pressure of the halter against his head. He would bring him to a stop and let Uncle Wilmer lead the mare away from him. Then, talking to the colt, Tom would keep him where he was until he was ready to take him to his mother. At first the colt would want to run to her, but Tom carefully held him down to a walk.

It was tedious and trying work teaching the colt to obey Tom's every command. And during the long hours, Uncle Wilmer talked more and more of the racing records of such horses as Billy Direct, Spencer Scott, Titan Hanover and others, for he had memorized much of what he had read in

The American Trotter. And he discussed bloodlines with Tom while they walked endlessly about the paddock with the mare and colt. He liked the Queen's breeding. She had Guy Axworthy's blood in her. He didn't think you could ask for more than that. "And it was a good idea breeding the mare to the Black, too," he told Tom. "The outcross to his Arabian blood might really do something for this colt."

That had been Jimmy Creech's idea, Tom could have told him. But he didn't, for he had learned that the less he mentioned Jimmy's name to his uncle, the easier it was to get along with him.

Letters came frequently from Jimmy and George Snedecker. After leaving the Bedford Fair, they had gone on to Butler, Ebensburg, back to Carlisle, and then on to the Lebanon, Youngstown and Mercer fairs. Jimmy finished in the money at most of the fairs, but he never brought Symbol home to win. There were several pictures of him in the latest issue of *Hoof Beats,* and Uncle Wilmer studied them critically.

"He's gettin' on," Uncle Wilmer said in a surprised tone. "Must be my age, all right."

"So are a good many of the others," Tom said. "Some of the best drivers are old men."

"Not *old men,*" Uncle Wilmer answered a little fiercely. "Just gettin' on. We can keep up with any of the young'uns, all right."

From that day, it seemed to Tom that Uncle Wilmer's attitude toward Jimmy Creech changed considerably. Once he even went so far as to claim that Jimmy Creech was "responsible for the good looks of the colt. It was him who bred the mare to the Black. He knew what he was doin', all right."

The first week of September approached and with it came the fair at Reading, just fourteen miles from the farm. Tom listened to his uncle and aunt discuss the many reasons why they couldn't afford to go this year; yet he knew that nothing would keep them from attending it. They hadn't missed one in the past forty-three years; Uncle Wilmer had told him that much. And Tom knew too of Aunt Emma's crock of mincemeat that had been standing for three months in the cellar. Aunt Emma was famous for her mincemeat pies, and certainly she would have one in the pie-judging contest this year as in previous years. The entry applications had arrived a week ago, and they had been signed and returned by Aunt Emma. Tom knew that, even if Uncle Wilmer didn't. And Aunt Emma's pie wouldn't be at the fair without Aunt Emma.

Monday was the first day of the fair and Aunt Emma and Uncle Wilmer were very definite about not going this year. "We always spend too much money," Aunt Emma said. "And when you've seen one fair you've seen them all."

Uncle Wilmer nodded his egg-shaped head in agreement.

On Tuesday, Aunt Emma went down to the cellar to taste her mincemeat. Returning to the kitchen, she looked for the program of activities at the fair which had come in the mail. She found it on the porch in her husband's hand. He was telling Tom, "Looks like they'll have some good races on Wednesday and Thursday, all right."

Aunt Emma took the program from him, read it quickly, then said quietly, "Thursday is pie-judging day."

"Heh?" Uncle Wilmer cupped his ear.

"Thursday," Tom shouted for his aunt. "It's the day they judge pies."

Uncle Wilmer took back the program, studied it, then said, "Thursday's races are better'n Wednesday's."

"I just might have some mincemeat down cellar," Aunt Emma said. "Wouldn't do no harm to try to—"

"Heh?"

But Aunt Emma said nothing, and Tom knew there was no need to tell his uncle about the mincemeat in the cellar.

"We really shouldn't go," Aunt Emma said loudly to her husband.

"Darn right," he returned. "We saw it last year—" He stopped suddenly, his head turning in Tom's direction.

And then the boy was conscious too of Aunt Emma's gaze upon him.

"But Tom didn't see it last year," Uncle Wilmer said.

"No, he didn't," Aunt Emma said, nodding her head in agreement.

"We oughta go for him. That's what we oughta do, all right."

"We certainly should," Aunt Emma said. "'Specially since he'll be goin' home soon. He ought to see the fair before he goes home."

The smile left Uncle Wilmer's face. "Tom goin' home? When?" He turned to the boy.

"Jimmy said he'd pick the mare and colt up soon now. I'm going back with him. I have to be back at school in two weeks," Tom said.

"I hadn't thought of your goin' yet," Uncle Wilmer said quietly. "Seems you only jus' got here."

Aunt Emma turned upon her husband. "What have you been thinkin' about, Wilmer! You know well enough he has to go to school!"

"Sure, I know it!" Uncle Wilmer returned defiantly. But

then his gaze fell. "I guess the summer's just about gone, all right. I guess it is. That always comes with the fair, too."

"Time goes awfully fast," Tom said. "It seems to me I just got here, too, But the colt is over two months old now. Uncle Wilmer. Even that's hard to believe."

When Tom left the porch after it had been agreed to go to the fair on Thursday for his benefit, Uncle Wilmer joined him.

"Where you goin'?"

"To the mailbox. I thought there might be a letter from Jimmy."

"I don't suppose he'd be racin' at the fair."

"He didn't say anything about it in his last letter. He was at the Mercer Fair then; that's a couple of hundred miles from here."

"That's purty far, all right. Guess he wouldn't come."

They walked to the mailbox together and found Jimmy Creech's letter. As Tom opened the envelope, Uncle Wilmer made it plain he was definitely interested in its contents. "Read it aloud, Tom," he said. "Good and loud."

"The season is just about over for George and me," Tom read. "We decided we'd kill two birds with one stone by racing at Reading, then pick up you and the mare and colt and come home."

Tom stopped reading and turned excitedly to his uncle. "You hear that? He's coming to Reading!"

Uncle Wilmer nodded his head vigorously.

"I entered Symbol in a race on Thursday; that's the day we'll get there," Jimmy wrote.

Tom stopped reading again to shout, "Thursday, that's our day!"

"We'll be there Thursday, all right," Uncle Wilmer said.

Tom turned back to the letter and continued reading aloud: "We'll go back to Coronet on Friday, and you can come back with us, if you want to—"

"What's he mean, 'if you want to'?" Uncle Wilmer interrupted. "When that colt goes you go, too. You belong with him, all right." But he didn't meet Tom's gaze when the boy turned to him. "What else he say?" Uncle Wilmer asked without raising his eyes.

"We got the picture you sent of the colt," Tom continued reading, "and he sure looks like everything you've written about him. George and I can hardly wait to see him in the flesh. Glad to learn everything has worked out so well with your uncle."

Tom glanced at Uncle Wilmer. "I told him you've been a big help to me," he said.

"That the end?" Uncle Wilmer asked.

"That's all, except he says he'd like to meet you," Tom replied, folding the letter.

Uncle Wilmer said nothing until they were well on their way down the hill. "I'd like to meet him, too, all right," he said.

"You will," Tom returned, "at the fair—Thursday."

Although it was only a little past eight o'clock, the traffic was heavy as they approached the fairgrounds Thursday morning. Tom sat in the front seat beside Uncle Wilmer, who had a firm, deathlike grasp on the wheel and whose body swung with his old car as he weaved it in, out, and around the other cars. Tom found himself moving with his uncle, gauging distances between cars and wondering if they were ever going to get to the fair at all. In the back, sitting in the middle of the seat, Aunt Emma held her carefully wrapped mincemeat pie and never said a word.

Tom relaxed a little when he saw the flags of the fairgrounds just ahead. Attendants of the parking lots solicited Uncle Wilmer's patronage by waving and shouting, but Uncle Wilmer kept his foot on the gas. "No need to pay those fellers," he said. "I know my way around, all right."

Two blocks from the main entrance to the fairgrounds, Uncle Wilmer swerved recklessly across the highway, bringing the oncoming traffic to a screeching stop. The drivers of the other cars shouted angrily at Uncle Wilmer. But unmindful of their critical blasts, Uncle Wilmer turned down a side street, where there was no traffic ahead of them.

Tom settled back in his seat, certain his uncle knew where he was going. A few minutes from now and they'd be inside. It seemed a very long time since they had gotten up. And it was, when he figured it out. Uncle Wilmer had awakened him at four o'clock to help with the chores, and Aunt Emma had been up even earlier getting ready. The mare and colt were in the paddock with free access to their stall and a rack full of hay. They'd be all right until he returned to the farm; and Jimmy and George would be with him to see their colt for the first time. And tomorrow? Tom faced tomorrow with mixed emotions. He'd miss his uncle and aunt, and life on the farm. But there was much to look forward to as well, for before very long the colt's real schooling and training for the track would begin. While he'd never have been able to do this by himself, he could watch Jimmy Creech, helping him while he brought the colt along and learning a great deal.

Tom felt that he had done the job Jimmy had expected of

him, for the colt could be handled and had complete confidence in human beings, which was what Jimmy wanted. And while his task in the months to come would be that of assistant to Jimmy Creech instead of having the colt all to himself, it was the way it should be. For the colt's professional life was about to begin and he would have a part of it. He'd learn with his colt. And who knew what the future would bring them?

Uncle Wilmer drove his old car down many residential side streets, and at last found a spot to park just a block from the main entrance to the fairgrounds. "Like I said," he mumbled when they left the car, "there's no sense in payin' those fellers. Not when you been comin' to the fair for forty-three years."

Walking to the main gate, Aunt Emma handed her pie to Tom while she straightened her good gray dress and the black straw hat that was trimmed gaily with white flowers. Uncle Wilmer, too, fixed himself up by buttoning the collar of his blue shirt and drawing up his tie. He wore his new gray hat, but like his everyday hat, it was much too small and sat high on top of his head.

Reaching the gate, Uncle Wilmer stopped Tom from paying his own way and struggled with his big change purse until he had enough money out of it to purchase the tickets.

In the early-morning sun, they walked down the already crowded avenues of the fair. Tom could feel the fair as well as see it. He had forgotten the smells, the sounds and the excitement of a fair. And now they all burst upon him—the throaty bellowing of the brown-and-white Hereford cows from the nearest open sheds, the sweet fragrance of freshly cut flowers coming from a Grange building as they passed its doors, and all about them the farm people, so much like his aunt and uncle, as eager and excited as they were.

Yet, unlike the other people who streamed in and out of the exhibits housed in the long, low buildings on each side of the avenue, his uncle and aunt never slackened their pace and cast only a quick glance into the doorways of each building while hastening by. They seemed to know where they wanted to go, and Tom followed, as anxious as they were, to get to his destination, which was the racetrack. In and out of the crowd they wound with Aunt Emma leading the way. Hawkers shouted their wares to them from small booths along the way; and even though it was early, the odor of caramel-treated popcorn balls filled the air, and fluffy cotton candy of red and white was waved in Tom's face as he hurried to keep up with his uncle and aunt.

Finally his aunt came to a stop before a building through the doorways of which wafted the spicy smells of pastry of all kinds. She turned to her husband. "I'll meet you right here, Wilmer, at four o'clock." Even before finishing her sentence she had turned toward the door again, the pie held carefully in her hands.

"Heh, Emma?" Uncle Wilmer cupped an ear.

She turned upon him, and Tom saw the irritable look on her face. "I'll tell him, Aunt Emma," he said quickly.

Nodding, she smiled tightly, and Tom knew there would be no relaxing for his aunt until the pie contest was over. She was on her way through the door, when suddenly she stopped to turn to Tom once more. "You bring your friends to supper, mind you, Tom. Won't be no trouble at all. The makings are ready."

Tom hurried to catch up to his uncle. There was no need

to ask him where he was going, for ahead and towering above the low exhibit buildings was the high-tiered grandstand of the racetrack. For a farmer, Uncle Wilmer showed only mild interest in the long rows of open sheds which housed the pedigreed cattle—the black-and-white Holstein cows, all with red and blue prize ribbons hanging proudly above them; neither did he stop when they passed the sleek black Angus steers, nor at the goat shed. Instead he made directly for the grandstand, and his eyes left it only for the flags flying over its red roof. "Time to see the cattle is later," he told Tom. "Right now they're working the horses, gettin' 'em ready for the races this afternoon."

Tom needed no urging.

They walked behind the grandstand toward the entrance to the paddock, through which the horses passed on their way from the stables to the track. "I always go there," Uncle Wilmer said. "You see more what's goin' on."

"I'd better go to the stables first," Tom said. "I want to find Jimmy."

"You think he's here now?"

"I'm sure of it," Tom replied.

They passed the grandstand and came to the bleachers. And now through the wire-mesh fence they could see the horses on the track. Just a short distance beyond was the paddock entrance and a little farther on were the long rows of stables.

Their paces quickened to the sound of hoofs on the track and the shrill neighs from the stables. Through the paddock gate passed sleek animals, pulling their light, two-wheeled racing sulkies behind them. Those going onto the track were charged with energy and their drivers guided them carefully past the sweated horses coming off the track from their morning workouts.

At the gate, Uncle Wilmer came to an abrupt stop. "Look'ut the roan mare, Tom. Just look at her! And that dark bay mare comin' off the track. She could be the Queen!" Excitedly, Uncle Wilmer passed through the gate and made for the rail, where grooms and drivers stood watching the horses as they went through their workouts.

Tom watched while his uncle secured a place at the rail, then he turned toward the stables, where he'd find Jimmy Creech. But he stopped suddenly, looking back once more at his uncle and then at the man standing next to him. That bald head, unprotected against the sun, and the blue coveralls could belong only to George Snedecker! And if it was George, Jimmy Creech was out on the track working Symbol!

Carefully, Tom made his way around the horses, loving their nearness, and wanting so much to be one of these hardened men who sat so casually and expertly close behind powerful hindquarters. Such men and horses were as much a part of a fair as the cows and steers and chickens—and Aunt Emma's mincemeat pie! It was a life Tom wanted very much to live.

Nearing the rail, he stopped a few feet behind the man he thought to be George Snedecker. Uncle Wilmer had turned to the man and Tom heard him say, "I got a good colt back at my farm, a darn good one. From the looks of him he'll go all right."

The man turned toward Uncle Wilmer, and Tom saw his face, tanned heavily by the sun. One stride of Tom's long legs took him to the man's shoulder. "And don't you think he's kidding, George!" he said.

George Snedecker threw an arm around Tom, while Uncle Wilmer stood watching them sheepishly. Now George pushed Tom an arm's length away. Shifting his chaw of tobacco, he said, "You put on weight, Tom. You're not such a tall bag of bones any more."

"My aunt's cooking did it," Tom said, turning to Uncle Wilmer. "And this is my uncle. He was telling you about *his* colt."

"Heh?" Uncle Wilmer asked, while George Snedecker clasped his hand.

"Looks like a good many people got an interest in that colt." George smiled. "He really looks good to you, Tom?"

"He does to me," Tom replied. "Wait'll you see him."

"We're lookin' forward to it," George said; then he added, "Here's Jimmy comin' around now off the backstretch."

Uncle Wilmer heard George, for he too turned to look at the track.

Jimmy Creech brought Symbol around the turn at a fast rate of speed.

"He's brushin' him this last quarter," George said. "Got the watch on him."

Off the turn came Symbol, his head stretched out, his legs working hard. Jimmy Creech held the reins high, urging Symbol to greater speed. They swept past the paddock rail, past the bleachers, and it wasn't until Symbol had gone by the judges' booth opposite the center of the grandstand that Jimmy moved back in his sulky seat. Tom's eyes had never left them.

"What do you think of Symbol?" George asked.

"Jimmy has done a lot with him, but he's too rough

gaited. He works hard but doesn't stretch out. And he'll break when the going gets tough. It's a wonder Jimmy has done as well as he has with him."

"You sure don't generalize, Tom," George said. "You never did." Pausing, he spat his tobacco juice on the ground. "All you say is true about Symbol."

"Does Jimmy know it?"

"Sure. He knew that the first time he worked him last year. But Symbol takes him to the races and he's certain of place money here and there. Call it old-age security, if you like." George smiled.

"But now he has the colt," Tom said.

"Yep," George agreed, "and I'm hoping the colt will help Jimmy more than the medicine he's been taking."

"I thought he was feeling better."

"He was," George returned, "up until a few weeks ago, then his stomach started acting up again. Maybe you could call it 'end-of-the-season jitters.' I don't know. Jimmy calls it indigestion. I don't wonder he's got stomach trouble. Never eats a decent meal during the day; it's always a quick hamburger, hot dog and a bottle of soda pop at a stand. Good hot meals are what he needs as much as anything, I think."

"I was hoping he'd be feeling well," Tom said quietly. "Maybe seeing the colt will change things," he added hopefully.

"Maybe so, Tom. But don't expect too much from him. It takes a long time to understand Jimmy Creech. Took me the fifty years I've known him." George spat on the ground again. "Looks like it was a mistake comin' to this fair, too. There are too many young fellers like that guy"—George nodded his head toward a man driving a dark chestnut stallion with light mane and tail—"and Jimmy doesn't like those young fellers. He says they take too many chances. That's a laugh, when I think of some of the races Jimmy drove years ago." He turned to Tom. "But he's sick, Tom, so let's just you and me go along with him and be patient. He'll come out of it."

Uncle Wilmer touched Tom's arm. "Here comes Jimmy," he said and there was a definite note of eagerness in his voice.

Jimmy neared the track gate and as Tom studied the thin, frail body he could tell that Jimmy hadn't gained a pound during the summer. His face was tanned, but there was a strange brightness in his eyes that Tom didn't like. From all appearances it looked as though George was right. He walked to the gate behind George, while Uncle Wilmer followed.

George unhooked the check rein that kept Symbol's head up and shouted to Jimmy, "Here's someone to see you!"

Holding the lines, Jimmy slid from the sulky seat and gripped Tom's outstretched hand warmly. "Good seeing you, Tom," he said. "Let's get over to the stable where we'll have some quiet."

Jimmy walked beside Symbol while George led the horse out the paddock gate. And as Tom walked with him he noticed that Jimmy ignored the greetings of many who called to him. That, he knew, wasn't like Jimmy.

Uncle Wilmer was with them and Jimmy had greeted him cordially. On the way to the stables Uncle Wilmer did most of the talking, telling Jimmy of some of the races he had seen at this fair twenty to thirty years ago. Jimmy pushed his soiled red-and-white sulky cap back on his head and listened to Uncle Wilmer while they walked along. Uncle Wilmer needed no more encouragement than that to continue his stories.

Tom's gaze moved over all three of them. They had much in common, he thought, being of the same generation. Physically they were much alike too, except that Jimmy was small-boned and very thin compared to stocky George and Uncle Wilmer. Temperamentally, though, they were very different. He couldn't imagine anything disturbing George or Uncle Wilmer from their placid, regular way of life. But Jimmy was as highly strung as any colt and his emotions would vary from day to day and from hour to hour.

"Is the colt as good as his picture, Tom?" Jimmy asked suddenly, turning to him.

"Better." Tom smiled. "And you'll probably see even more in him than I do."

"I hope so," Jimmy said, and eager anticipation came to his hazel eyes with the speed of a camera shutter. "I sure hope so. I'd like to have a great one before—" He stopped abruptly and the enthusiasm left his eyes. "If only it didn't take so long."

"It's not so long, Jimmy," Tom said earnestly. "A little more than a year from now and we'll be getting him ready to go."

Jimmy Creech smiled grimly, saying, "Sure, Tom, I know. Maybe we can do it."

Reaching the stables, they went down the long shed row until they came to Symbol's stall. With all four men working on Symbol, they had his harness off, the sulky put away, and the horse washed in a matter of a few minutes. After Symbol had been walked by George and Tom, they put him in his stall; then they all sat in the chairs and talked.

For a long while Jimmy was cheerful, telling of the fairs where he and George had raced; then Tom noticed that his gaze turned more and more often to the brightly colored awnings set up in front of some of the other stables, and to the neatly arranged piles of fine blankets, the well-oiled and expensive harness, the water heaters and tack trunks and sulkies and training carts and spare wheels—all freshly painted and expensive. Then Jimmy's gaze would sweep back to their seats in the sun, to his one sulky and little tack; and once he removed his racing cap and looked at it. Tom noticed for the first time how soiled it was.

"Sure getting to be a fancy business," Jimmy said finally, and there was much bitterness in his voice. Tom and Uncle Wilmer turned to him, but George kept his gaze focused on the ground and chewed his tobacco.

"Look at that van. How'd you like to travel in that, George?" Jimmy indicated a large green-and-white-painted van that had the picture of a horse's head drawn on its side. Beneath it was lettered: *Ray O'Neil's Stables*—ROOSEVELT RACEWAY—*Westbury, Long Island.*

"It wouldn't be much different from riding in Sadie." George grinned, pointing to the dilapidated Ford horse van that was parked in front of them. "Sadie gets us there. That's all we want."

"But George, they have sleeping quarters in that one," Jimmy said sarcastically. "And maybe a kitchen, too."

"Nothin' wrong with sleepin' in a spare stall," George replied. "Been good enough for me for a long time now."

"Yes, but things have changed, George," Jimmy said even more bitterly. "Harness racing is big-time now. They got night raceways just outside of about every big city. They don't need the fairs no more—or people like us," he added slowly.

"Cut it, Jimmy," George said a little angrily.

But Jimmy Creech only turned to Uncle Wilmer and continued, "You wanta know why this guy Ray O'Neil who owns that fancy van came out to Reading Fair this week instead of staying at Roosevelt night raceway?"

Uncle Wilmer pulled his chair closer to Jimmy Creech, his eyes never leaving the man's lips.

"Wanted to get some sun, that's all," Jimmy said. "That's why he's here." He laughed loudly. "Take a day off and get some sun at a fair for him and his horses."

"You're not being square, Jimmy," George interrupted. "They live one life at night raceways and we live another at the fairs. But it's all harness racing. This Ray O'Neil is a good driver from all I heard. He topped 'em all at the raceways last year."

"Young squirt," Jimmy said. "He can't drive. Why, I—" Jimmy's hand went suddenly to his stomach and his face was white beneath the dark tan. It lasted only a few seconds, and when the pain had gone, Jimmy spat the chewing gum out of his mouth and opened another stick of gum. "Indigestion," he said casually, conscious of the anxious eyes upon him.

"Stop getting yourself all excited about the raceways and guys like Ray O'Neil an' you'll be all right," George said.

But Uncle Wilmer didn't let the subject drop. "No young feller ever could hold the lines as well as us old-timers," he told Jimmy. "You're sure right about that. It takes age, and that's what young fellers ain't got. You'll show this Ray O'Neil this afternoon, Jimmy. You'll show him, all right."

"He'll have his chance," George said. "O'Neil is in the first race, and that's our race, too."

"Jimmy'll show him, all right," Uncle Wilmer said again. "He sure will."

And it was only then that Tom was able to change the subject. But he was worried about Jimmy, more worried than ever before. Jimmy wasn't in any condition to race.

Racing Wheels

9

"Good afternoon, ladies and gentlemen," the announcer said over the public-address system. "Welcome to the races at Reading Fair." Pausing, he waited a moment while the huge throng in the grandstand and bleachers turned its attention to him. "It's another beautiful day and as usual your fair committee has arranged another fine day of racing. We've had some stirring races every day this week and I'm certain today will be no exception. It's two o'clock and the horses are now leaving the paddock for the post parade of the first race on your program."

While the eyes of the crowd turned to the horses and the drivers dressed in their colorful silks, the announcer continued, "For your information, this race is restricted to horses having won one thousand dollars or more but less than twelve hundred dollars during their racing careers. And now here they come down for the post parade, ladies and gentlemen. Your attention, please, while I introduce horses and drivers according to post position, reading from the top of your program down. Number one, who will race in the pole position, is Sandy Hanover, a gray horse by Spencer out of Jean Hanover; owned by Mr. Leo Hofeller of Butler, Pennsylvania, and being driven by professional reinsman Roy Moyer. Number two is Princess Holly, a dark bay mare by His Excellency out of . . ."

The people stopped reading their programs to take a quick look at each horse and driver as he was introduced while filing past the judges' stand. Beyond the stand, the track infield lay green and beautiful in the sun. Across the backstretch of the half-mile track were the red carnival cars of the fair's midway, while high above them circled a Ferris wheel, its silver paint glistening as it caught the sun's rays.

"And in number six position," the announcer was saying, "is Crusader, a dark chestnut horse by the very famous stallion, Volomite, and out of Lady Luck; owned by Mr. C. H. West of New York City, and driven by the leading driver of the night raceways, Ray O'Neil.

"Number seven, racing on the outside position, is Symbol, a black gelding by Direct Hollyrood and out of Mary K; owned and driven by Mr. Jimmy Creech of Coronet, Pennsylvania." He paused, while Jimmy Creech, the last in the parade to pass the booth, tipped his red-and-white cap to the crowd. "The horses will take two warm-up scores in front of the grandstand and then face the starter."

The drivers released their horses from prancing walks and moved quickly down the track to the first turn. There they stopped and then came back past the grandstand. Reaching the bleachers, they turned cautiously to avoid one another's sulky wheels and horses and went down the stretch once more, moving faster now. Each repeated this fast scoring warm-up, then filed around the turn and down the back-stretch, ready to come in behind the mobile starting gate awaiting them just off the back turn.

"Your attention, please, ladies and gentlemen," the announcer said. "For those of you who have never had the opportunity of watching the mobile starting gate in action, I'd like to explain briefly how it works. Our starter, Mr. George Reed, is riding in the back of that open convertible you see awaiting the horses just off the turn out there. You will notice the long poles to each side of the rear of the car and extending across the track. Behind these 'wings,' as we call them, the horses will come into their post positions. Mr. Reed will have his driver start the car moving away from the horses as they come up behind the 'wings' of the starting gate. By means of a microphone which is about his neck, and a loudspeaker at the rear of the car, he is able to instruct the drivers as to their position, conduct and speed while they all come down toward the starting line. He will bring them down the stretch, slowly at first, then faster as they approach the starting line directly in front of this booth. He will keep them together until he sends them off; the 'wings' of the mobile starter will swing away from the horses as they cross the starting line, and Mr. Reed will pull away from them and around the track. The race will then be on, ladies and gentlemen. The horses are now fanning out as they round the back turn and move toward the starter. This is the first heat of the first race on your program; the race will be for the best out of three heats and the second heat will take place just about one hour from now. Keep your eyes on the starter and the horses, ladies and gentlemen. They're coming behind the gate, and Mr. Reed is moving away from them."

Tom, his fists clenched around the paddock rail, stood beside George, and the skin over his knuckles tightened until it was white as he saw Jimmy take Symbol to the outside position close beside Ray O'Neil, driving Crusader. "Does Jimmy know how to get away behind these mobile starting gates, George?" he asked tensely.

"They had one at the York Fair; that's the only time he's been behind one," George replied. "He did all right. It doesn't take Jimmy long to learn anything. But he hates 'em," he added, "—just like he does anything else that's different from what it was forty years ago. Modern, silly gadgets, he calls 'em."

"But these mobile starters get the horses away better," Tom said, "and faster, too. The old way, when they come down to the starting line by themselves, they're usually never together and are called back to start all over again. This mobile gate makes certain they get off the first time. It's easier on everyone, it seems to me—the horses, drivers and the people watching. They know the race is on when they come down now."

"Sure, I know," George said. "But like I said, Jimmy don't like any changes. He likes to keep the sport the way it was. Some of his criticisms of this mobile gate are good, too. He says the horses don't like those 'wings' and the car in front of 'em; and then the wheels of the car usually throw dust in their faces. Yep, there's a lot to what Jimmy says. But here they come now. Watch 'em, Tom."

The horses were in position, pushing their heads toward the barrier in front of them as the car moved away, increasing its speed. Jimmy's face was taut, and Tom saw him bring Symbol ever closer to Crusader. Ray O'Neil glanced at

Jimmy but said nothing; yet he kept his position, and their spinning wire wheels were dangerously close.

George Snedecker's hand left the rail to rest on Tom's arm as their gazes followed the pounding horses, going ever faster down the stretch toward the starting line.

"Don't come any faster, gentlemen," they heard the starter warn the drivers. "Keep your horses back. Don't charge the gate! Hold your positions now. Not so fast on the outside there. Mr. Creech, keep your horse back! Mr. Creech, don't crowd Mr. O'Neil! All right now. Keep it that way! We're coming down. GO!"

Tom and George leaned far over the rail as the crowd yelled to the quick thunder of unleashed hoofs. The line of horses drove as one down the stretch for the turn. The silks of the drivers blended into a large indistinct mass of colors as they bunched, moving toward the rail. For a second, Tom could make out Jimmy's red-and-white silks, then he, too, moved toward the inside; a flash of green went with him and Tom knew Ray O'Neil and Crusader were going with him in an attempt to reach the turn first. He could make out nothing now of what was happening; he'd have to wait until they came around the first turn.

George muttered, "Symbol's got the early speed. Jimmy might get away with it. But he's takin' a chance—a big chance."

Suddenly, from the top tiers of the grandstand, came a sharp cry. From the moving mass on the turn, a horse swerved abruptly toward the outside rail and behind him careened the sulky with its driver trying desperately to stay in it and stop his horse at the same time.

The announcer's voice came quickly over the public

speaker. "Accident! Left wheel of sulky broken! It's number seven; Mr. Creech's entry. But there's no danger. He's stopping his horse. Will Mr. Creech's groom go to his assistance, please! Keep him on the outside of the track, there's a race going on! And now going in to the backstretch we have Crusader on top, followed by Sandy Hanover and tucked in the third position is . . ."

George and Tom had jumped the rail and were running down the track past the grandstand. Jimmy was off the broken sulky and was standing at Symbol's head, awaiting them.

"I didn't think he could get around all of 'em," George said. "He shouldn't have tried."

"Crusader went up with him," Tom said.

"Yeah, it could have been O'Neil who did it to him," George said. "Crusader is fast at the break and O'Neil is no dumb bunny—even though he is a lot younger'n Jimmy. Jimmy probably thought he could force him back, and he got the worst of it." They were only a few yards away from Jimmy now, and George added, "He's goin' to be mad. Careful what you say, Tom. Let him do the talkin.' "

Jimmy's face was filled with rage. But he said nothing when they joined him, only nodding toward the wheel, which was smashed beyond repair. George lifted the sulky's axle off the ground, and they moved up the outside of the track, with Tom leading Symbol while Jimmy walked beside him.

They were passing the grandstand when the horses came down the stretch for their first trip around the track; they had one more lap to go for the mile distance and the finish of the race.

"Crusader with Ray O'Neil three lengths on top at the half," the announcer said. "Princess Holly closing fast on Sandy Hanover. Flash Count is coming up on the outside. He's moving fast! Here they come!"

As the horses passed them, Jimmy Creech glanced only at Crusader, leading the way. He muttered something to himself, but said nothing to Tom. When they reached the bleachers, the attention of the crowd was focused on the race now being staged on the backstretch, but a few people turned to Jimmy and clapped lightly, attempting to let him know they shared his misfortune. Jimmy touched the peak of his cap, but Tom noticed his face redden and realized the people's applause had served only to make him more angry. Jimmy needed a rest, a long rest. He was sick mentally and physically. The immediate future was going to be hard on all of them, Tom knew, for there was no telling what Jimmy would do in his present state. And there was the colt to think about. He wouldn't want anything to happen to the colt or the Queen.

They were leaving the paddock gate when the horses entered the homestretch for the finish of the race. Turning, Tom saw that Ray O'Neil had Crusader five lengths in the lead. The sound of hoofs died beneath the roar of the crowd as the race ended; then the announcer's voice came clearly to them, "First, Crusader; second, Princess Holly; third, Flash Count; fourth . . ."

Jimmy Creech, his head down, gave no evidence of having heard the results.

It was well after four o'clock when they left the fair for the farm. Jimmy sat beside Uncle Wilmer; Tom and George were in the back with Aunt Emma, who once more held her mincemeat pie, minus three pieces which the contest judges had eaten. Tom hadn't asked her how she'd made out. He didn't have to ask; he had only to look at that sober, lined face and he thought he knew. That's why he was so surprised when he saw the red ribbon tucked away in Aunt Emma's pocketbook when she opened it to get her handkerchief. "Y–You—you won a prize!" he said in amazement.

His aunt shrugged her shoulders, and turned again to look out the window of the car. "Only second," she said. Tom thought she had finished until he heard her mumble half to herself, "To think they gave first prize to Mrs. Yoder." She snorted. "Young enough to be my *granddaughter*." Aunt Emma snorted again, then was silent.

Uncle Wilmer was the only one who cared to do any talking, and he couldn't say much now that he was driving through Reading's downtown traffic. Even George was alone with his thoughts. Tom sat back in his seat and thought bitterly, *A great day at the fair! Everyone feels swell for it. Sure. Jimmy and Aunt Emma are angry because younger people did something better than they did. George is worried about Jimmy, and I'm worried about Jimmy, the Queen and the colt. But perhaps Jimmy will snap out of it; he's had spells like this before. He'll be able to take it easy now that the racing season is over and he can go back to Coronet.*

George told me, Tom continued thinking, *that a good hot meal tonight and seeing the colt will make Jimmy see things in a different light. With Aunt Emma's cooking, Jimmy is certain to have the best of meals. And when he sees the colt he'll know he's the best, too. But it's funny that Jimmy shows such resentment toward anything new in harness racing, especially the night raceways and the men who race there. This Ray O'Neil seems to be a very nice guy, and he's not so young as Jimmy makes him out to be. He's in his thirties. Jimmy was driving at that age. But he doesn't think of that, not Jimmy. And O'Neil can drive, there's no doubt about that. He hadn't let Jimmy force him back, and had gone on to win. Then, after the heat he'd been nice enough to come around to offer Jimmy a spare wheel to use in the second heat of the race when he heard Jimmy didn't have one. But Jimmy had given him a curt refusal, and said he was withdrawing from the race. That's what Jimmy had done. He hadn't even gone out for the second heat. And that wasn't like the old Jimmy, either—to quit a race.*

"What's the color of the colt, Tom?"

It was Jimmy's voice and Tom lifted his gaze to find the man turned around in his seat, looking at him. "He's a bay, Jimmy," Tom said. "Black mane and tail, what there are of them now," he added, smiling. "But it's hard for me to tell what shade of bay he's going to be, because he's still covered with furry baby hair. Maybe you'll know. But it doesn't look as though he's going to be that dark mahogany brown like the Queen. I think he's going to be lighter, much lighter, maybe even a red bay."

"You mean a blood bay," Jimmy corrected.

"Same thing," George interrupted. "Red or blood bay."

"But blood bay is better," Jimmy said. "I've never had a blood bay before," he added quickly, and a sudden, eager light came into his eyes. "You like him, Tom? You see nothing wrong?"

Tom responded fast to Jimmy's enthusiasm. "He looks wonderful to me, Jimmy. But I'm not—"

"You got a good head for horses," Jimmy said. "If you say he looks good, he'll look good to me, too."

"And Jimmy's not foolin'," George said.

Tom turned to George Snedecker and saw the relief in his face too at Jimmy's interest and sudden enthusiasm. *That's Jimmy for you,* Tom thought; *on again, off again;* but this man so interested in his blood bay colt was the real Jimmy.

Less than a half-hour after leaving the fair, they turned down the lane leading to the farm. While the car careened over the rocky route and all of them bounced hard on the springless seats, Jimmy said, laughing, "Y'ought to get a new car, Wilmer, or build a new road!"

"Heh?" Uncle Wilmer asked.

But Jimmy didn't repeat his statement; instead he turned to George. "We'll see him in a minute, won't we, George?"

"Sure will, Jimmy."

They emerged from the woods and the barn was ahead of them. As they crossed the brook, the Queen came from her stall and into the paddock at the sound of the car. She raised her head, whinnying to them. From inside the stall, the colt echoed her whinny. As they stopped the car, there was a rustle of straw from the stall, and Tom said, "I'll bet he was down, sleeping."

Jimmy was out of the car first and went to the mare. But no sooner had he reached her than the colt came bolting out of the stall, head high, ears pricked, eyes searching, and seemingly covered completely by straw entwined in his coat. He had been down, all right.

Tom climbed through the rails of the paddock fence to go to him, but Jimmy and George stood still, content at first to look at the colt from a distance.

Quickly the colt came to Tom, nuzzling his hands and pockets, while the boy talked to him and ran his hands over the hard body, removing the straw. Then he scratched him on the spots he knew the colt liked best. For a long while Jimmy and George just stood there studying the colt. And the colt turned his large, wondering eyes toward them, trying to figure them out, too.

Finally Tom took him by the halter and led him away from the Queen and to the far side of the paddock and back. He did it, he told himself, so Jimmy and George could see the colt's beautiful walk, as light as though he could step on eggshells without cracking them. But Tom knew well enough he had another reason for leading the colt around as he was doing. He wanted Jimmy to see that he had done a good job, the job Jimmy had expected of him.

Jimmy noticed, for he said, when they approached him at the fence, "You did it, Tom. We won't be havin' any trouble with him."

"And he's what you said about him," George added.

"Is he, Jimmy?" Tom turned to him for his opinion, too.

"And more, Tom," Jimmy said, "Much more."

"I believe it," Uncle Wilmer spoke for the first time. "You won't find none better."

"No," Jimmy said, "I don't think anyone could find a better-looking colt."

"And he'll have the speed, too, Jimmy," Tom said convincingly.

"We'll see," Jimmy said. Turning to the Queen, he added, "He should have it, with the Queen for his dam and the Black for a sire." His hand stayed on the mare, stroking her while he turned again to the colt. "He's goin' to be a blood bay, all right, Tom. I wouldn't know where he gets that color. But I know just from looking at him that he's got the

Queen's good temperament—that's in his eyes. They're hers, all right. But there's a lot of the Black in his body. He's going to be big, maybe sixteen hands. And the quarters are the Black's an' the chest, too. So's the head; it's going to be fairly small and sets well on his neck. That neck is the Queen's, though. That much we can all see," he added quietly. "What's inside of him is another story, and that is most important. The will and drive to win is what I hope he has."

"He'll have it, Jimmy," Tom said eagerly. "You should see him in the pasture. He'll go from morning to night. Why, he'll . . ."

And for the next hour and a half all three stood there, listening to Tom give an account of his colt and watching him while he played about the paddock. It came to an end only by Aunt Emma's shattering call to come to supper.

To make the round kitchen table as large as possible, Aunt Emma had inserted all her extra leaves. On it, Tom knew, was her best rose-bordered tablecloth, but you couldn't see much of it, for it seemed that every platter and bowl she had was on the table, each filled with good things, smoking and steaming hot.

Jimmy took one look at the platters of fried chicken, the bowls of gravy and giblets, the pork sausage, the potato filling studded with chopped onions and celery, the steaming plates of hot corn, peas and noodles, and all the hot rolls waiting to be eaten; then he turned to Aunt Emma in amazement. "My gosh!" he said. "What a spread of food! You did it all now—while we were at the barn?"

Aunt Emma turned from the hot wood stove, her face flushed from its heat. "Land sakes, Jimmy. Why, this is nothing," she said. But she smiled and her eyes lighted at Jimmy's appreciation of her well-filled table.

Motioning them to the straight-backed chairs around the table, Uncle Wilmer said, "When a farmer eats, he eats."

"It sure looks like it," George said, taking his seat. "It's hard knowin' where to start."

"Start here," Aunt Emma said, passing him the fried chicken.

They spent a long time at the table, and as Jimmy Creech ate, his spirits rose higher. Very often George would catch Tom's gaze and nod his head as though to imply that he had been right all along when he had said that all Jimmy needed were the colt and a good, hot meal.

Eagerly Jimmy discussed the potentialities of the colt and how he would go about training him. He even went so far as to ask Uncle Wilmer if he'd like to take care of the Queen when he was ready to wean the colt from her a few months from now. "I want a good home for her while I'm busy with the colt," he told Uncle Wilmer. "And I won't be able to breed her again until I make enough money to pay the stud fee. You know, I didn't pay anything for the Black's service. My old friend, Henry Dailey, arranged that for nothing. He knew I couldn't pay. I'll pay him back one of these days."

"The colt will help you do that," Tom said, helping himself to another ear of corn.

"I hope so, Tom." Jimmy turned to Uncle Wilmer again. "Would you like the Queen, if I send her back in December?" he asked. "I'll be able to pay you a little for her keep."

"No need to pay me anything," Uncle Wilmer replied, taking a long inspired reach across the table for the platter of chicken. "I'd sure like to have that mare around, all right;

they don't come none better. An' I got a buggy in the barn; she'll save me enough gas money to more'n keep her for nothing."

"That'll be good," Jimmy said. "She'll need the work to keep from getting soft."

Tom's gaze was on his plate of food. He'd miss the Queen, but he knew Jimmy was right in finding a good place for her. It would be easier weaning the colt with the mare out of sight; and then, too, it wouldn't do her any good just to stand in her stall at Coronet. There weren't any fields around Coronet like Uncle Wilmer's pasture. The Queen would be happier here. And Uncle Wilmer would take good care of her; Tom was more certain of that now than ever before.

Aunt Emma had served her mincemeat pie when George said, "If I'd been judge, you'd have won *first* prize."

Tom was eating his second piece when he first became aware that Jimmy had been silent a long while. Looking at him, he saw the sudden tightness come to his face; Jimmy bit his lower lip and Tom knew he was in pain.

"Jimmy," he said quickly. "You all right?"

The man managed a grim smile. "Just a stomach ache; it'll go away." Then turning to Aunt Emma he added, "I'm not used to such good, wonderful food." But his hand went quickly to his stomach and he held it there.

George rose from his seat to go to him, but Jimmy pushed him away. "You know it's indigestion, George," he said. "It'll go in a minute."

But George turned to Aunt Emma. "Would you have any bicarbonate of soda? It helps."

"I have baking soda—same thing," she said, hurrying to the corner cupboard. "Maybe he should lie down a while.

Wilmer, show George where the spare bedroom is!"

Jimmy made no protest when they guided him upstairs.

An hour later Tom and George returned to find the dishes washed and his uncle and aunt sitting in their chairs.

"How is he?" Aunt Emma asked with concern.

"He's sleeping. He'll be all right in a little while," George replied.

"Jimmy should see a doctor," Aunt Emma said.

"I believe it," Uncle Wilmer agreed.

"We have seen them," George said, "—a couple of times in different towns. They say it's indigestion or acid stomach an' give him powders; bicarbonate of soda is all it is. He's only had this stomach trouble a few times this season. The docs say it's livin' the way he does. Always on the go or worryin' about something. He'll be all right now that the racin' season is over, I guess; it usually works that way."

"I hope so," Aunt Emma said. "But you keep your eye on him, Tom," she added, turning to the boy. "You make it your job to watch Jimmy. It isn't right he should have those pains."

Tom nodded. "I guess I'll go upstairs and pack," he said. "We'll be starting early tomorrow, won't we, George?"

"Yeah, Tom. Jimmy wants to get back to Coronet before dark."

"Why don't you two sleep here tonight?" Aunt Emma offered. "We have room."

Uncle Wilmer nodded, and Tom noticed for the first time that his uncle wasn't having any trouble hearing what was said, even though they hadn't raised their voices. "I'll drive you over to the fair just as early as you want to pick up your truck and Symbol; then we can come back here for Tom and the mare an' colt," Uncle Wilmer said.

"All right," George said, "if it won't be too much trouble."

"Trouble?" Aunt Emma asked. "It won't be no trouble at all."

A little later Tom finished his packing. He was closing the lid of his suitcase when the stairs creaked and Uncle Wilmer appeared at the head of the stairs.

"Just finished," Tom said, and then he noticed the book and magazines his uncle was carrying.

"You forgot these," Uncle Wilmer said.

Shaking his head, Tom said, "They're yours. I'm leaving them for you."

"You take them." But Uncle Wilmer still held the books and magazines close.

"I want you to have them," Tom insisted. "I have too much now to carry."

Uncle Wilmer turned back to the stairs. "All right," he said. "I'll keep them for you, if you got too much already." As he reached the top step, he turned again to Tom. "You take good care of that colt, Tom."

"I will, Uncle Wilmer."

"An' you write to me, mind you, same as you did to Jimmy. I'll want to know, all right."

His uncle was descending the stairs when Tom called out, "Uncle Wilmer—"

"Heh?"

"I had such a good summer with you."

"Heh?"

"*I said I had such a good summer with you and Aunt Emma!*" Tom shouted.

Uncle Wilmer started down the stairs again, and without turning around he said, "It was good havin' you, Tom." Three more steps, then he stopped and looked back at the boy. "And Tom—"

"Yes, Uncle Wilmer?"

"You git Jimmy to race the colt at Reading Fair, won't you? I'd sure like to see him race, all right. I sure would."

"I'll get him to Reading some way," Tom said. "I want you to see him, too. And it won't be long, Uncle Wilmer. He'll be here before you know it. Time passes fast with a colt like that. And I'll let you know every week how he's doing until you see him for yourself."

The Weanling

10

For Tom, it was difficult getting used to Coronet again. As he walked from his home in the small mining town across fields studded with high, iron frames of wells that had plumbed the earth in search of natural gas years ago and now were forsaken for surface coal mining, he thought of his uncle's farm with its acres of green, unravaged fields. And he missed it all very much for a while. But his days and weeks were filled with activity, so it wasn't very long before he had forgotten the farm.

The Queen and her colt were, of course, stabled in Jimmy's shed at the track. Every morning before school, Tom would leave his home early enough to go to the stables; there he would help George clean the stalls and feed and water Symbol, the Queen and the colt. Later in the afternoon he would return to play with the colt in the dirt paddock in back of the long sheds. He saw Jimmy Creech only on Saturdays, for Jimmy was taking it easy now that the season was over. Jimmy jogged Symbol only every other day, for the aged horse needed little work to keep in condition. And there wasn't much to do with the colt except to continue leading him about the paddock and handling him; and Tom took care of that.

"We'll let him nurse the mare until the middle of December," Jimmy told Tom. "That'll be long enough, just about six months. I don't like to keep a colt on a mare longer'n that. Takes too much out of the mare, an' doesn't do the colt any good; he becomes too dependent on her. Besides, the colt is eating enough oats and hay now to keep him goin' without the mare's milk. He's growing every day, Tom, isn't he?"

And whether it was Jimmy's enthusiasm for the colt or the regular, non-hectic life he led now, the man's health improved considerably. Jimmy put a little weight on his small bones; he had good color in his face and his eyes were bright; there was no more stomach trouble, and as October and November passed and December came, George and Tom forgot that Jimmy had ever been sick.

The first snow fell in the middle of December and although it was only a light fall, Jimmy had Symbol's shoes changed, putting edged shoes on him, which would hold better on the ice-spotted track. The snow made Tom think of Christmas and in his next letter to Uncle Wilmer he included the subscription to *Hoof Beats* magazine, which he had ordered for him. Uncle Wilmer wrote occasionally, but only to ask for more pictures of the colt and when Jimmy was sending the mare to him.

The Queen would leave for the farm any day, so Tom spent more and more time with her and the colt in the large box stall. It was crowded, for the colt was getting too big to share the Queen's stall and to nurse her. Tom knew it was time for the colt to be weaned. He told himself over and over again while he stroked the Queen that he couldn't ask for a better home for her than the one she'd have with Uncle Wilmer; that it was far better than staying here, for she belonged on a farm, where there would be fields of grass to roam in the spring. Coronet was a training track; it had facilities only for horses getting ready to race. And that's why the colt belonged here; in a short time his real work would begin.

The following Saturday morning, Tom as usual was helping Jimmy and George hitch Symbol to the two-wheeled training cart in preparation for his three-mile jog on the track. He hooked the check rein from Symbol's head, then stepped back, blowing on his fingers to warm them before putting on his gloves. It was cold in the shed and colder outside. Jimmy had his fur-lined cap pulled down about his ears and a brown muffler around his neck. George and Tom were dressed just as warmly. But Jimmy had to go outside, to sit in the training cart while the wind whistled about him.

George went to open the shed doors, and Tom took Symbol's bridle.

"Tom." It was Jimmy.

"Yes, Jimmy." The boy turned to him, but all he could see of Jimmy was his beaked nose, for he was walking on the other side and behind Symbol.

"Come back here."

Tom left Symbol's head to join Jimmy. "Take these," the man said, handing him the long lines.

"Th-the reins?"

"Lines, let's call 'em, Tom," he said. "You've been want-ing to drive, haven't you?" The tiny pinpoints of light flick-ered in his eyes at the incredulous look on Tom's face. Then Jimmy turned away, saying simply, "We'll start today, then." He went to Symbol's head to lead him from the barn while Tom, holding the long lines in fumbling hands, walked behind.

Jimmy stopped Symbol outside the shed, and the sharp wind coming across the track was icy cold on their faces. There were three other horses and drivers already circling the track.

Turning to George, Jimmy asked, "You figure Tom has done enough work around these stables to warrant learning to drive now, don't you?"

George smiled. "As his Uncle Wilmer would say," he re-plied, " 'I believe it.' "

"You won't mind the cold?" Jimmy asked, turning to Tom.

The boy shook his head without saying anything.

"Get up, then, and go to it," Jimmy said.

Tom felt awkward lifting a leg over the seat as he'd seen Jimmy and other drivers do thousands of times. The lines, too, felt clumsy in his hands, and he had trouble finding the foot stirrups on the shafts of the cart. But finally he was ready and sat tense and waiting, his eyes on Symbol's black hindquarters and the long tail falling between his out-stretched legs.

"Take the hand holds," Jimmy said, and Tom's hands moved forward until they had reached the loops in the lines. "Thumb and index finger over the top. That's right, you know that. Got the end of the lines under you? You don't want 'em trailing on the ground to get caught in your wheels."

"I'm sitting on them good." Tom spoke for the first time.

"Get goin' then," Jimmy said. "He's hard mouthed. Keep a good hold, but don't tear his mouth. Just jog him three miles—six laps."

Tom took Symbol onto the hard track, the light cart bouncing over the ruts. Before his eyes, Symbol's hindquarters quickened and his hind legs moved faster. Tom didn't feel the cold; he felt only a new and surprising sense of power as he looked at the hindquarters of the horse pulling him. He felt small and low, as though Symbol could whisk him and the cart off the ground if he moved much faster. Tom glanced toward the sheds they were passing and only then realized that Symbol wasn't flying but going at a very slow trot. He gave him more line, knowing full well Jimmy wanted to have Symbol worked faster than he was going now. He couldn't see over the high haunches before him, so he looked to the left and then to the right of Symbol to make certain the track was clear. It was, so he sat back in his seat again.

He hadn't gone very far around the track when he realized the lines no longer felt so clumsy in his hands. Even more surprising, he could actually feel Symbol's mouth through the long lines. It seemed he could tell, too, each time the horse took the bit or wanted to go faster. It came to his hands as though the signals traveled over telegraphic wires instead of leather lines. Self-confidence came with this sensitivity of hands, and his tense body relaxed a little.

Tom clucked to Symbol when they came into the backstretch the first time around; and when they passed Jimmy and George, who had remained in the cold, watching them, Jimmy shouted, "That's good, Tom. Keep him at that speed."

It took but one more lap for Tom to feel very much at home behind a horse. And he knew for certain that he wanted to make driving and training horses his lifework. He wanted to be like Jimmy Creech. His love for horses and this wonderful sport of harness racing was in him deep, and he knew he'd never change. No more than Jimmy Creech would.

Symbol wanted to go faster, but Tom spoke to him through the lines with a slight touch whenever he felt Symbol's urge to go. The touch at the precise second, he learned, was all that was necessary to control the horse.

When they had gone a mile and a half, Tom found himself taking time to glance at the other horses and drivers on the track. Ahead of him were Si Costa and Frank Lutz; they were men from the same mold as Jimmy and George, just as all the others here were. Men you'd always find wherever there was a county fair.

Turning to the far side of the track, Tom watched the only two-year-old colt on the track. Behind the colt sat Miss Elsie, huddled well within the raccoon coat she wore while driving in the winter. Miss Elsie was one of them in every respect except one—or rather two, Tom corrected himself, since she was a woman.

But Miss Elsie had all the money in the world; that was the big difference. You'd never know it to look at her, though. She drove to the track every single morning, no matter what the weather, in an open jeep. And she'd never been sick in all the thirty years Jimmy and George had known her. The track and stables and the big white house and barn sitting high on the hill overlooking the track—all belonged to Miss Elsie. Her father had built the track, and when he'd died he left Miss Elsie everything, including the coal mines on the other side of Coronet. Miss Elsie didn't care about coal, just horses, like Jimmy and the rest of them here. She must be in her forties, Tom figured. Miss Elsie had ten colts in two sheds, and she worked every one of them, even though she had a lot of help. Next year, she would have a new group of colts from the big barn on the hill where she kept her broodmares and her stallion, Mr. Guy. Mr. Guy had been a famous racehorse ten years ago, and Miss Elsie wanted to breed and raise another like him. But with all her money, she hadn't done it yet. Every year she would sell her two-year-old colts, knowing that in them she didn't have another Mr. Guy. She'd been right, too, for no colts she'd sold ever had become as fast and as famous as Mr. Guy. Miss Elsie knew her horses, all right; everyone was agreed on that.

And they all liked Miss Elsie, for she was one of them; she understood their financial problems even though she did have a lot of money herself. She never loaned money to anyone, and every person at the track knew better than to ask her. But she helped them in other ways that were more important. She charged but a dollar a month for the use of her stables and track, and that included electricity; she sold them their hay for practically nothing, and it was the best of hay, having been raised on her farm, the only unspoiled land within a radius of twenty miles of Coronet; and there was a building at the track which she had built just for the men, where they could sit and rest, even live there, if they wanted to do so.

Tom was taking Symbol into his last half-mile when Miss Elsie drove her colt alongside. Symbol's ears pricked up at the colt's nearness. Tom touched the lines and the black horse responded by slowing down again.

"Good to see you out here, Tom," Miss Elsie called.

Tom turned to the fur-coated figure. All he could see of Miss Elsie's sharp-featured face beneath her peaked cap and raised collar were her horn-rimmed glasses and large teeth, even more prominent now since she was smiling. "Thank you, ma'am," he said. "It's good being out here."

Miss Elsie flicked the lines and the colt stepped away, with Miss Elsie humming to him; she always hummed to her colts. And as her voice drifted back on the wind, Tom too started humming. Symbol bolted forward, eager to move after the colt. Tom touched the lines just in time to slow him down again. Once more Symbol tried to get away, and again Tom was able to stop him.

When Tom brought Symbol back to the shed, Jimmy Creech said, "You did much better'n I expected, Tom." Then, taking the boy's hands in his own, he turned the palms upward and slapped them lightly. "From what I saw you might have the kind of hands most of us give our eye-teeth for; and you'd be the luckiest kid in the world. You never acquire the feeling in the hands that I'm talkin' about. You're born with that kind, and very few are lucky enough to have them." His eyes left Tom's hands and traveled to his face. "I'm not saying you have them—so don't get all excited. But I know I couldn't have kept Symbol down to the speed you were goin' without keeping a good hold on him all the time. You didn't have to do that. You touched him at the right time. He knew you had him outguessed; that much I know."

George reached for Symbol's bridle. "Don't build him up so much, Jimmy," he said. "Might be different next time."

"Yeah," Jimmy replied, "maybe it will. But what I saw looked good."

Tom followed them into the shed, wondering why Jimmy and George were making so much fuss just because he could tell through the lines exactly what Symbol was going to do. It seemed that anyone should be able to do that; yet Jimmy said *he* couldn't—and that was most surprising of all.

Tom looked forward to the following Saturday and possibly driving again until Jimmy Creech told him that he had made arrangements to send the Queen that day to Uncle Wilmer. He stopped looking forward to Saturday then.

But the day came, and it found him standing quietly beside the Queen while Jimmy blanketed her dark-brown body and got her ready to be loaded into the van which waited just outside the door. Tom was glad that it was a closed van, for it was very cold that morning. He was glad, too, that the driver was the same man who had taken the Queen to the farm last summer; Tom could depend upon him to take it easy with the Queen.

While Jimmy hooked the straps of the blanket about the Queen, her colt kept close to her side.

"They both know somethin's up," George said, leaving the stall.

"Yeah," Jimmy replied, "they know, all right. 'Specially the Queen; the blanket tells her she's going to move."

Tom was silent, standing close to the mare and colt. He thought he had become reconciled to the Queen's going, but it was much more difficult now that the time was here.

Running his hands through the short black mane of the colt, he said, "It's going to be all right, boy." Then he turned to Jimmy. "He *will* be all right, won't he?"

"He'll miss her today and tomorrow, and the mare will miss him. But in two days they'll have forgotten each other. That's the way it goes, Tom."

"You're sure, Jimmy?"

"I'm not sure about anything, Tom," Jimmy said quietly. "But you'll find that the colt will settle down in two days. You'll see for yourself. It's all a part of growing up," he added when he met the boy's troubled eyes. "The Queen will be better off at the farm, as we both know, and the colt belongs here. Each has a separate life from now on."

Tom nodded. "You're right, Jimmy. I know that."

They took the Queen from the stall, closing the door between her and her colt. She nickered several times but obediently followed Jimmy. "You stay with him, Tom," the man said. "He won't like being left alone and I don't want him to hurt himself. George and I won't have any trouble loading the mare."

They went out the shed doors and Tom was alone with his colt, whose short, shrill neighs came frequently as he moved back and forth in the large stall, his ears pricked and eyes large and startled. Tom went inside the stall to comfort him, but the colt ignored him.

Outside the shed there were a few neighs from the Queen, then came the sound of her hoofs on the wooden ramp leading into the van. Tom was glad he wasn't out there. He heard the doors close and the Queen's neigh again, now muffled. The van's motor was started.

Frantically the colt moved about the stall, his shrill cries never ending. Tom stood beside the half-door of the stall, wanting to comfort him but knowing he could not take the Queen's place. Suddenly the colt moved quickly to the door and his forelegs rose in an attempt to get over. Tom's arm went beneath the hard body in time to stop him, then held him until he was able to pull the struggling legs from the door. When he had him down once more, Tom hurriedly closed the wire-mesh screen above the half-door.

It was then that Jimmy and George returned to the shed and stood just outside the stall. The shed rang with the colt's incessant neighs while Jimmy went to the grain box and returned with a quart of oats. "Put this in his box, Tom," he said.

But the colt would have none of the grain, and his eyes never left the shed's closed door as he watched for the Queen to return.

"You might as well come out an' take it easy, Tom," Jimmy said. "This will go on all day, and you're not goin' to help him any. We just have to keep our eye on him, that's all, to make sure he doesn't hurt himself."

But Tom shook his head and stayed with the frantic colt, and finally Jimmy and George left to get Symbol ready for his morning workout.

All day long Tom spent in the stall, leaving it for only a short time around noon, when George told him to come out and have a sandwich with him. He hadn't been able to comfort the colt, just as Jimmy had said he wouldn't. The colt waited only for the Queen.

It was late afternoon when the colt's cries lessened and he turned to Tom. The boy ran his other hand over the red furry winter coat and talked to him softly. Tom took him by the halter and attempted to lead him to the corner feedbox

and the rack of hay. For a minute the colt refused to go and
his eyes were frightened; he turned his head toward the door
and neighed again. Then he followed Tom to the feedbox.

"He'll be all right," George said, standing outside the
stall. "The worst is over for him. You'll see. He won't hurt
himself now."

"But tonight, George?" Tom asked. "What about
tonight?"

"I'm sleepin' here," George returned, shifting his chaw of
tobacco. "But he'll be so exhausted from all the moving
around he's done that he'll sleep. They all do."

"I'll stay with you," Tom said quickly.

"Your folks would worry about you. Besides, we've got
only one cot. I promise you he won't get hurt, Tom. There
really isn't any need for my bein' here. He'll be quiet."

Jimmy had gone home after noon, but returned around
four o'clock. He came into the shed, carrying a large envelope. "Come on into the tack room, Tom," he said, stopping
outside the stall. "The colt will be all right now, and I want
you to help me with something."

Seeing that the colt was interested in his hay, Tom nodded
and left the stall to follow Jimmy into the tack room.
George was there, sitting beside the small electric heater.

Opening the envelope, Jimmy withdrew a long application blank and set it down on the table before him. He took
off his cap, baring his gray, almost white head, then un-
wound his muffler from about his neck. Sitting down at the
table, he took out a pen and said, "We're goin' to register
the colt with the Association, so we can race him."

Looking over Jimmy's shoulder, Tom saw the outline
drawings of a horse's body profiles and head. On them,
Jimmy was to put any of the colt's identification marks, but

his pen didn't touch the drawings. "No marks on our colt," Jimmy said. "He's as clean as they come . . . no stockings, no blaze, no star, no nothin'."

When he came to the line below he started writing. "*Color:* Blood Bay"; then he encircled *"Horse"* from the selection headed, *"Horse, Gelding, Mare."* He stopped to look at George and Jimmy when he came to *"Name Selected."* "We don't have a name for him yet. We'll let that go until we finish the rest of the application."

Turning again to the paper, he continued writing. *"Foaled:* June 26; *Bred by:* Jimmy Creech, R.D. 2, Coronet, Pennsylvania; *Name of Sire:* The Black; *Name of Dam:* Volo Queen; *Sire of Dam:* Victor Volo; *Name of Second Dam:* Hy-Lo; *Sire of Second Dam:* Hollyrood Bob. . . ." Jimmy Creech went on writing for a long while before he had finished giving all the pertinent information required for the colt's registration.

"Why are we doing this now?" Tom asked George. "His racing days are a good way off."

"He'll be a yearling on January first," George said. "It costs only five bucks to register him now but fifteen once he's a yearling. Jimmy's figurin' on savin' that money."

Tom's brow furrowed. "But the colt will actually only be about six months old on January first," he said.

"For the records and racing he'll still be a yearling," George said, removing his cap to scratch his bald head. "An' the following January first when he's eligible to race he'll be a two-year-old. Yep, and some of the early colts—those born earlier in the year than ours—will have some months on him when they all go to the post."

Jimmy looked up from his writing to say, "But the colt is goin' to be as big and strong as any of the early ones. I know

that just by lookin' at him now." When he had finished filling out the last line of the application blank, he turned to
them again. "A name. We've got to have a name for him.
That's all we need to finish this thing."

"A good name," Tom said.

George nodded. "Yeah, it's gotta be a good name, one
that fits."

The colt was striking the wood of his stall, so Tom left
the tack room to look at him. Finding him all right, he returned quickly, for he wanted to help select a name for his
colt.

Jimmy said, "He's goin' to have a black mane and tail and
a red body. So how about calling him Red and Black?"

Shaking his head, George said, "Naw, Jimmy, that's too
long. Let's get something good an' short. How about just
naming him Red?"

Jimmy and Tom shook their heads simultaneously.

"Whatever we call him," Jimmy said, "let's all agree on it.
He belongs to all of us."

"Red Prince," Tom said. "He's out of a Queen."

"Not bad," Jimmy returned. "But I'd like to give him just
one name, if we can think of something good."

"How's just Prince?" George suggested.

"No, that's not right, either," Tom said.

"Robin?" Jimmy asked. "He might fly like one."

"I don't like it," George answered.

"He's going to be big," Jimmy said, getting up to leave
the tack room to take a look at the colt. When he returned
he suggested, "Big Red?"

"You jus' said you didn't want two names," George
muttered.

"Yeah, so I did. Well, Let's keep on thinking. I want

to mail this application tonight."

For another hour they continued submitting names for one another's approval, but came to no agreement. As though in the hope of helping matters along, they separated frequently, walking down the long shed to look at the colt or to do odd jobs which weren't necessary.

The winter sun was setting rapidly when George decided to burn some crate boxes that had accumulated in a corner. "I'll do my thinkin' outside," he told them, leaving the shed.

Tom went into the colt's stall to handle him while Jimmy walked into the tack room. The colt still neighed for the Queen, but only at long intervals. Tom changed his water, and while the colt drank he scratched him on the forehead. His eyes took in the short black mane and whiskbroom tail, the red furry body. *When his winter coat's gone,* he thought, *he'll be so red he'll seem to be burning in the sun. And that, together with his black mane and tail, which will be long then, should make him a very beautiful-looking colt. He'll need a name worthy of his looks and the fire that I know is burning inside of him.*

"How about just King?" Jimmy Creech called from the tack room.

"I don't think so," Tom yelled back. "There are a lot of horses named King."

Jimmy was silent for a long while and finally Tom left the colt to go into the tack room again. He found Jimmy looking out the small window at George, who had the fire going a good distance away in the track's infield.

Jimmy said quietly, "George always goes what seems miles away from the sheds to build his bonfire. He never takes any chances of starting a fire around here. A careful guy, George is—and you couldn't find a better friend," he added quietly.

But Tom wasn't listening to him. Instead he said to himself, "Bonfire." He liked the sound of it. You didn't hear that word much any more; people usually just said "fire." There was a tattered dictionary on the shelf above the table. Going over to it, Tom took it down from the shelf.

"What're you doing?" Jimmy asked.

Tom didn't say anything until he had found the word he wanted. Then he read to Jimmy from the dictionary: "Bonfire—a large fire in an open place, for entertainment, celebration, or as a signal." He looked up from the book. "As a signal, Jimmy," he repeated, "—our signal to everybody *now* that he's on his way, starting today. *Bonfire!*"

"Bonfire," repeated Jimmy, and the way he said it and the light in his eyes gave Tom the approval he wanted. Together they turned to look at the flames, leaping brightly toward the darkening sky. "A signal to all," Jimmy added, "—just as you said. Come on!"

Minus hats and mufflers they rushed from the shed to join George, and together they shouted, *"Bonfire!"* George just grinned and shook his head in approval without taking his eyes from the flames, so careful was he to see that no flying embers found their way to the sheds.

In his stall, the subject of it all sniffed the corners of his feedbox, cleaning up the last bit of oats; then he stretched his long, supple neck to the hay in the rack above him.

Bonfire was learning to be on his own.

First Bridle

11

It didn't take very long—only two or three days, just as Jimmy had said—before Bonfire ceased neighing for the Queen. Uncle Wilmer wrote, telling them that the mare had arrived safe and sound and "liked her old stall, all right." He said too that he had hitched her to his wagon and had driven the Queen into town for his weekly supplies. "She's a fast stepper, all right," he wrote. "Lester Eberl rode in with me and he says she's the fastest mare in Berks County. I believe it."

"The work will do the mare a lot of good," Jimmy said, after reading the letter.

January came, Bonfire was a yearling, and Jimmy Creech spent more and more time with him. On nice days the colt was put into the paddock to romp and play and get all the exercise he needed. When the weather turned bad, Jimmy kept him in the stall and started breaking Bonfire to bridle and harness. Each lesson was taught so slowly and patiently that Tom's respect for Jimmy's thoroughness knew no bounds.

"They don't break colts better than Jimmy breaks 'em," George said. "He talks about not havin' patience. But he's got all the patience in the world when it comes to schoolin' a colt. There aren't many left like Jimmy."

And it was true, Tom knew. For weeks Jimmy tied Bonfire in his stall or at the paddock fence for a few minutes each day, teaching the colt to stand tied and to respect the rope holding him. Tom watched Bonfire, fearful at first that he might try to get away. But the colt hadn't fought the rope, and Tom's eyes had shone with pride when Jimmy said, "The work you did with him at the farm is payin' off, Tom. Makin' it real easy for me, it is."

He repeated this compliment to Tom's early work time and time again. Jimmy put a light bridle and bit on Bonfire and the colt did nothing but play with the bit while he moved about his stall. As the days went by he got so used to it he even ceased playing with it. Jimmy nodded in approval, and during February he placed the light racing harness on the colt's back. Bonfire didn't take to the harness as quickly as he had the bridle, but Jimmy was patient with him and within a few days the colt moved about his stall complete with bridle and harness.

And that, together with daily handling of the colt's body, especially his feet, was all that was done during the winter months.

With the coming of spring, Bonfire shed much of his winter coat under Tom's daily grooming. He was a tall colt, standing almost fifteen hands now, and still growing.

George remarked, "Jimmy said he was goin' to be over sixteen hands, an' he's goin' to be. He's filling out, too."

There was no doubt about that, for even now fine, hard muscles stood out prominently beneath his sleek red coat.

George turned to Tom while the boy pulled his brush through the black mane, which now fell halfway down Bonfire's neck. "And you're growin' with him, Tom," he said. "You're puttin' on weight yourself."

Tom's frame was gaunt no longer and there was a full, healthy look to his face. Going to the colt's tail to brush it, he laughed and said, "It's the hard work, George."

"You've sure made things easier for us," George admitted, taking a plug of tobacco from his pocket. "When you get our age, y'need young hands around." Then, seeing Jimmy drive Symbol past the shed, he added, "We'll be needin' your help even more now with spring here. Jimmy'll start workin' harder now, and worryin', too, about the season ahead of us."

During the weeks that followed, Tom understood more and more what George had meant. For Jimmy worked tirelessly and became quieter and, at times, irritable. Symbol's workouts were stepped up, and Tom stopped driving him on Saturdays, for Jimmy was attempting to lengthen the black horse's stride. He changed Symbol's shoes often and tried heavier toe weights to encourage a longer stride; but all this was of no avail, and Jimmy's drawn face was evidence of his anxiety about the fast-approaching races.

At the same time, he spent many hours with the colt, very often leading him around the track with one hand while he drove Symbol with the other. Bonfire's strides were low, and beautiful to watch, but even they didn't comfort Jimmy just now.

"He couldn't ask for more than a colt like that," Tom said, watching Bonfire's effortless stride behind the uneven, ponderous-gaited Symbol. "He should feel wonderful."

"He does feel good about the colt," George said. "But there'll be time enough next year for Jimmy to get real excited about Bonfire. Right now he's thinkin' of the season comin' up ahead of him, and wondering whether or not he can make enough money to buy feed and hay to keep us going for another year. It's always been that way for Jimmy this time of year," George added with concern. "Sometimes I wonder why he keeps goin' on his own. He could have had all kinds of jobs trainin' and racin' for other people; then he'd have no money worries."

"But it wouldn't be the same to him," Tom said quickly.

"No," George admitted. "It wouldn't. Jimmy wants his own horses. He wants it the way it's always been for him. But it's tough making a go of it these days, an' he knows it."

The month of May came and with it an early hot, summer sun. Even so, Jimmy Creech was reluctant to open the shed doors or to remove the heavy muffler from about his neck. It was, Tom thought, as though Jimmy didn't want to accept the fact that the racing season was drawing near, as though he knew that Symbol wasn't ready for it and neither was he. Tom's knowledge of horses told him that Symbol never would be ready again, and he was convinced that Jimmy knew this as well as he. Yet Jimmy was going out with the black horse, and Tom could only hope for the best.

One Saturday morning Jimmy experienced the first stomach pains since his attack at the farm. He was in the colt's stall with Tom, working over Bonfire's feet, when suddenly he went down on his knees and clutched his stomach.

"Jimmy!" Tom dropped down beside him while the colt moved away, then came back to shove his soft muzzle against Jimmy's head. Tom pushed him gently away while helping Jimmy to his feet.

"Just indigestion again. Something I ate," Jimmy said, as they left the stall.

George came running up, took one look at Jimmy's distorted face, then shook his head sadly at Tom. "I knew it would come," he said, "—just like last year, same time."

"Nothing's come," Jimmy mumbled, but his eyes were glazed. "I'll be all right in a minute. It's just uncomfortable, that's all. I'll need some bicarbonate of soda, George," he added, meeting his friend's eyes.

"You need more than that," George answered quickly. "We tried that last season. We're not goin' to have another attack like that one. We're goin' to see Dr. Morton now— like we shoulda done last year." George's voice and face were adamant. He wasn't going to listen to any objections from Jimmy.

Tom knew that Dr. Morton was a stomach specialist in Pittsburgh, twenty-five miles away, and that George had tried without success to get Jimmy to see him months and months before.

Whether Jimmy realized that George was determined to take him to Dr. Morton, or the stomach pains were more severe than he pretended they were, Tom didn't know; but for one or both reasons Jimmy followed his friend obediently to his car. George got behind the wheel.

"Can you stay until we get back, Tom?" George asked while starting the motor.

Tom nodded. Jimmy didn't say anything until the car was moving, then he said, "I didn't get to feed the colt, Tom. You do it, please."

Again Tom nodded. He stared after the car long after it had disappeared down the road. Poor Jimmy. It was one thing on top of another. Finally Tom turned and went inside the shed.

He fed Bonfire, stood beside him while he ate, then took the colt to the paddock behind the row of sheds and turned him loose.

He was watching him go about the paddock, noticing the sun picking up the brilliant red of his coat and making it glisten. But Tom's thoughts weren't with the colt just now, for he was worrying about Jimmy. So he was startled when he heard a voice say, "He's a grand-looking colt, Tom. Jimmy is proud of him, I'll bet."

Turning around, he saw Miss Elsie. As usual, this time of year, she wore her gray sweatshirt, faded and turned inside out, the same kind as the one Tom wore. And like him she was hatless, her brown hair cut short and bristling.

"He's proud of him, all right," Tom said. "But he's sick again, Miss Elsie. George just took him in to a Pittsburgh doctor."

"I was afraid he'd be sick again," she said, shielding her horn-rimmed glasses from the sun the better to see Tom. "Jimmy's getting on—and it's too bad this had to happen, because we need men like Jimmy Creech," she added soberly.

Together they watched the colt for a long while. He was moving swiftly about the paddock, enjoying his freedom, and his mane swept back from his red neck like a black flame.

"You like him?" Miss Elsie asked without taking her eyes from the fast-moving colt.

Tom nodded but said nothing.

"You like him?" Miss Elsie asked again.

"He's the best," Tom said quietly. "The very best that ever was."

"You're generalizing, Tom," she said. "And I've always told everyone around here that Tom Messenger was good on detail, and that's why he was going to make a fine horseman."

Turning away from the colt, Tom saw the challenge in the woman's gaze. He turned back to Bonfire again and said, "He's pure-gaited. He's got good control of action and never leaves his feet when going at top speed. He's only a baby, but even now he never shifts or changes a beat as long as he's out there. He's it for Jimmy . . . and for George and me," he added.

"That's better . . . and more like you," was all Miss Elsie said.

Tom was silent for some time before he asked, "Did you find a future Mr. Guy among your two-year-olds?"

"No," Miss Elsie replied, and she tried to draw her upper lip over her prominent teeth with no success. "I don't have him in this year's crop."

"You'll sell them again—all of them?"

"I think so, Tom. I'll know better next month." She smiled as she added hopefully, "But maybe next year I'll have the one I've been waiting for. I have a yearling up at the farm who looks as good as yours. It's a filly, so maybe she'll be a female Mr. Guy. She's black except for four white stockings and a blaze." Miss Elsie pushed herself back from the paddock fence, laughing as she said, "I call her the Princess with the four white stockings. She looks like the best I've ever had."

And with all the colts Miss Elsie had bred, raised and

trained, Tom never had heard her say that before. He didn't think anyone else had, either. Miss Elsie knew horses, and she wouldn't say anything like that unless she honestly meant it. Her black yearling filly would be something to see.

Miss Elsie was leaving when she said, "I'll have my filly down here at the track this summer. You'll see her." She paused. "You are going to be here, aren't you, Tom?"

"Yes, Miss Elsie," Tom replied. "I'm taking care of Bonfire while Jimmy and George go out to the fairs."

Tom watched Miss Elsie climb into her jeep and go bouncing down the road; then, after spending a few minutes more with his colt, he went into the shed to clean Bonfire's stall and bed it down for the night. He decided he'd stay there until Jimmy and George returned.

It was almost dark when Tom saw Jimmy's car come down the road. Jimmy was sitting beside George and Tom felt relieved to see him, for he had been afraid that Jimmy might have something seriously wrong and be hospitalized.

They left the car and as they came toward him Tom searched their faces. Jimmy grinned. "Nothing wrong with me at all," he said.

"Don't let him kid you," George muttered. "He's got an ulcer. He's had it for years."

"The doc said a lot of people had 'em," Jimmy retorted. "Nothing for you to get all upset about."

"*You* were the one who got upset when he told you to live a quiet life with no more excitement," George reminded him. "That would mean giving up racing, and hopping from one fair to the next, wearing yourself out."

"That's silly," Jimmy said angrily. "I might as well be dead as to give up the fairs."

"Then you got to follow that diet he gave you and take it

as easy as possible," George returned. "And don't get upset about anything. We'll get along all right."

"Who's upset?" Jimmy shouted angrily. "I never get upset. You're the one who gets all excited about everything." He stalked into the shed, still bellowing.

George stayed with Tom at the door. "Sure," he said. "I'm the one who gets upset, all right."

"How serious is his ulcer?" Tom asked.

George spat his tobacco juice on the ground, thought a minute, then said, "The doctor wasn't too worried about it. Says there's a lot of people like Jimmy walking around with one and they don't even know it."

"What do you mean people like Jimmy?" Tom asked.

"Guys who've worked hard all their lives an' have a lot of worries like Jimmy has had, 'specially the last few years. About makin' ends meet, I mean. That and never sitting down a moment, and taking all the responsibility, thinkin' no one else can handle a horse like he can. All those things, plus never takin' time to eat a decent meal when we go to the fairs, all add up to ulcers—that's what the doc said, anyway."

"And he wanted Jimmy to quit?"

"Sure, for a season or two, anyway. Jimmy wouldn't have any more pains if he took it easy and rested."

"But he won't do it."

Shaking his bald head, George said, "No, and I guess we couldn't expect Jimmy to give up the fairs. The doc knows that, because he's known Jimmy from 'way back. So he gave Jimmy a long list of things he could eat and things he couldn't eat and some medicine to take. He told Jimmy to stick to that diet or he'd have more pains which would get

worse in time. An' he made Jimmy promise he'd try hard not
to get excited about anything. An' Jimmy promised he
would . . . that's all there was to it, except Jimmy's got to
see him again as soon as we get back from racin'."

"Do you think Jimmy will do all the doc made him promise to do?"

"Guess so," George said. "Jimmy don't like those
pains . . . that attack he had today was pretty bad. An' the
doc scared him by telling him they could get worse than
that, much worse." George smiled, adding, "He sure made
Jimmy mad when he told him no more gum chewing.
That's bad for Jimmy, the doc said. And Jimmy likes his
gum as much as I like my tobacco. But Jimmy said he'd give
up gum. Jimmy said he'd do a lot of things today, an' I'm
only hoping he will." Putting his arm around Tom, he said,
"Let's get Jimmy and close up shop. It's getting late and we
all oughta be home."

Together they walked into the shed, each wondering what
the months to come would bring for Jimmy Creech.

The few weeks before Jimmy and George left for the fairs
were good in many respects. Jimmy seemed to be more relaxed and had no more attacks. School closed for the summer, and Tom was able to spend every day at the track,
helping George and Jimmy even more than before. And
Jimmy, surprisingly, allowed Tom to take more responsibility off his shoulders by letting him work Symbol every other
day. They taught Bonfire to work on the longe, encircling
them at the end of the long rope.

And finally they hitched the colt to a training cart. Bonfire felt the shafts against his sides as Jimmy turned him by
pulling gently on the lines. Tom stood near the colt's head,

ready to quell any fear Bonfire might have of the cart he drew behind him. But there was no sign of fear, no fractiousness while the colt springily walked about the track, his eyes clear and large as he watched the track ahead, his ears pricked up and only shifting when Tom spoke to him. The boy was aware of Bonfire's eagerness to step out, yet the colt did not pull and awaited Jimmy's commands through the lines.

Tom turned from the colt to tell Jimmy, "He's taking to it like an old-timer!"

"The Queen was like that. And he's soft-mouthed like she was," Jimmy called back. "But you're just as much responsible for makin' it this easy, Tom. You taught him early to have full confidence in us, and that's most important of all."

They walked around the track twice, and Bonfire never once made an attempt to pull away. Neither did he kick the two-wheeled cart he pulled so close behind. It was as though he knew that this was the beginning of his career on the track, and was eager to be on with it.

Later Jimmy told Tom, "Now until George and I get back, I want you to do just what we did today. I don't want you to get in the cart and have him pull you yet. I don't believe in rushin' a colt like that. All we're doin' is getting him used to the cart and track. He's only a yearling and there'll be plenty of time later on for the real work. To get most of his exercise let him use the paddock, and work him on the longe, too, so he won't forget what he's learned. Take him out to graze every day, too. I want him to have plenty of grass."

Jimmy stopped talking until he was certain George was out of hearing distance. "I've decided to cut the season short this year if I can make enough money during the first couple of months to tide me over for the year. We should be back sometime in August. I don't want George to know just yet. He might think I'm gettin' soft or thinkin' too much about my—" Jimmy pointed to his stomach. "And it isn't that, Tom, I just want to get back to work with the colt. Not that I don't think you're capable of handling him, Tom," he added hastily. "You know what I said about your hands when I first saw you drive Symbol. Well, I'm sure of it now. You got more in your hands than I ever hoped to have. I know I'm not goin' to make you cocky by telling you this because you love horses and you're sincere in your desire to make them your lifework—just like I have. There's a lot more to learn, and I can teach you all that. But I never could have given you the hands you got; you were born with those."

Tom said nothing when Jimmy had finished. It wasn't necessary to tell Jimmy how he felt. Within a few days he'd be alone with his colt again. How well he remembered his anxiety and lack of confidence at Uncle Wilmer's when the colt had come! There was no doubt in his mind now but that he could do exactly what Jimmy wanted him to do during the next few months. And it was a good and wonderful feeling. He and Bonfire had grown up.

Tom Messenger,
Trainer

12

Jimmy and George left for the fairs with high hopes for a successful season.

"If Jimmy only sticks to his diet," George told Tom, "he'll feel well; then maybe we'll have the fun we used to have at the fairs."

They put Symbol in the old van, Sadie, and left for Indiana, Pennsylvania.

For Tom, it was good having Bonfire all to himself again. He worked with him as though he alone was the trainer of this blood bay colt and was getting him ready to race the following season, to drive and share with him his first competition. Temporarily he forgot Jimmy Creech, professional trainer and driver.

Yet instinctively he followed Jimmy's instructions, walking to the side of the two-wheeled cart while Bonfire pranced around the track, eager to go but responsive and obedient to the lines. Often Tom thought of the joy it would be just to sit behind him a few minutes, to have those supple hindquarters working so smoothly between his outstretched legs. But always he resisted the temptation, well remembering that Jimmy didn't want him to do it. He let the colt get his exercise in the paddock and while working him on the longe. And for many hours each day, he stood beside him while Bonfire grazed in the infield of the track.

There were times, too, when Tom added his own training lessons to those Jimmy had given him. He walked Bonfire up and down the wooden loading ramp, getting him used to entering and leaving a van, which would be so much a part of his racing life. And he walked him in and out of other sheds, now empty except for those of Miss Elsie, because Bonfire must get used to strange stalls and barns. And the colt followed, having full confidence in the hands which led him. Tom took him too to Miss Elsie's two-year-old colts, allowing Bonfire to nuzzle, neigh, and snort angrily occasionally at the other horses. Getting used to strange colts both in the stable and on the track was very necessary.

And whenever Tom brought the colt in from pulling the cart about the track, he would work over him the very same way as he would have done had Bonfire had a strenuous workout or race. Removing the harness and bridle, he would wipe him clean and rub him down, although there was no sweat or dirt on the colt's smooth red coat. Then he would throw a cooling blanket over him and walk him. It would all be a part of Bonfire's life, and it was important that he accept it now so that later Jimmy would only have to concentrate on bringing out the colt's speed and building stamina.

Tom wrote Uncle Wilmer regularly, telling him of Bonfire's progress and asking about the Queen. His uncle wrote back, telling him, "The mare never looked better, all right, and she's the best there is. Too bad Jimmy didn't have the money to breed her again. I'd sure like to see her have another colt. Maybe next year, huh? Maybe Jimmy will make some money this season. Where's he at now? I seen in *Hoof Beats* that he took a third at the Indiana Fair, but nothing since then. Is he coming to the Reading Fair this year? Hope so. Sure like to see him, all right, so would your aunt. We miss you, Tom, but know how busy you must be with the colt and all. You send more pictures of him. . . ."

Tom took more pictures of the colt and then sat down to write Uncle Wilmer. "I don't think Jimmy and George will make the Reading Fair this year. Jimmy's figuring on cutting the season short so he can get back here by late August . . . that's if things go well for him. He wants to work Bonfire. But next season I'm hoping we'll all be at Reading, and you'll see our wonderful colt go!"

Tom stopped writing at this point to look out the tackroom window. After a while he went on with his letter. "I don't know where Jimmy is right now. He wrote me after the Indiana Fair, but I haven't heard from him since. I'm not worried because I know how busy he and George must be. I figure they ought to be at the Clearfield Fair by now. . . ."

Tom finished his letter and sealed the envelope. But he was worried. Jimmy might be too busy to write, but it wasn't like George not to keep him posted, knowing how concerned Tom was about Jimmy. And here it was well into July, with at least four fairs behind them, and still no word. He would feel a lot better if only there had been some mention of Jimmy Creech in *Hoof Beats*—just so he'd know Jimmy was all right and racing. But there was nothing.

A week more went by, and still there was no word from

Jimmy or George. Two large vans pulled up to Miss Elsie's shed and Tom saw her supervise the loading of her two-year-old colts. Miss Elsie hadn't found what she was looking for in this group, just as she'd suspected she wouldn't months ago. And this year, the same as last year and the year before, Tom watched the colts leave for the big summer sales in Kentucky. He liked Miss Elsie very much, but he couldn't understand how she could breed, raise and train colts year after year, to get to know them so well, and then send them away to the sales. Maybe she just wouldn't let herself fall in love with any colt—not until she had found the right one. Tom didn't know or understand. Maybe the black filly with the white stockings would be *the* one for Miss Elsie.

For the next few days only Tom and Bonfire roamed about the empty sheds and worked on the track. Tom would have been lonely had it not been for his colt.

It was during this time that George's letter came.

Bedford Fair
July 29

Dear Tom,

I know I should have written long before this, but I thought you'd worry even more if I told you what I got to tell you now. I've been waiting and hoping things would get better for Jimmy, but I don't think so now. And they could get worse.

Jimmy has been sick quite a few times—the same trouble. Symbol ain't been racing good at all, and Jimmy started worrying when he started using his savings, what they are, to make ends meet. It's the first time I ever wished I had a lot of money, just so I could loan it to him. But then again, he most likely wouldn't take it, anyway.

He got so mad at the trouble he was having that he had stomach pains one night. That made him madder, and he threw away the list of foods that he should eat and did everything the doc told him not to do. And now he's worse than ever, hardly getting any sleep at all and looking almost like he's dead.

I been trying to get him to go back home. The colt and rest would fix him up again, I know. But he won't listen to me and is going to keep racing. I don't think we'll be back early like Jimmy planned. I only hope things don't get worse. Jimmy is in no shape to race. He's careless when driving, and I'm afraid for him and for the others in the race. And the dangerous part of it is that Jimmy don't know how careless he is.

I'm hating myself for telling you all this about Jimmy. But you got to know sometime, and I couldn't very well cover up what's wrong. I'm real worried, Tom.

Your letters have reached us, and I read them all to Jimmy, hoping they'll help. Keep sending pictures of the colt and keep writing. The only time Jimmy perks up at all is when we hear from you.

Your friend,
George

George's letter only made things worse for Tom, and he turned to Bonfire for comfort, spending every minute of the day with him and keeping busy. He tried hard not to think about Jimmy. He couldn't do anything for him at the fairs, and it only made him more miserable to think about him. He had a job here, and the best he could do was to teach Bonfire his lessons so well that Jimmy would have less to do when he returned to Coronet.

A few days later, Miss Elsie moved her group of yearlings

from her farm on the hill to the track. Their presence and the renewed activity made it a little easier for Tom, and he managed at times to forget Jimmy Creech. He saw the black filly and knew that she was everything Miss Elsie had said of her. Like his colt, she was clean-bodied and her legs were good-boned and shaped well, with four startling white stockings running up to the same height on all legs—to the hocks on the hind and to the knees on the fore.

The black filly was as feminine in appearance as his colt was masculine. She was slim, lithe and delicate of line, and her every movement was graceful and beautiful to watch. Her head was small and set finely on a long, slender neck. And running from her forehead down to her nostrils was a white, narrow blaze, the only other mark besides her stockings.

Tom watched her effortless, birdlike action while Miss Elsie worked her on the longe; then he went to Bonfire. And because it was his nature, he looked at his colt a long while, pointing out to himself the different physical characteristics between colt and filly.

In many respects they're alike, he thought. *Each has the same fineness of line, but the filly is so graceful she gives you the impression that her feet are scarcely touching the ground. My colt is graceful, too, but not as graceful as the filly. Bonfire gives you more the impression of power. He's taller and more muscular— maybe that's why. The filly glides and you get the feeling she might take off and fly. Maybe she will when Miss Elsie starts working her. On the other hand, my colt's stride is smooth and regular, and there's a feeling of power you get when you watch him that overshadows anything else—even his control of action.*

"My colt's neck is more muscled and more arched at the

crest than the filly's," Tom said aloud. "And his head is smaller, too. He probably gets both those characteristics from his sire, the Black. From what Jimmy has told me about the Black, I'd guess that."

Bonfire came to the door of his stall and shoved his muzzle into Tom's armpit. "There's a girl your age down the row," Tom said. "You'll be seeing a lot of her pretty soon now. She looks good—maybe the best Miss Elsie ever had. Only time will tell that."

And Tom knew, too, that only in time would they know what speed his colt possessed. A lot of colts and fillies looked good as yearlings, but failed utterly later on when their trainers asked for speed.

The days passed and Tom enjoyed Miss Elsie's company, especially when they went around the track together. For Miss Elsie had broken all her yearlings to bridle, harness and cart at the farm, and now at the track she followed very closely Tom's methods with Bonfire. But the woman worked longer and harder than Tom, for she had eleven yearlings in her sheds and she wouldn't let anyone else, even Tom, help her school and exercise her colts and fillies. Only she knew the kind of horse she wanted to take Mr. Guy's place.

It was two weeks since Tom had received George's letter, and there had been no further word. While Tom walked to the side of the cart as Bonfire pulled it around the track, he was thinking about Jimmy and wondering what was happening at Bedford.

So concerned was Tom with his thoughts that he didn't see Miss Elsie leave her shed, walking behind the Princess. Neither did he hear the filly's hoofs as she drew close. But he felt the light touch of Bonfire's mouth on the bit, and knew immediately that Miss Elsie was behind him. His colt always acted this way when another horse was on the track; he threw his head up a little, so eager was he to move out of his nimble walk. But the signal for which he waited so patiently didn't come.

Tom turned to find the filly's head, her white blaze shattering the blackness of her face, directly behind him.

Laughing, Miss Elsie turned the filly away and let her draw up alongside Bonfire. The colt didn't turn to the filly nor did the filly take any notice of Bonfire. Yet two pairs of ears pricked forward and strides lengthened until filly and colt felt the unspoken commands of their drivers through the lines. They slowed to a walk again.

"They're all business out here," Miss Elsie told Tom.

The boy nodded. "When I take Bonfire into your shed, he'll play and nuzzle the filly. But not here. He's serious about this," he added, smiling.

"And so is the Princess," Miss Elsie said, removing one hand from the lines to adjust her glasses. "I've named her Princess Guy, Tom," she added quietly.

Tom said nothing, but he knew full well that never before had she named any of her yearlings after Mr. Guy.

"You think she's it, then, Miss Elsie?"

"I think so, Tom. I know it's too early," she added quickly, "what with all the work ahead. But there's a feeling here." She raised the lines in her hands. "It's different somehow with Princess Guy than with any colt I've ever had. She looks good, but it's more than that. I feel this filly—for some reason I do. And she could be the one."

"I hope so, Miss Elsie," Tom said, his gaze on the red coat

and moving black tail and mane of his colt. And he thought, *if she's really it, she'll have Bonfire to reckon with.*

They were halfway down the backstretch when Tom asked, "If Princess Guy is the one you've been waiting for, what'll you do now that you've found her?"

"I'll go to the races with her, Tom," she returned quickly. "I always said I'd go out if I found another Mr. Guy."

"You'll drive her?"

"Of course, Tom. I drove Mr. Guy, didn't I?"

Miss Elsie didn't say anything more, becoming absorbed with every movement of the black filly for which she had waited ten long years. Finally she gave Princess Guy more line and left Tom behind.

The boy saw his colt gather himself and felt the burning desire of Bonfire to catch and pass the black filly. Tom's fingers moved on the lines, comforting Bonfire and letting him know that it wasn't time—not yet.

When he led Bonfire into the barn, he saw the rolled newspaper lying on the tack-room table. It was a daily Pittsburgh paper to which Jimmy subscribed and which Tom forwarded to him every day.

He didn't pick up the newspaper until after he had rubbed and walked Bonfire and put him in the paddock. Then, taking a pencil, he crossed out Jimmy's Coronet address and wrote, "c/o Race Secretary, Bedford Fair, Pa." He tossed it to one side, planning to take it to the Coronet post office on his way home. The paper rolled until it came to a stop against the wall of the room. And it was then that Tom saw the black headline of a story at the bottom of page one.

Quickly, frantically, he reached for the paper and tore the brown wrapper from about it. Then he read the story.

CORONET REINSMAN NARROWLY ESCAPES DEATH IN BAD SPILL AT BEDFORD FAIR

Jimmy Creech, Veteran Driver, Hospitalized After Race Collision

Bedford, Pa.—Jimmy Creech of Coronet, Pa., veteran of more than forty years of harness racing, collided with twenty-nine-year-old Frank Lunceford, of New York City, well-known night raceway driver, in the third race of today's program at the Bedford Fair.

Lunceford escaped injury when sulkies hooked wheels, but Creech was thrown, striking his head heavily against the ground. He was removed to the Bedford Hospital while still unconscious.

X-rays taken later showed that miraculously there was no brain concussion or skull fracture. Creech regained consciousness two hours after the accident. He will remain in the hospital a few days under close observation, doctors said, and should have complete rest when he's discharged.

Track officials stated that had Creech worn the new protective helmet liner beneath his sulky cap—worn by all other drivers in the race—he would have suffered less injury or might not have lost consciousness at all. He had been asked to wear the liner before the race by officials, but had refused.

Anguish for Jimmy was very evident in Tom's pale face when he finished reading. Yet he couldn't help thinking, *That's just like Jimmy. He wouldn't wear a good protective liner because they didn't wear them in the old days. And Jimmy won't stand for any changes—not Jimmy.*

But he'd be coming back to Coronet now, early in August, just as he'd planned. Yet for a different reason. Jimmy Creech couldn't go on racing this season, even if he wanted to, not after a spill like that. Tom wondered where it would all lead, and what Jimmy would do about the blood bay colt. Not so long ago, when Jimmy was in bad health and in need of money, he almost sold the Queen before her foal came. Tom didn't want to think of what Jimmy might possibly do now. Jimmy wouldn't, couldn't sell Bonfire! Or could he?

Tom wasn't certain of anything that Jimmy Creech might—or might not—do.

Dizzy Speed Ahead!

13

Two weeks later Jimmy returned to Coronet, his head swathed high with bandages, his face very pale. George helped him from the van, but Jimmy pushed his hands away. "No need for that," he said brusquely; then he greeted Tom as though nothing at all had happened.

The boy tried to smile but couldn't, not while looking into Jimmy's thin, drawn face and the eyes that burned hot within black, sunken pits.

Jimmy turned away. "Just a cut, that's all I have, Tom," he said angrily. "I've had 'em before, lots of 'em. And I'll have more before I'm through. Don't look so scared. Just a lot of bandages, I tell you." And with that he walked into the shed, mumbling, "The colt . . . I want to see the colt."

Tom stayed behind with George. "How bad is it, George?" he asked.

"Just a cut like he says," George returned, "—but a bad one. He's lucky. He coulda been killed, easy." George turned toward the shed. "It's his stomach I'm worried about more.

We got to get him to the doctor again."

George was walking toward the shed when Tom stopped him. "We ought to get Symbol out of the van first, shouldn't we?"

"No Symbol in there," George said quietly. "Sadie's empty."

"Where is he?"

"Jimmy got rid of him."

"Sold him?"

George shaded his eyes from the hot sun as he looked at the boy. "No. Jimmy figured on doin' that while he was in the hospital. He needed the money. But then a young farm kid from outside Bedford came to see him. The kid had been around the fair track an' Jimmy knew how much he wanted a trotter to hitch up to an old buggy he had an' drive around the country roads. So Jimmy just ups and gives him Symbol then and there."

Taking a chaw of tobacco, George shoved it in his mouth. "More'n the money he needed, he'd rather see Symbol get a good home. He knew that anyone who bought Symbol might race him. And he figured, I guess, that Symbol was more than ready to be retired. That's Jimmy, all right, knowin' when it's time for a horse to quit the races, but never realizing he oughta quit, too."

They had seen Jimmy standing before the colt's stall all during their conversation, but when they walked into the shed, Jimmy turned and went into the tack room.

George stopped to run his hands through Bonfire's black mane. "He ready, Tom?"

The boy nodded. "For anything, George. All Jimmy has to do is to get into the seat and drive him. Bonfire never makes a wrong move. And he knows that it's all business when he's out on the track."

Inside the tack room, they found Jimmy seated at the table, holding his head between his hands.

"The cut bother you?" George asked.

"No . . . just thinking," Jimmy returned. He rose to move nervously to the door and back. "When I remember how Lunceford fouled me up on that turn, it turns my stomach," he said bitterly. "I was going to win that race, and the five-hundred-dollar purse would have pulled me out of a hole. Now I'm back here without hardly enough to keep the colt in grain, let alone race him next year. And all because a fair-haired boy of the night raceways took a day off and spent it at a fair for the laughs he could get out of it—laughs and a bit of sun! They oughta stay where they belong," he added, bellowing. "If they want the raceways they ought to stay there . . . and keep their dirty driving there and not bring it to the fairs!" Jimmy's face was flushed with rage.

"Sit down, Jimmy!" It was George, and his voice was angry and no longer that of a friend.

Both Jimmy and Tom turned to him, and the paleness returned to Jimmy's face while he listened to George's hard words, spoken with neither pause nor sympathy.

"I been listening to you long enough. Now listen to me. I saw what happened on that turn. I was there, right when and where it happened. You pulled into Lunceford, Jimmy. I don't even think you know it, but you did. And maybe the same thing happened that day at Reading when you and Ray O'Neil hooked wheels. I don't know about that. I was too far away then. But I know what happened at Bedford. You tried to force Lunceford closer to the rail so you could get

by. You knew Symbol didn't have the finish to go around
him. But Lunceford didn't give way, an' you hooked wheels,
and you got the worst of it again, just like at Reading. Only
this time you pretty near got killed with those horses coming up behind an' just missin' you. You were lucky, and you
might not be so lucky again. You fouled Lunceford, Jimmy,
and if the judges didn't see it, I did."

George paused then, and his voice was a little softer as he
added, "An' like I said, you don't even realize you did it.
That's the pity of it, Jimmy. And it's the dangerous part of
it, too. You don't even know how reckless you are. You got
no business racing in that shape."

Jimmy said nothing when George had finished. He sat in
his chair, hurt and beaten. Tom bit his lip and turned away.
He couldn't look at Jimmy now; it took too much out of
him.

The room was quiet for a long while. Then Tom heard
Jimmy speak and the weak, shaking voice didn't seem to be
Jimmy's at all.

"Y–You mean I pulled into him, George? I fouled Lunceford? He didn't pull over on me? You saw it? You're sure?"

"I'm sure," George said. "I know." George's voice was
gentler now. "I wish that it wasn't true. But it is, and I have
to tell you, because you can't go on this way, Jimmy."

Jimmy Creech said no more, and Tom only turned away
from the window when George spoke again.

"You want to get better, don't you Jimmy? You want to
drive the colt, don't you? Tom said Bonfire's ready for anything you want to do with him."

"You know I do," Jimmy said weakly. "If I could have
just one good horse . . . to see him—" He stopped, his

gaze fixed on the table. "But it's no go, George," he added. "It takes money to feed and race him. And I haven't much left."

"But I've a little more," George said. "We can do anything we want if you just stop worryin' about it."

"And I have a hundred dollars in my savings account," Tom said. "It's yours, Jimmy."

"I don't want to take—" the man started to say. But George stopped him, his voice firm again.

"The colt is ours as much as yours. We're not giving *you* anything. We're thinkin' of the colt, aren't we, Tom?"

The boy nodded while Jimmy said, "Yes, he belongs to both of you . . . as much as he does to me."

"Then if he's ours we share responsibility with you," George said quickly. "And none of us are goin' to do any more worryin' about anything. You're going to get better, Jimmy. From now on you're listening to Tom and me jus' like we have to listen to you about training the colt. And I'm sayin' that you're going to see Doc Morton with me tomorrow. We're goin' to get that list of food you should eat an' the medicine. You're goin' to listen to us, Jimmy. We're taking over, startin' now. Spit out that gum you're chewin'. You know you shouldn't be doing it."

A flush rose quickly to Jimmy's face, but he removed the gum from his mouth and threw it in a pail. "Okay, George," he said quietly. "We'll try it your way from now on."

The following day Jimmy obediently accompanied George to the office of Dr. Morton in Pittsburgh. And late that afternoon, George returned to the stables alone.

"I sent him home early," George said, seeing the startled look on Tom's face.

"What'd the doctor say?"

"He said the X-rays of his stomach showed that Jimmy needed complete rest, either in a hospital or at home."

"But Jimmy wouldn't listen?"

"No, nothin' the doc said would keep Jimmy away from here for a good long time like the doc wanted. And I couldn't ask him to do that either. But he was scared, so he said he'd stay home a few days each week. And that was more'n I expected to hear Jimmy say."

"Jimmy must be scared," Tom said. "He really must be."

This was even more evident during the weeks that followed, for when Jimmy came to the stables he let Tom do all the work with the colt, and was content to tell him what to do with Bonfire and to watch them. His admiration for the colt and Tom's handling him, together with the strict diet and less work, were responsible for Jimmy's better health. He had stomach pains but his attacks were less severe and at longer intervals.

A week before school opened, Jimmy told Tom to sit behind Bonfire.

"It's time to start going with him," Jimmy said, turning over the lines to Tom. "But just jog him. Nothing more."

"But, Jimmy, it's his first time. Don't you want to—"

"You mean you're afraid of what he might do, Tom?"

"Oh, no, Jimmy," the boy returned quickly. "I know him too well for that. He won't make a wrong move. It's just that . . . well, I mean . . . it'll be so good to sit behind him, to be the very first one. You should—"

Jimmy shielded the softness that came to his eyes by sweeping his hand over the small bandage which now was the only evidence of his accident. "Sure, it'll be good," he

said with forced harshness. "That's why I want you to be behind him. He's yours as much as mine . . . maybe even
more. You're both learnin' together and I'll be happy if I can
do a good job on each of you." Going to Bonfire's head, he
added quickly, "Get goin' now an' I'll be watching. Make it
two miles at a slow jog. We'll start him easy an' later work
up to six miles. We'll concentrate on building up his wind
and stamina now and go for speed in the spring."

Tom took his seat. He said nothing to Jimmy, and spoke
only to Bonfire through the long lines.

"You set, Tom?" Jimmy asked impatiently.

The boy moved his head in agreement; then Jimmy released the colt and Bonfire moved onto the track at Tom's
unspoken command.

He took him the wrong way around the track, the same as
he'd always done, well knowing that the only time they'd
turn him the right way around would be for a speed-work-
out. Bonfire would then know that turning meant racing
and all-out effort.

Tom felt the colt's surprise when the lines told him that
he could move out of his walk for the first time. His strides
lengthened and they were low, even and effortless. There was
no indication that having Tom in the seat was any different
from pulling an empty one; it was as though he had expected to pull the boy's extra weight in time, and this was
the time.

Bonfire was eager to go faster, but Tom kept him at the
jog which Jimmy had ordered. They came around the first
lap and passed George and Jimmy. George called and nodded his head to Tom in approval. But Jimmy had eyes only
for the colt and his every movement.

Tom sat back a little more comfortably in his seat and gloried in the feeling of riding behind his colt. He thought of the day Bonfire had been foaled; he remembered the days that followed, his handling him at the farm, the tight halter, the hours spent together in the pasture, the Queen, Uncle Wilmer and finally Coronet again and Bonfire's weaning. There were so many wonderful things to remember—all leading to this moment! Yet there was so much more to come, too. With his colt, Tom looked forward to all that was ahead.

Bonfire was starting his last half-mile when Tom saw Miss Elsie come onto the track with her Princess Guy.

The colt snorted but kept to a jog at Tom's command. Yet the distance between filly and colt lessened rapidly until Tom was opposite Miss Elsie; then she let Princess Guy out a little more and the two yearlings went along as a team.

"How's Jimmy this morning?" Miss Elsie called.

"He's feeling better, thanks."

"Anything I can do?" she asked when they entered the backstretch.

Tom was comparing the action of her filly to his colt, but he turned to Miss Elsie and said, "You've done enough. George and I appreciate it very much."

Pulling her peaked cap further down over her head, Miss Elsie said, "I haven't done anything, Tom." She clucked to Princess Guy and started moving away from them.

The colt was impatient to follow and Tom's fingers tapped on the lines before he called out to Miss Elsie's back, "George and I found two hundred more pounds of oats than we paid you for." But the woman only clucked louder to her filly. "And there was more than an extra ton of hay, too," Tom shouted.

Miss Elsie pulled rapidly away, and never even turned her head in Tom's direction.

Jimmy and George were still in front of the shed when Tom brought Bonfire off the track.

Jimmy's eyes were only for the colt as he said quietly, "He's all I could ask. He's *it* for us."

George smiled. "Just like the black filly with the white stockings is *it* for Miss Elsie?" he asked.

"Yeah," Jimmy said, without taking his eyes from Bonfire, "about the same, I guess. Nobody 'round here ever saw the like of these two yearlings. Nobody. What's inside of 'em will come out in time; then we'll know more."

They took Bonfire into the shed and were removing the harness from his sweated body when Tom asked, "Then you think we'll have him ready in time to race next season?"

Jimmy said, "We'll see, Tom. I think so now, but I don't want to rush him any. He looks like he'll take the work, though. He's big and ready."

"And maybe we'll even get him to Reading?" Tom asked eagerly. He was thinking of Uncle Wilmer's last letter in which his uncle had told him how much he wanted to see the colt race next season.

Jimmy removed the bridle from Bonfire's tossing head before saying, "Depends on how much money we have by that time, Tom. Reading is pretty far east."

George said quickly, "Money problems are my worry, Jimmy. You think only of the colt. Get him ready for us. That's all Tom and I ask."

Jimmy smiled and turned to Tom again. "You're thinkin' of your Uncle Wilmer seeing him. Is that it, Tom?" And when the boy nodded, Jimmy added, "Then you write and tell him it looks like we'll be there."

Happier than he'd been in a long, long time, Tom ran the wet sponge quickly over Bonfire's hard body, cleaning his nostrils well and squeezing the water from the sponge until it ran down the colt's face. Bonfire liked that. Things were looking up, Tom thought. Next season would be different, much different, for Jimmy Creech and for all of them.

Through September and October, life was everything Tom could have asked of it. He drove Bonfire regularly, sharing the colt's workouts with Jimmy. Bonfire was kept at his jogging, and as much as Tom and Jimmy, too, wanted to put the watch on him they resisted the temptation in the best interests of the colt and spent their time building up his stamina and staying power. Bonfire thrived on the work. His body became very strong and hard, his legs even more developed.

Occasionally, perhaps once a week, Jimmy let Tom sprint the colt for very short distances of no more than two hundred yards. Tom opened him up only a little, but each time the effect upon the boy was that he was being picked up and hurled forward by some unseen force from behind; yet he knew this power and fairly dizzy speed was directly ahead of him.

Jimmy said, "He's got more sprinting snap than any horse I've ever seen. If he can carry it through he'll be unbeatable."

During these weeks Jimmy spent as much time schooling Tom on driving technique as he did with the colt.

"You got the hands. We know that, Tom," he said. "An' you got strong arms and a good back. They're natural gifts and more important to you than you realize now."

"He's got the head, too," George interrupted, chawing

thoughtfully on his tobacco while listening to Jimmy.

"Yeah," Jimmy agreed, "as George says, you got the brains and understand horses. The colt, for example, senses how you feel about him. He has complete confidence in you. He'll make any move you want him to—"

"Tom's got an even temper. Never gets excited," George interrupted again. "That's important, too, for any driver to have. Jimmy knows that."

Jimmy looked at George, but his friend's gaze was turned away. "Yes," Jimmy said, "George is right. You got to keep cool in a race. That way your judgment is better and you think faster when you get in a tight spot. Knowing how to handle yourself and your horse in races is an art in itself, Tom. It only comes after years and years of racing experience. But I aim to tell you all I can just in case—" Jimmy stopped talking.

"Just in case what, Jimmy?" Tom asked with concern.

"Just in case nothing," Jimmy said. "I only meant there's no sense takin' what I know to the grave with me." He laughed. "We all have to die someday. And like George says, 'We're old fogies.' So I just plan to start telling you what I know now. As I said, it'll take a long time anyway, Tom."

And that's the way Jimmy Creech had left it. Tom thought from what Jimmy had said about dying that maybe he was feeling worse. But in the weeks that followed Jimmy looked better than ever and had only one bad attack. It happened early in November, after Jimmy read the story of the Yearling Fall Sales held at Harrisburg, Pennsylvania.

His face became livid with rage, and he threw the copy of *Hoof Beats* hard against the table of the tack room.

"Forty-eight thousand dollars for a yearling!" he bellowed,

walking up and down the room. "Where do they get that kind of money?"

George tried to quiet him, but Jimmy pushed him out of the way; then he picked up the magazine.

"Listen to this, Tom," he shouted, his voice shaking in his fury. " 'An all-time record for the Harrisburg sales was set when the gray colt Silver Knight was sold at auction for forty-eight thousand dollars. Spirited bidding lasting more than two hours ended with the successful bid of Phillip Cox, wealthy Pittsburgh clothing manufacturer.' "

Jimmy stopped reading and turned savagely to the boy. "You think Phillip Cox bought that colt, Tom? Well, he didn't! The Phillip Cox Clothing Company bought Silver Knight!"

George said quietly, "But maybe this Phillip Cox likes horses."

Jimmy paid no attention to him. "This guy Cox knows nothing about horses, Tom," he went on shouting, "and maybe he likes 'em less. Silver Knight will be expected to publicize the Cox Clothing Company. I can just see the company name on his blanket every time he sets a hoof near where people are watching. He'll just be another name on the company payroll—publicity, advertising, that's all it amounts to! Just like last year the Cox Clothing Company had a group of midget auto racers and the year before racing motor boats. I read about all of them! I know! And now this year it's horses. But we won't see 'em at the fairs, Tom. Don't worry about that! The Cox Clothing Company will race its horses at the night raceways where there are lots more people to see its name . . . and where they'll get a lot more publicity. Big business, that's harness racing today,

Tom. Everybody, just *everybody,* is climbing aboard!" Only then did Jimmy's voice soften as he sat down wearily in his chair. "And it might be the end of a grand, wonderful sport, Tom; it might, if we can't some day get it back to the fairs, where harness racing belongs."

That night Jimmy had his bad attack, and he stayed at home resting the remainder of the week while Tom worked the blood bay colt.

Hard Fists

14

While Jimmy was home in bed, George told Tom, "I know Jimmy must sound awfully bitter to you. He's sick, but y'got to remember he's sincere about 'most everything he says. He's sick to his stomach with that ulcer an' sick to his head when he realizes what's happening to his sport—*our* sport," George added quietly.

It was early morning and they were cleaning Bonfire after a long workout. "Wipe his nostrils clean, Tom," George said. Going to the colt's tail and lifting it, he sponged the sweated hindlegs.

Tom was working on Bonfire's small head and couldn't see George. But the man's voice came easily to him.

"You got to remember, too, Tom," George went on, "that Jimmy and I were brought up in the old days. To sit behind a fast horse and to set out for town in a buggy was like some guy today ridin' around in a blue convertible. On the way to town, we'd never let anyone pass us—not if we could help it. That's how harness racin' started, just tryin' to

get to town with your horse before another guy. We lived
for our horses and we still do, Jimmy 'specially. I don't do
anything but help him. But I understand all right how
Jimmy feels."

Tom ran his sponge down Bonfire's neck, and now he
could see George. The colt's tail was hanging over the man's
bald, bared head while he went on cleaning the horse.

"I guess I'm jus' more adaptable than Jimmy is," George
continued thoughtfully. "Maybe you can call it that. Anyway, what I mean is I seem to be able to accept a lot of
things that Jimmy can't. He's too mad to accept any change
in harness racing. Lots of what Jimmy Creech says about
night racing, the raceways an' even the Phillip Cox Clothing
Company may be true. Don't you forget that," he added
emphatically.

"But there are other things Jimmy should remember, an'
he won't. The way I see it, harness racin' has to have its
progress jus' like everything else in this world today. It's
getting big because a lot of new folks are learning what a
grand sport it is. You wouldn't have raceways if a lot of
people didn't want to see our horses go. Our sport don't belong only to the farmer and country folks—not no more, it
don't. City people who never saw a fair now can watch our
horses go at a raceway track . . . and that's good in many
ways. But Jimmy can't see it. Not for the life of him, he
can't."

George came around to the other side of the colt and
looked over Bonfire's back at Tom. He took a chew of tobacco before continuing.

"It's good because it means that a lot more people all over
the country are becoming interested in our sport. It means

bigger purses than you'll ever get at most fairs. Jimmy in his best years at the fairs never made much more than enough to pay his feed bills and have a little left over. An' that's not right, Tom. Jimmy says it's all sport with him and that's the only way it should be. But I say it's his lifework too, an' he should have more to show for it after fifty years of it than he does!" George's voice rose so high that he swallowed a little tobacco juice. He coughed and then was quiet for a moment while Tom threw the white cooling blanket over Bonfire.

George followed when the boy led Bonfire outside into the cool November morning. While they walked the colt, George continued.

"And don't forget, Tom, that with more people interested in our sport it means more and better horses, too, because the competition is a lot keener than it was, and that always means improvement. But it doesn't mean," he added quickly, "that the little guy like Jimmy Creech is bein' shoved out of the picture. With Jimmy's horse sense he's got just as much chance of breeding a champion as any guy with money to burn. Look at Bonfire—there's your answer to that. An' look at Miss Elsie, with all her money, just waitin' and waitin' year after year for the good colt she wants."

They turned Bonfire around at the end of the row and walked him back again.

"Maybe this Phillip Cox won't do anything with that forty-eight-thousand-dollar yearling, either," George said. "An' then again maybe he will. It's a gamble for him jus' like it is for the rest of us—Miss Elsie, Jimmy and hundreds of others—whether we're gettin' ready for the raceways or the fairs. You jus' never know when the good colt will come along."

George seemed to have finished, so Tom spoke for the first time. "But do you think Jimmy is right about what he said of this Phillip Cox, that he'll only use Silver Knight to publicize his clothing company?"

"Maybe so, maybe not, Tom. Maybe Jimmy's only half right. Phillip Cox may like horses all right an' just figures that if Silver Knight comes along and races well he'll get a little extra publicity for his company. I don't know. After all, Silver Knight might not even get to the races. A lot of high-priced yearlings don't."

"I know, George," Tom said thoughtfully. "But I certainly agree with Jimmy that a person should be in this sport because he loves it and not because his company might get some free advertising out of it."

"I do, too, Tom, and I'm hopin' with Jimmy Creech that folks don't lose track of the fairs with all this new popularity of the night raceways." George paused, then said with deep sincerity, "I only wish more people would come to our fairs. They'd get the feel of the horses then just as we do. You can't get that feelin' at any night raceway."

"How do you know, George? Have you ever been to a night raceway?"

"No, but I know it's not the same as watching 'em go at a fair. I just know it."

When Jimmy returned to the track the following week, he looked a little pale but was in better spirits than Tom thought he'd be. That was Jimmy, all right, just as George said—up one moment, down the next. Jimmy never mentioned Phillip Cox and his high-priced gray yearling; in fact, he seemed to have forgotten all about them. Besides, there were other yearlings to think about now. He watched Miss Elsie work her black filly faster and harder.

"She's it for Miss Elsie, all right," he told Tom. "Miss Elsie can turn that filly off an' on just like you do with the colt. But they're different. That filly don't even seem to be trying, but she's flyin', Tom. While with our colt—"

"He just makes you dizzy watching him," Tom finished for Jimmy. "You know something is happening when he sprints."

Jimmy nodded. "Yeah, that's what I mean. Two different kinds of yearlings to watch, but each havin' a world of speed." He stopped, then added, "But Miss Elsie is bringing her filly along fast—too fast for me. I like to give them more time to grow than Miss Elsie does."

During the rest of November, Jimmy redoubled his efforts to teach Tom everything he could about driving in a race. Tom listened long and hard to Jimmy's instructions, and when he was alone with Bonfire, either in the stable or on the track, he went over and over all the lessons Jimmy was teaching him. There was a lot to learn, too much to absorb even in a few months or a few years. As Jimmy said, "It takes long years of practice and experience, Tom. Even I'm still learning. Something new is always coming up when you're in a tight spot."

But there were fundamental lessons, and these Tom concentrated upon and learned quickly, for they were based on natural instinct and knowing your horse. His skill in handling the lines behind Bonfire increased under Jimmy's careful eye. His hands, wrists, arms and back developed and were strong. He learned to rate the colt's speed, taking him a quarter of a mile in the time Jimmy wanted; and never did he carry a stopwatch. He listened long to Jimmy's talks on track strategy during a race, and when he was alone with Bonfire on the track he pictured other horses racing against them. With the colt only jogging, he visualized all kinds of tight racing situations and then tried to get out of them. He took his colt up behind the imaginary lead horse, yet kept his eye warily on those coming up behind. And when he knew he might be pocketed by them, he pulled Bonfire out and made his drive for the wire. There were times when he let the colt set the pace and other times when he came up from behind and around. In his mind, he tried everything Jimmy told him he might expect in a race; and he repeated them over and over again until he was racing Bonfire even while he slept.

Jimmy and George watched him with the colt and nodded their heads in approval. Everything was going well again, and everyone was happy. Then it happened.

The first day in December they watched the huge red-and-white horse van drive down the road and stop at the next shed. Jimmy, George and Tom saw the lettering on the van at the same time. It was such large lettering that they had no trouble reading it:

COX CLOTHING COMPANY STABLES

"Phillip Cox," George muttered. "What's he doin' here?"

Jimmy said nothing, but when Tom turned to look at him he saw that every bit of color had been drained from his thin face. Yet Jimmy never left the doorway of their shed while the van was being unloaded and four yearlings, including the valuable Silver Knight, were taken into the shed. Jimmy's eyes blazed with anger as he watched everything.

He saw Miss Elsie and the other drivers at Coronet gather

around during the unloading. He saw the long, low, blue convertible come down the row and stop behind the van. Miss Elsie went to meet the tall, middle-aged man wearing an open camel's hair coat and a brown hat. He saw Miss Elsie smile at the man and shake his hand. He said nothing when George mentioned that "Probably that guy is Phillip Cox. Looks like what you'd expect of a clothing manufacturer."

As he watched the man take his hat off to Miss Elsie, he noticed that his hair was dark and heavy, with no trace of gray. He saw them go over to the big colt with the tossing gray head. He knew that was Silver Knight, just as George and Tom did.

The groom pulled back the fine white blanket with the red borders. The lettering across it read, "Cox Clothing Company." Miss Elsie stepped back to get a better look at Silver Knight; then they covered the colt again and all followed him into the shed.

It was only then that Jimmy Creech spoke, and he never turned to Tom or George as he said, "Goin' home for a little while. Stomach."

They let him go without a word, knowing that nothing they could say would help. When his car had gone down the road, George said with more bitterness in his voice than Tom had ever heard before, "It's not enough that Phillip Cox is here. He had to go an' pick Jimmy's racing colors, too."

Tom glanced at Jimmy Creech's worn red-and-white blanket hanging in the sun and nodded sadly.

A short while later, the blue convertible left with Mr. Cox at the wheel.

"That's the blue convertible I told you about some time

ago," George said, "—the kind Jimmy and me never knew."
Then he saw Miss Elsie walking alone toward the track. "I'll
find out what it's all about," he said, leaving Tom.

He was back in a few minutes.

"Miss Elsie said that Phil Cox's father was a friend of her
father's," George said. "He needed a place to keep his colts
until he goes to Florida for training January first. He
couldn't get away from his business before then."

"He'll only be here a month, then," Tom said thoughtfully. "Maybe it'll be all right, George. Maybe it will. A
month isn't very long."

"It depends on Jimmy," George said. "It all depends on
how he takes Cox's being here at all."

Tom learned how very long a month can be when you
begin dreading each day and the next—for thirty-one days.
Jimmy seldom talked and he just withdrew into his hard,
embittered shell. Tom and George pleaded with him to stay
home, but he came every day as though attracted despite
himself to the shed next door with its newly painted red-
and-white tack trunks, its gleaming sulkies and soft black
sets of harness. Always the fine white blankets with their
bold red lettering, "Cox Clothing Company," would be
hanging on the lines to air, to wave in the breeze as though
to taunt Jimmy Creech still more.

Jimmy walked by Cox's shed once a day to look through
the open doors and see the colts' nameplates, lettered black
on golden brass, hanging above the stall doors. Yet he never
said a word to anyone who worked for Phillip Cox—even to
his trainer or the grooms, who were friendly and nodded to
him when he walked past.

Phillip Cox seldom came to the stables and for that Tom and George were grateful.

Each morning they would stand beside the track to watch Cox's trainer work his colts, for they had been broken before arriving at Coronet. When the gray colt swept by, Jimmy would never ask Tom what he thought of him; it was as though Jimmy's whole being was now completely absorbed by his bitterness for Phillip Cox and his kind.

Jimmy's face became more haggard than Tom had ever seen it, and he lost weight until he was nothing but skin and bones. Tom didn't think Jimmy could get any thinner or look worse. But Jimmy did both, and Tom was the cause of it.

Early one morning, two weeks after the arrival of Phillip Cox, Jimmy reached the track in time to see Tom leaving the shed next door. His eyes blazed in anger, yet he said nothing to the boy and turned away from him.

"I only wanted to see Silver Knight close," Tom called after him. "That's all I did, Jimmy!"

But after that Jimmy ignored Tom completely, and when he had anything to say to him he would direct his remarks to George. Moreover, Jimmy took over all the work with the blood bay colt, and Tom didn't drive any more. It was then, too, that Jimmy started chewing gum again and worked hard from early morning until dark. The stomach pains came again, both at the track and at home. But Jimmy kept working.

It was Saturday and the day before Christmas when Phillip Cox arrived at the track with another yearling he'd bought. A few hours later Cox and his trainer took the new dark bay colt, wearing bridle, harness and lines, but pulling no cart, onto the track.

There had been no snow and the weather was still mild, so George and Tom stood outside their shed while Jimmy sat in the tack room. They could see his face pressed hard against the closed window, watching the new colt as intently as they were.

George said, "That's the baby they've been expectin'. He hasn't had much breaking, and they're aimin' on doing it before going to Florida, I guess."

Tom watched while Cox held the long lines behind the colt and his trainer had the bridle. Anyone could see that the dark bay was nervous and fidgety. He didn't quite know what was expected of him.

The colt stopped, refusing to go forward, and Tom said, "They shouldn't rush him. He doesn't know what it's all about yet."

Phillip Cox snapped the whip in his hand but did not touch the colt.

George muttered, "I heard Cox say he'd worked with a lot of colts. You'd never know it to look at him now."

Phillip Cox snapped the whip again, but the sound of it only made the colt more nervous and he shifted uneasily without moving forward.

"Why doesn't the trainer take the lines?" Tom asked. "He ought to know how to go about it better than Cox."

"He does," George returned. "But Cox is his boss, an' maybe the guy don't want to lose his job."

The dark bay colt half-reared; his trainer brought him down and started talking to him and stroking him. But Phillip Cox only snapped his whip again, and more sweat broke out on the colt's body. The trainer turned to Phillip Cox, his eyes worried, but he said nothing to his employer.

The colt reared again, higher this time, and when he came

down he felt the sharp sting of the whip on his haunches. Startled, he rose again and his dark body was wet with lathered sweat.

Phillip Cox's whip was raised again to strike the colt when Tom shouted and ran toward them; behind him he could hear George's footsteps.

The colt never stopped at the height of his rearing this time; he went over backwards, his fear of the whip causing him to lose his balance. When he went down he stayed down, and felt the cut of the whip—once, twice—on his hindquarters.

Tom threw himself on Phillip Cox's back. But even as he did he felt the man being torn from his arms, and Tom landed heavily on the ground. Rolling, he turned over quickly to find that Jimmy Creech was clawing and tearing with maniacal fury at the tall, heavy body of Phillip Cox.

There was nothing fair about Jimmy's tactics. He lunged, gouged and kicked Cox, who sought to get hold of his crazed opponent. Jimmy had him down and together they rolled on the hard ground of the track. For two or three minutes no one stopped them, and then they all moved upon the fighting mass of arms and legs. When they got them apart, both faces were bloody and torn. They pulled them away from each other and half-carried them to their sheds.

George and Tom got Jimmy into the tack room and set his battered, beaten body down on the cot. But his eyes still blazed and he made several attempts to get to his feet before lying back. After a while he opened his eyes again and found Tom watching him. He smiled grimly and nodded his head. "Did it, Tom," he mumbled through swollen lips. "And I'd do it again. He's a—"

"He'll be all right," George said quietly, bringing a basin of hot water. "He got no more than he gave Cox. An' Jimmy's body is hard . . . hard as they come."

But a little later, Jimmy's face became agonized in pain. Quickly Tom went to him. "What hurts, Jimmy? What is it?"

The words were hard in coming, and Jimmy fought to make himself heard, "Stomach, Tom. My stomach. Doctor."

It was then that Jimmy Creech went home to stay.

Let the Speed Come!

15

Dr. Morton told George and Tom that Jimmy wouldn't get well unless he stayed home in bed and had nursing care. Only with complete rest, strict medical treatment, and freedom from worry of all kind could he be helped; if Jimmy didn't follow instructions the ulcer would get worse.

The practical nurse Dr. Morton sent came to live in Jimmy's small, white-frame house on the outskirts of Coronet. If Jimmy wondered where they'd get the money to pay for her services, he never asked. He only sought relief from the severe and frequent pains that racked his stomach and twisted his face in agony. It wasn't until early spring that any great amount of relief came to him. it was only then that he asked about the blood bay colt.

Tom's eyes turned from the racing pictures, which were the only things that relieved the bareness of the walls of Jimmy's bachelor quarters, to look at the small, flat body beneath the bedsheets.

"Bonfire's a natural, Jimmy," the boy said. "He has all

the speed we expected from him. I brushed him a quarter in thirty-three seconds this morning."

George moved across the room to Jimmy's bedside. "But Tom held him in all the way," he said. "We never let him go faster than that 'cause we didn't think you'd want us to."

"No," Jimmy said in a weak voice, "that's fast enough for him now. I don't want to rush him. Let the speed come to him. Don't force him. It'll come."

"I've brushed him up to a half-mile, too," Tom said, "but without pushing him. Then I hold him down for the last half. But he wants to go, Jimmy," he added eagerly. "He really does."

"That's good, Tom," Jimmy said, his eyes lightening a little. "He knows what it's all about. He's got the will to win. And that's what I was hoping for when I bred the Queen to the Black. The Queen didn't have that. The Black gave it to the colt." He paused for a moment, resting. The nurse, a small gray-haired woman, stood near the door and watched Jimmy with concern. But Jimmy wasn't through talking.

"Keep the colt down, Tom," he said. "Remember that . . . no rushing him. Go along just as you have." Jimmy turned his head toward the doorway. "Mrs. Davis, leave us alone for a moment, please."

The nurse nodded; but her eyes pleaded with George and Tom not to stay too long.

Jimmy waited until the door closed behind Mrs. Davis. "Where's the money coming from to pay her?" he asked.

"We got it," George said quickly. "Don't worry about it. I'm the business end of this outfit." He smiled for Jimmy's benefit. "She doesn't charge much. She needed a home, an' you're givin' her that."

"But—" Jimmy began, only to be silenced by Tom.

"When you put all our money together, it makes more than you think," the boy said. "As George said, there's nothing to worry about."

"But how long will it last?" Jimmy asked, his sunken eyes upon them. "How can we manage to race the colt, to pay for feed, equipment, even gas for the van?"

"I've fixed up the sulky and all the harness, everything," George said. "We don't need to buy a thing. It's all like new."

"And the colt will make money for us, Jimmy," Tom said. "Once he gets going everything will be all right."

"I hope so, Tom," Jimmy smiled weakly; then he closed his eyes and they thought he was asleep until he said, "It's been a long time, a very long time . . . since I had a good one."

Leaning over him, George said, "You'll be driving him, Jimmy. The doc said you're getting better fast. Just do everything he says an' don't worry about a thing. Then you'll be up behind the colt soon."

"Sure, George," Jimmy mumbled; but he didn't open his eyes.

George lifted his bald head away from Jimmy. When he and Tom left the room there were tears in their eyes.

As usual, early the next morning before school, Tom had Bonfire out on the track. The sun felt good on his back and he knew the red colt liked it too, for Bonfire neighed repeatedly while Tom jogged him the wrong way around the track, loosening him up.

Through the lines he talked to his colt, telling him to bide his time. *That's the way Jimmy wants it,* he told him. *Get your legs and body so strong and hard that no racing will ever bother them. Let the speed come slow and easy, Bonfire. We have time . . . all the time in the world.*

But each time Tom jogged Bonfire past the shed which Phillip Cox and his high-priced yearling had occupied, he said to himself, "It's not fair . . . somehow it isn't fair." And for the first time he felt the embitterment that Jimmy Creech had lived with so very long.

"Jimmy doesn't have all the time in the world at all," he told the colt. "You and I have time, but he doesn't. We've got to speed things up for him. He needs you, Bonfire . . . not the money you'll make for him, but the satisfaction you'll give him. Jimmy wants to know that he's still an important part of his sport. He wants to know that it still requires understanding and knowledge of horses to make a champion, rather than how much money you've got in the bank. Let's go, Bonfire!"

Turning the colt around, Tom opened him up. Long, muscled legs moved with the power and precision of a mighty machine. So fast was Bonfire's sprint that in a matter of a few yards Tom, as always, felt that the wheels of his sulky would leave the ground. Bonfire's strides were far-reaching and came with the swiftness of wings. Yet the blood bay colt never pulled on the bit, and drove down the stretch well within himself, waiting for the signal Tom might give him this time.

They swept by the quarter pole, then the half, and Tom, his face flushed with the velocity of Bonfire's speed, let him go. He touched the lines and the colt responded with a burst of extreme swiftness that took the boy's breath away. The colt's black tail swept hard against his face and he heard himself shouting, "Fast for Jimmy, Bonfire! Fast for Jimmy!"

Then Jimmy Creech was with him.

"Don't rush him, Tom. Remember, don't rush him."

The boy's fingers moved along the lines again; the colt responded immediately, and slowed down. Tom brought him down to a jog, then turned him around.

Miss Elsie came onto the track while Tom was still jogging Bonfire. She drove her black filly up beside Bonfire, then said to Tom, "He's more sweated than you usually have him, Tom. Working him harder?"

"Just a little," Tom admitted. "Jimmy says . . ."

Miss Elsie smiled, and her large teeth were startling white in the sun. "Jimmy never would work a colt as hard as he should be worked, Tom," she said, "especially this colt; he's ready for it."

Tom said only, "Jimmy's the boss."

"How is he, Tom? Any better? I dropped in on him last week. He didn't look very well."

"He's a little better," Tom said quietly.

"If there's anything I can do, Tom . . ." Miss Elsie paused and glanced away. "Well, you know how I feel about Jimmy. We need men like him."

"Thanks, Miss Elsie. But we'll get along all right. And you've been kind about giving us the feed and the hay."

"That's nothing, Tom," she said quickly; then, changing the subject, she said, "I've got Princess Guy down to a very fast mile. She's more than ready for the fairs."

"Bonfire will be ready, too," Tom said a little defiantly as though in justification of Jimmy's training methods. "What fairs are you going to, Miss Elsie?"

"I'm going out to Ohio, Tom," she returned. "That's where I went with Mr. Guy." Her eyes shone with eagerness, but she said no more. That she had raced Mr. Guy in Ohio ten years ago was all the explanation necessary as to why she chose Ohio fairs in preference to those held in her own state.

Tom watched her pull away, singing to the black filly with the white stockings. She was almost out of hearing distance when she called back, "The Ohio fairs first, then I'll decide where we go from there." And it seemed to Tom that Miss Elsie's words were meant only for herself.

Bonfire neighed after the filly and tossed his head. Tom turned him in the direction of the shed, where George was waiting for them.

If Miss Elsie stuck to her plans to go to the Ohio fairs, Bonfire and Princess Guy wouldn't meet on the track during the coming season. In many ways Tom was sorry, for he had all the confidence in the world that his colt could beat any other two-year-old in the country. Yet he'd never let him out all the way.

George was holding two letters in his hand when Tom reached him with Bonfire. "They're for you," George said, taking the colt. "Postman was just here."

Taking the letters, Tom said, "One's from the Association; the other's from Uncle Wilmer." He opened the first and held the certificate up for George to see.

"Your license to drive," George said, squinting his eyes in the sun. "It's good it's come, Tom." He turned away to lead the colt into the shed before adding sadly, "Maybe we'll be needin' it this season. Maybe we will."

Tom knew full well what he meant, for he and George had discussed his racing Bonfire in case Jimmy didn't get better in time to go out. And just now, with only a few weeks to go until the first fair, it didn't look as though Jimmy would be ready.

"Maybe it's just as well he don't go out—even if he does get better," George had said when they'd filed for Tom's driver's license. "It might not do him any good, even with the colt. And this time Jimmy has to get completely well, the doc says—or be an invalid the rest of his life."

Tom walked behind the colt while George took him inside. He looked long and hard at the license, for it meant he could drive his colt in the races. And while he knew the joy it would be to begin his lifework the same time that Bonfire started his, he realized the responsibility that would go with it, for they'd be racing for Jimmy. He knew too the danger he would face with no racing experience behind him or his colt. They were both untried.

George said, "I'll take care of the colt. Get goin' to school or you'll be late again."

But Tom opened Uncle Wilmer's letter and read it aloud to George.

"The Queen's in good shape, all right," Uncle Wilmer wrote. "Been on grass for a couple of months now. Never looked better. Your aunt and me are sorry to hear Jimmy's been so sick and ain't better by now. You see he gets good care. Ain't no better man around than Jimmy. He should have been a farmer. Then he wouldn't get sick like he does.

"Glad the colt's coming along like I said he would. You race him, Tom, if Jimmy ain't in shape. You can do it all right. That colt knows you better'n anybody in the world. He'll go for you. I believe it.

"And you come to Reading in September! I want to see

that colt go. Beat them all, he will. You come. You remember us to Jimmy and George. Your Uncle Wilmer."

When Tom had finished reading he put the letter away.

"Do you think we'll make the Reading Fair, George?" he asked, helping to remove the harness from the colt.

"I don't know," George said, reaching for the sponges. "The money's going faster'n I let Jimmy know. And Reading's a long time off, Tom—September. A lot can happen before September." He brought the wet sponge down on Bonfire's sweated neck and added, "Depends on the colt, Tom. It all depends on him."

Tom stooped to pick up the other sponge in the water pail, but George stopped him.

"You get goin' like I said," the man told him. "You only got a couple more weeks 'fore school closes. Then your work will really start. Race drivin' is no cinch."

Tom left for school, realizing that what George had said was true.

The days passed, school closed for Tom, and Miss Elsie left with her black filly for the Ohio fairs. It was time for Bonfire to leave too for his first race, and George and Tom knew that Jimmy Creech wasn't going along with them.

"There's a little improvement in his condition," Dr. Morton told them. "But he's still worrying about his financial problems and that's keeping him back more than anything else. I don't know what we can do for him. I mentioned that as an old friend there'd be no bill from me, and I told him that Mrs. Davis is more than glad to have a home. She's a widow, you know, and a little too old to get many jobs. She's just right for Jimmy. Yet he worries about paying all of us in spite of what I tell him."

"Jimmy don't want anybody to give him somethin' for nothin'," George said. "That's been Jimmy's trouble all along, never wanting a favor from nobody."

Then Tom said, "It'll be different when he has his own money—and the colt will make it for him. That and being so proud of Bonfire will do it for Jimmy."

George said, "I hope so, Tom. But it won't be easy. Nothin's easy these days."

"We don't expect it to be easy," Tom replied.

He and George packed for their departure from Coronet. The leather, black and well polished, was put into Jimmy's battered but newly painted red-and-white tack trunks, along with the pails, brushes, sponges, rolls of bandages and cotton. The last thing to be packed were Jimmy's faded but clean red-and-white silks. On top of old Sadie, the van, was the training cart, heavier and not so narrow as the racing sulky which rode in front of it. Both were covered with tarpaulin to protect them from sun and rain. The inside of the van was well bedded down with straw for Bonfire.

Before loading the blood bay colt, Tom and George went to see Jimmy. Mrs. Davis met them at the door and she said angrily to George, "*You* left that racing magazine behind you last time. He's been reading it and I can't get it away from him!"

When they entered Jimmy's bedroom he waved the copy of *Hoof Beats* at them, his face red from his excitement and exertion. Tom and George saw that it was an old issue—one that had come back in March.

"Did you see this?" Jimmy sputtered, opening the page. "Let me read you this. It's from Florida, where Cox and his kind go because they can't stand a little cold!" Then Jimmy turned to the magazine and read aloud: " Phillip Cox's gray colt, Silver Knight, set a new track and season record for colts in training here when the two-year-old stepped the mile in 2:17 with a final quarter in 31 seconds, sensational time for a colt of this age and at this time of year. Mr. Cox bought Silver Knight as a yearling at the Harrisburg Sales last November for the record price of $48,000. But it seems now that this price was not too much to pay for a colt possessing the speed Silver Knight is showing so early. Obviously Mr. Cox knew what he was doing when he bid $48,000 for this gray colt."

Jimmy struggled to sit upright in bed, and it only served to weaken him more. George pushed him back against the pillow. "Take it easy, Jimmy," he said. "You'll make yourself worse."

But Jimmy wouldn't stop talking. "Cox doesn't know a good colt from a tuxedo," he shouted as loud as he could. "Working a colt that fast in March! Nobody in his right mind—"

Mrs. Davis grabbed the magazine from Jimmy's waving hand but he caught her and took the magazine angrily from her. "I ain't through with it," he bellowed. "Not yet I'm not!" His fumbling hands turned the pages, then he held up a picture for them to see. "Look at this, Tom," he said, directing his attention to the boy. "It's the immortal Greyhound, the fastest horse that ever pulled a sulky. Take a good look at him! Look at his hoofs! They're painted red, Tom! Red! They've put red nail polish on those hoofs that set about every record in the book! You know why?" Jimmy paused a moment, breathing heavily, and then he said sar-

castically, "He's too old to race any more so they're going to
have him give exhibitions at the *night raceways*! They're
going to make him pretty as a picture and let him go up and
down before the grandstand. He's going to be seen by city
people so they paint his hoofs red so they'll like him better."
Then Jimmy shouted louder than he had in months. "As if
it wasn't enough just to see this great horse! What do they
think they're doing, putting red paint on those hoofs like
they'd paint up an old woman before she goes on the stage?
Bah! I'm sick of it all!"

Only then was Jimmy through talking and content to lay
his head back on the pillow. Mrs. Davis took the magazine
from his hand.

Their faces grim, Tom and George stood there a long
while. Jimmy's breathing became more regular and finally he
slept.

George touched Tom's arm. "We better go," he
whispered.

"Leave him?" Tom's gaze never left Jimmy.

"We can't do anything for him here," George said.
"Maybe we can at the fairs. I'll let the doc know where we'll
be all the time. He'll let us know."

Tom turned to Mrs. Davis. "When he wakes up, tell him
we're on our way. Tell him that George, the colt and I will
be racing for him. And we'll do our best, all of us."

Then they left for the Washington County Fair.

Bonfire's First Race

16

Awaiting the first race at Washington County Fair, Tom and George sat in their rickety canvas chairs in front of Bonfire's stall. Behind them the blood bay colt pushed his head over the stall's half-door and stretched to nuzzle Tom's hair. Turning to him, the boy fondled Bonfire's red-braided black forelock.

All they had to do now was to wait. In an hour's time their race would be called. He had worked the colt early that morning, and then he and George had rubbed him down well. After that had come his mid-morning feed, oats mixed with a little bran. No hay . . . not until after the race. And no more grain until afterwards too. Wearing the worn white sheet with the red borders, Bonfire had nothing more to do until the call came. He would just wait—as they were doing.

George said, "The crowd's startin' to come."

The stables were just off the first turn and Tom could see the people moving leisurely through the fair's main entrance. The grounds were much smaller than at the Reading

Fair. But the atmosphere was the same; there were the mooing of cattle, the snorts of hogs, and above it all the shrill
crowing and clucking from the poultry sheds just a short
distance away. But the majority of the people passed the exhibits by just now, to walk in front of the small, wooden
grandstand and continue on toward the stables to see the
horses.

"Just havin' races only one day here makes 'em all come
over," George said. "This is their early fair, Tom. Later on,
in September, they'll have a bigger one and a whole week of
races."

"Will we be back for it?"

"Maybe we will . . . maybe we won't. Depends on how
things go."

"The purse money isn't very much," Tom said, thinking
of Jimmy's need for money. He opened the small blue race
program and George leaned over to study it with him.

"Like I told you," George said, "they never are. Jimmy
never got rich racin' at the fairs. Three races today and the
purse money we'll be after is the most—one hundred
bucks." His gnarled fingers pointed out the first race; there
were four horses listed and the last was "Bonfire . . . Owner,
Jimmy Creech . . . Driver, Tom Messenger."

There it was for the first time, and Tom looked hard and
long at it before asking, "What do they mean by calling it a
classified race?"

"The fair's racin' committee picks horses at the track
which they think are about the same speed at this time of
year and able to compete on an equal basis," George replied.
"There are no races jus' for two-year-olds at most of the
places we'll be goin', Tom. They'll be classified races jus' like
this one is."

"Then most of the other horses Bonfire will be racing will be older than he is. Is that it, George?"

"That's it, Tom. They'll be older, all right, with most of 'em 'has-beens' like Symbol was. Too old for real fast competition, so their drivers bring 'em to small fairs like this where they'll have a chance to make some money. Our colt should keep up with 'em, all right, and the racin' committee here knows it, so Bonfire goes in this race."

George stopped talking to wave to some people coming down the stable row, then he rose to meet them. Tom stayed behind, reading the program.

Their race, he saw, was a two-in-three heat plan. That meant to win first place Bonfire would have to win two out of the three heats, and each heat was a mile long. Tom realized more than ever why Jimmy had insisted that they build up the colt's strength and endurance before going after speed.

His thoughts turned to Jimmy again when he read the way in which the one-hundred-dollar purse would be divided. Fifty dollars would go to the winner; twenty-five dollars would be given to the second horse; fifteen dollars to the third; and ten dollars to the fourth. It wasn't much money, as George had said, but they were certain to make something with only four horses in the race and four prizes. The colt's entry fee had been two percent of the purse—costing them only two dollars of their savings.

Tom knew it would be a long, long time before they could help Jimmy Creech financially if they raced in small-purse races such as this one. But it was the way it had to be, and Jimmy knew what they were up against. *Anyway,* Tom thought, *today Bonfire and I will be out to take first place and make fifty dollars for Jimmy Creech.*

He looked up from the program to find hundreds of people, practically everyone at the fair, now milling around the stables. Many of them were pushing close to Bonfire's stall; very young children and old men and women were reaching to touch the blood bay colt. Tom rose from his chair.

A man lifted a little girl in his arms so she could pet Bonfire. "He won't bite, will he?" the man asked.

"No . . . not him," Tom replied, holding the colt's head still while the little girl moved her small hand up and down Bonfire's face. Finally she touched the braided forelock. "He has a red ribbon just like yours," Tom told her, "and for the same reason . . . to keep the hair out of his eyes."

The little girl giggled and the man laughed as he put her down and lifted another child to Bonfire. The crowd pushed closer and Tom asked them to step back just a little to give the colt some air. They obliged willingly, as though they understood.

A short and very plump lady spoke. "A two-year-old, isn't he?"

"Yes," Tom said.

"I've always liked blood bays," she went on. "He's tall for his age. He must be close to sixteen hands."

"A half-inch short." Tom smiled. "He's fifteen, three and a half."

"And he's still growing," someone in the rear said. "What's his breeding?"

"By the Black and out of Volo Queen."

There was a deep murmur from the crowd.

"He gets his size from the Black, then," a lady said. "I saw his picture. He's a giant of a horse."

"And that head's the Black's too," a man said. "Broad forehead and long, thin nose. That's him, all right."

The small, stout woman in front spoke again. "But don't you go forgettin' Volo Queen. That neck's hers, so are the eyes. The Queen could go, all right. I saw Jimmy Creech win with her."

"That colt belong to Jimmy Creech?" another man asked. Tom nodded.

"Where's he, then?"

"He's been sick," Tom said.

"Old Jimmy Creech sick! Why, he ain't missed a fair here in . . ."

And that's the way it went until Tom sent Bonfire back into his stall for some quiet, and George returned.

"It's gettin' near post time," George said. "Come on in with Bonfire a minute. I want to tell you something."

The colt came to them when they entered the stall, and Tom put his hand beneath the white sheet to rub him.

"Far as I can figure it out from talkin' to the other guys, it's this," George said while cleaning his bared head of sweat with his handkerchief. "Sam Kossler is the only one who should give us trouble. He's got an aged, dark chestnut gelding that's in pretty good shape. Jimmy beat Sam an' that same gelding last year an' the year before with Symbol. So he shouldn't be much to beat with our colt. But Sam's tricky," George added cautiously. "He won't pull no rough stuff, but he's smart. He's been drivin' as many years as Jimmy. So he knows what it's all about. You're drivin' against another Jimmy Creech, Tom, when you race against Sam Kossler. And that same thing goes pretty much for the others in the race an' maybe for all the rest of the season. We meet old-timers where we go. So be on your toes, today and every day you go out."

Tom nodded; and at that moment they heard a loud clap

of thunder. They looked out the stall to find that the sun had been blanketed by heavy clouds.

"I was afraid they'd move over this way," George said.

Then the rain fell heavily; people hurriedly sought shelter beneath the eaves of the stable sheds and the roof of the grandstand.

"Will they call off the race, George?"

"They will if the rain keeps up."

After a few minutes, the downpour stopped as suddenly as it had begun. Once again the lone group of clouds in a blue sky moved away and the sun shone brightly again. The people left their shelters and the fair was on.

"This sun will dry the track out enough, Tom," George said. "We'll be racin'."

A man came toward their stall, and Tom recognized the fair's race secretary. Handing a letter to Tom, he said, "It's from Jimmy Creech, special delivery. Thought I'd better get it to you. Know how worried you and George are about him."

While Bonfire nuzzled his neck, Tom opened the letter and held it to one side for George to read with him.

Dear Tom,

I'm sorry I didn't get to say good-bye to you and George. I wanted to tell you one last thing before you drive our colt in his first race. So I'm writing this now, right after I woke up and found you two gone.

I get the idea—more from the way you and George look while you're here than what you say—that you might be fig-uring on pushing the colt just to make money for me.

I don't want you to push him any more than he wants to go.

And even *if he wants to go what you think is too fast for early in the season, you hold him in, even if it means losing races! Don't you ruin a fine colt by rushing him just so you can make money for me. I'd rather kick off now than have you do that.*

Remember, Tom, what I've said.

Your friend,
Jimmy

And Tom and George knew that Jimmy Creech meant every word he'd written. His horses always came before he did. They always had and always would.

"Let's hook Bonfire up, Tom," George said quietly. "We've got eight minutes before race time."

There were more people all around the rail of the half-mile track and standing on the hill close behind it than there were in the wooden grandstand, where admission was charged. The public-address system wasn't working properly, and the announcer's voice would fade, then shrill loudly as he introduced the four horses in the post parade for the first race.

But when the announcer said, "Number four in the outside position is Bonfire, a two-year-old colt racing for the first time on any track. Owned by Jimmy Creech of Coronet, Pennsylvania. Driven by Tom Messenger, who, like his colt, is racing for the first time," Tom's face flushed and his heart pounded crazily. He was here behind Bonfire; *it was happening . . . he was here!* And while he talked to the blood bay colt through the lines, he saw the much-too-short sleeves of Jimmy's racing silks—the silks he wore for Jimmy Creech. Jimmy Creech was here . . . every move Tom made, even to the slightly bent shoulders, was Jimmy's.

He warmed Bonfire up before the grandstand, loosening the colt's strong body. Only once did his eyes leave his colt for the others; the three men were as old as Jimmy Creech and like Tom were unsmiling now that the race was at hand. He picked out Sam Kossler from the others only because he drove the dark chestnut gelding and was in the pole position. For a second Tom thought, *There are no Phillip Coxes here. There never have been and never will be. It'll always belong to men like these.*

Coming down the stretch for the last warm-up, Tom opened up the colt a bit. The footing was wet and muddy, but Bonfire seemed to hold to it without any trouble; his stride lengthened quickly and his fast sprint brought loud clapping from the grandstand and rail when Tom slowed him down and turned him back for the start of the race.

They walked past the judges' booth and the starter told them, "Take your horses down to that pole two hundred feet from here; turn them together and come down in your positions. I'll send you off if you're in position and together."

There was no mobile starting gate here as at the Reading Fair; this was the way Jimmy Creech liked it—the way it had been.

Tom turned Bonfire with the others, and they came down toward the starting line in position. The colt's eyes and ears were pointed straight ahead of him, and Tom felt his eagerness. This is what Bonfire had been bred, raised and trained to do. This was it!

Not too fast, Tom told his colt through the lines. *Not yet, Bonfire . . . not yet. Stay with the others. We're coming to the start. Just a second now.*

The four horses gained speed in unison; as a team they made for the starting wire, their drivers silent and tense. Tom took a quick look at Sam Kossler; the man wasn't keeping the chestnut gelding very close to the pole. Quickly Tom decided upon his racing strategy. He'd let Bonfire all out at the start; he'd get around all the horses and get the pole position away from Sam Kossler going into the turn. He could count on the colt's blazing sprint to get him to the turn first; old Sam Kossler was leaving the pole wide open—just ripe for him and his colt to take! Once he got the pole he wouldn't let Bonfire go any faster than was necessary to win the heat. That would be following Jimmy's orders not to let the colt extend himself yet. And there would be another heat coming up; two miles were enough for Bonfire's first day of racing.

"GO!" the starter shouted to them.

As one the horses shot forward, their drivers shouting. But Tom just moved his hand and said nothing aloud to his colt. Bonfire burst away from the group, his black mane and tail whipping like lashes in his breathtaking spurt.

Tom let him go straight ahead until he was clear of the horses beside him, then he started moving over as they swept into the turn. Only Sam Kossler was there to challenge him, and Tom knew that in another few yards he too would be beaten. Nothing could stop his colt. Nothing!

But he did not need the few extra yards to get in front of Sam Kossler and close to the pole, for the old man suddenly slowed down his chestnut gelding, allowing Tom to move in quickly to the pole. Tom's surprise at Kossler's strategy was forgotten in his exhilaration at being out in front. It lasted only a second, though, for suddenly he found out why

Sam Kossler had kept away from the rail. Bonfire's hoofs sank heavily in the deep mud that was there, for the rain had drained from the track to the inside of the rail! Tom was frantic. He could sense that the colt felt strange and uneasy. Bonfire pounded harder, but he only slipped all the more and the sulky wheels turned heavily in the mud.

Tom sought to get away from the pole, to get Bonfire's feet on the drier track just a yard away from the rail. But Sam Kossler was there, content to keep his aged gelding alongside Tom's sulky. And Bonfire couldn't get up enough speed in this mud to draw ahead of Kossler. Only the slowing down of the gelding would enable Tom to get Bonfire back on firm ground. Tom waited in vain for this break to come all the way down the backstretch, around the back turn and past the grandstand for the first time.

George yelled something as he passed, but Tom couldn't make out the words. They went around the first turn again. Down the backstretch, Tom realized that Sam Kossler's gelding wasn't going to slow down; he plodded awkwardly, heavily, but he stayed beside Tom's sulky.

Furiously Tom asked himself why he hadn't noticed the heavy mud on the inside. It was too late now! Sam Kossler had tricked him just as George said he might.

Bonfire was furious too, and Tom felt his fury. The colt slipped constantly, but he never stopped trying for more speed in the bad footing; heavy clods of mud covered the sulky wheels, slowing the colt, pulling him down.

And it was then Tom knew he was beaten. Bonfire had had more than enough of this kind of going. Nobody could ask any more of a colt. He touched the lines and Bonfire slowed down.

But even at this slow speed, Sam Kossler didn't make any

attempt to take his gelding past them until they came off the back turn into the homestretch. He moved up alongside Tom then, and grinned before going on past. He had known all along he'd had nothing to fear from the others in the race, and they followed in a line directly behind one another. There was no room between any of them for Tom to break through to the good footing; and as each driver and horse passed him, Tom realized that they had known all along what Sam Kossler was doing. They had bided their time with Sam, and only now made any attempt to catch up with and pass him. But Sam Kossler had the race well under control as he went for the finish wire.

When the last horse had gone by, Tom guided his colt away from the rail. But he made no attempt to catch up with any of the others; it was too late for that, for Sam Kossler was already under the wire. Tom wiped the mud in gobs from his face and silks. Sam Kossler had beaten them this time, but there was still another heat to go—and the next heat would be a different story.

George said, "Clean yourself up, Tom. I'll get the mud off the colt."

"How long before the next heat? How long, George?" Tom's voice was clipped, eager.

"More'n half an hour. Take it easy." George removed Bonfire's harness. "The colt needs a rest, if you don't."

That sobered Tom. "You're right, George," he said quietly. "He worked hard and got nowhere in that slop." Removing his sulky cap, he ducked his head in a large tub of rain water. When his head emerged, he said, "I should've dropped back the moment I found myself in that stuff. Don't you think so, George?"

"You shouldn't have gotten in there so close to the rail in

the first place," George said. "But it's my fault as much as yours. I noticed it an' shoulda told you. Jimmy would've told you. We've both got a lot to learn."

"I should've slowed Bonfire down right away," Tom insisted. "Let them all pass me and then come around them on the outside. They're not in the same class with Bonfire when it comes to speed. I lost the heat for him."

Sponging the colt's legs free of the mud, George said, "Your slowin' him down early wouldn't have worked either, Tom. Sam Kossler would have slowed down, too . . . and so would've the others, even if you went down to a walk. They jus' figured on keepin' you right up against the rail and in the mud for the whole mile."

"A dirty trick," Tom said angrily.

"Not dirty, Tom. Jus' driving smart, that's all, because they knew you had all the speed in front of you. Maybe they taught you your first lesson . . . and you'll think a little more before doin' what you do after this."

"They taught me, all right," Tom said.

George looked up from Bonfire's hoofs to smile. "We can still make expenses by winning the next heat," he said.

Almost an hour later Tom drove Bonfire onto the track for the second heat. Much to Sam Kossler's surprise, the boy nodded to him and smiled as he passed. They took their warm-up scores, then went back to start. Sam had the inside pole position again, for he was the heat winner; and Tom was on the outside, for he had finished last in the first heat.

Grim-faced, the others turned their horses without so much as a look at Tom or his blood bay colt. It was as though they knew it would be difficult to outsmart the boy and colt again. Once more they came down to the start as one and were off.

There was no sprint by Bonfire for the first turn, for Tom held him close and dropped him behind the others. He kept away from the inside, and the footing, though a little wet, was good. Bonfire liked the feel of the track. His body trembled with his anxiety to be let loose, and his ears cupped backwards frequently, awaiting Tom's words. But Tom spoke only through the lines, telling him to bide his time.

While rounding the turn, Tom saw Sam Kossler glance back in his direction; every other driver did the same thing. They were worried and wondering when and how Tom would come up to them; they knew the blood bay colt would come. Coming off the turn and going into the backstretch, they left their single-line formation as though to take up as much of the track as possible to prevent Tom's breaking through with Bonfire.

But the track was wide and Tom knew there'd be plenty of room to get by with his colt when he chose to use it. Just now he was content to let them worry and wonder about him.

They went the first lap of the track, the drivers ahead looking back at Tom constantly. They'd wanted him to make a move long since, for their straggling positions halfway across the track meant a longer distance for their horses to go. Only Sam Kossler and Tom were taking the short distance around.

They went into the first turn again and Tom heard George yell, "Good, Tom!"

Bonfire was getting impatient; he didn't pull, but Tom could sense how he felt by the movements in mouth and body. Tom knew that the pace Sam Kossler was setting in front was easy on the colt. It would mean about a 2:20 mile for him, and that was just what Jimmy wanted for Bonfire this early in the season. Tom touched the lines. Bonfire was going to win this time.

And coming off the turn, entering the backstretch of the last lap, it happened. Later, the people who saw it found it difficult to explain exactly what they saw and felt. The nearest they could come was that the colt's speed coming down the stretch and past the others set them afire; never had they seen such sudden power and breath-taking speed. For them, it was like being picked up and carried with him in his almost frightening, whirlwind flight to the finish. Sam Kossler said too that he'd never seen a colt turn on such speed so fast and for so long. Maybe one or two older horses during all the years he'd been racing, but never a two-year-old colt.

Bonfire didn't come out for the third heat. It was to have been a race between Sam Kossler's chestnut gelding and the colt, for each had won a heat, to decide which horse would be the winner. Tom and George had gone to the judges' stand and had conceded the race to Sam Kossler, claiming that another mile would be too much for the colt this early in the season.

They were racing Bonfire as Jimmy Creech would have raced him.

"So we get second money instead of first, Tom," George said, when they returned to the stable. "Jimmy said not to push the colt just to make money for him. We're off now, Tom. And we're twenty-five dollars to the good."

But Tom didn't hear George, for he was in the stall with

his colt, watching him while he ate his bran mash. He wasn't thinking of the money won or of Jimmy Creech. He was thinking only of his colt and the speed he'd shown that last time around. He and Bonfire had started their careers together, and the first race was usually the toughest. Next was the Indiana County Fair—and with his colt he looked forward to it eagerly.

Racing the Fair Circuit

17

Unless a person was a regular reader of the weekly racing publications which devoted some of their space to the results at the smaller fairs, or unless he had attended the Pennsylvania fairs at Indiana, Clearfield, Bedford, Dayton, Mercer and Port Royal during the months of July and August, he never would have known of a blood bay colt by the name of Bonfire. For Tom Messenger never allowed his colt to go faster than a 2:19 mile. And there was nothing exceptional in a two-year-old racing in that time, especially when this was the year of such top ones as Princess Guy and Silver Knight.

The weekly racing publications gave a large portion of their space to summaries of races won by Miss Elsie Topper's black filly, Princess Guy, at the Ohio fairs as she broke one track record after another in amazing times ranging from 2:09 to 2:04. Just as much space was given to the startling speed being displayed by Silver Knight as he improved with each successive night race at the Roosevelt Raceway and brought his record down to 2:05.

Hoof Beats was published monthly, and regularly there would be an article discussing "the extreme speed of Silver Knight and Princess Guy." The magazine hoped that "Miss Elsie Topper and the amateur sportsman, Phillip Cox, would see fit to race their exceptional filly and colt against each other before the season ended . . . as we feel certain that such a race would lower Titan Hanover's world record of 2:03 ½ for two-year-olds on a half-mile track."

George snorted, "Humph."

Tom said, looking at his colt, "If I just let him out once, just once, they'd all know."

But he never did. At one fair after another, race after race, he rated Bonfire carefully behind the others, trailing the field until near the end of the race when he made his move. And, as in their first race at the Washington Fair, it was these sprints that people talked about long after Bonfire had gone. Yet their talk of the blood bay colt's blinding sprints that "pick you up and set you afire even though you're sitting in the grandstand" stayed within the small-fair circuit and never reached the outer world.

"It's the way Jimmy wants us to do it," George said. "We're not rushin' him at all."

And Tom realized as the season progressed the value of Jimmy's orders. Bonfire was stronger than ever, his legs and body were as hard as steel and never was there any sign of lameness or stiffness. Moreover, the colt knew what racing was all about now. He and Tom had learned quickly.

Only twice did Bonfire lose a race, and then only because Tom was outsmarted by the older drivers and couldn't get through in time to win. At every fair except one, the colt raced against aged horses, the same as at Washington. The

Dayton Fair had a race solely for two-year-old colts and Tom and Bonfire had the easiest time of all, winning in 2:19.

The purse money won accumulated and George took care of it.

"Eleven races an' nine hundred dollars," he said, adding it up. "Jimmy never had it this good. And Tom, think what it would be if we were racin' for more'n two- and three-hundred-dollar purses divided up among the first four horses! But no sense thinkin' about that," he added soberly. "Purses never have been more an' never will be in this circuit."

From the money won, they deducted their expenses and sent the rest home to Jimmy Creech. They figured that Jimmy should feel a lot better having this money coming in to pay his bills. But he didn't; his letters were few and far between and his handwriting, a weak scrawl difficult to read, was that of a sick man. Dr. Morton's letters to them didn't help either, for he wrote that "Jimmy's condition is the same, but I'm surprised that he isn't in better spirits since Bonfire is doing so well."

George said, "I figure he's still worried about payin' the doc. Jimmy didn't have no idea he'd be sick this long."

Tom and George worried about Jimmy even more as they moved farther and farther away from Coronet, going eastward where the fairs were larger and the purses a little better.

It was early September when they arrived at the York Fair. Reading and Uncle Wilmer's farm were less than a hundred miles to the north and east. They would be at the Reading Fair in a week's time and Uncle Wilmer and Aunt Emma were expecting them. Eagerly Tom looked forward to seeing them and the Queen again; he knew too how much his uncle wanted to see Bonfire go.

They found the York Fair to be as large as the fair at Reading; there was a great cement grandstand and bleachers, and there were just as many people milling about the exhibit buildings and stables.

"Just look at this purse we're racin' for today," George said excitedly. "Six hundred and fifty dollars! Let's see now. That's—" He figured a moment, then went on, "Three hundred and twenty-five bucks to the winner! If we'd known the purses were going to be that big, Tom, we woulda come here earlier in the week. Here it is the last day of the races."

"There's Reading ahead of us," Tom reminded him. "The purses will be just as large there."

The boy turned to look down the long row of stables. He didn't know any of the men here, but they were no different from all the others he'd met and raced against at the fairs. Hardened, well-lined old faces—the Jimmy Creeches of this sport. There were no big stables, no raceway drivers, for the purse money, while good, could not be compared with that given at the night raceways. They had to work harder at the fairs for their money, Tom thought, for each race meant driving two and sometimes three heats, while at the raceways they went what they called a "dash," which simply meant just one race of a mile with no heats.

That was another thing Jimmy Creech had against the raceways. He didn't like those "dashes." He believed a horse should have stamina and endurance as well as speed, and how much he had of both could be decided only by racing in heats—the way it always had been done.

Some people crowded near to look at Bonfire in his stall, and George and Tom talked to them until it was time to get ready for their race. He enjoyed having the people come to their stall, as they had at all the fairs. Most of them knew something about fine breeding and were genuinely interested in the sport. That's what made the fairs, and that was one of the reasons, Tom knew, why Jimmy would never desert them for the raceways. George and Jimmy said it wasn't the same at the raceways, that it couldn't be. Tom didn't know, but he guessed they were right.

They brought Bonfire out of his stall, and his red coat burned bright in the sun while they put the light racing harness on him.

The track marshal came down the row, telling those who were getting their horses ready, "We're going out in a few minutes. Get 'em all set."

After hooking up the sulky, George stepped back to look critically at Bonfire. "Why don't you take him down to two fifteen today? He's ready for it, easy. An' from what I hear that ought to win for us. That three hundred and twenty-five first-place money looks pretty good."

"He's ready, all right," Tom agreed. "And I'll take him faster than two fifteen if necessary. Even Jimmy would say it's all right now." He put on Bonfire's bridle and adjusted the head number on top. It was of light plastic and stood up straight; there was a white figure 3 on a black background. "Pretty fancy today." Tom smiled. "Head numbers and everything."

"We got a mobile starting gate today, too," George said. "It's Bonfire's first time with one of those. Hope he don't give you trouble."

"I don't think he will," Tom answered.

The horses in the post parade passed the grandstand and bleachers. Tom felt a little nervous before so many people, and his nervousness communicated itself to the colt. Bonfire tossed his head, and the head number flashed in the sun.

Then Tom calmed down. "It's just another race," he told himself, "the same as at any of the fairs. More people here, that's all." And he told the colt. Bonfire relaxed with him.

"The number three horse is the only two-year-old colt in the race," the announcer said to the packed throng over the public-address system. "Bonfire, a blood bay colt, sired by the Black and out of Volo Queen. Owned by Jimmy Creech of Coronet, Pennsylvania, and driven by Tom Messenger."

The announcer's voice droned on until he had introduced all seven horses in the race. They went down to the first turn and came back. "The horses will take one warm-up score, then go into their respective positions behind the mobile starting gate awaiting them at the head of the stretch."

Tom warmed up Bonfire faster and farther down the track than he did usually. The colt sensed the change, for he snorted while going along; that was unusual for him, too.

The horses went around the track, jogging into position as they neared the mobile starting gate. Tom was glad he had drawn the number three spot, for with seven horses in the race the track was crowded and the going would be difficult at the start. But in his position he would be able to get to the turn first without having to go around any of the others. He had been lucky in the drawn for position. He hoped his luck held with $325 at stake.

Coming off the back turn, they spread out into position behind the wings of the mobile gate. The car began moving and the starter, dressed all in white, stood in the back of the open convertible, talking to them through his small microphone.

"Slowly now," he cautioned them. "Don't rush your horses. Come together. That's it. Stay together. Not too close, Mr. Wilson. Keep your horse back from the gate, Mr. Wilson! That's it. Mr. Read, come up a little with the others. You too, Mr. Messenger. Bring your horse up with the others."

The car was halfway to the starting line now and moving faster; the horses went along with it, pushing their noses close to the barrier.

"You're coming up too fast, Mr. Messenger. Keep that colt back from the gate!"

Tom was having more trouble than he'd expected. Bonfire wasn't sure about that pole extending across the track in front of him. He didn't know what it was going to do. And the strange voice blaring in front of him didn't help; neither did the speeding car's wheels that sent the track dust into his nostrils. Tom kept him close to the fast moving gate, for he wanted to get away with the others; he didn't want to lose his good position before reaching the turn.

Like an onrushing wave the horses came to the starting line, and the starter yelled, "GO!"

But just before the starter's cry sent them off, Bonfire touched the metal barrier with his nose. The gate's vibrations swept back through the colt's body; Bonfire threw back his head, breaking the check rein, and then stopped short.

Tom was thrown against Bonfire's hindquarters, but he regained his seat and sought to calm the colt. Bonfire responded when he heard Tom's voice, and the boy let him go again. But Tom made no attempt to catch up with the field, for by this time they were halfway around the track, and it would be better to save the colt's energy for the next heat.

He jogged Bonfire around the outside of the track, then took him back to the stables.

"I was afraid of this," George said, leading the colt. "Just as Jimmy says," he added angrily, "these new-fangled contraptions!"

"I shouldn't have kept him so close to the gate," Tom said, rubbing Bonfire's neck while he walked beside him. "Not his first time before it. I should've known better. I was just so busy thinking about getting away fast."

"We'll get them next heat," George said. "Take that one and the third an' the race is ours."

"I hope so," Tom returned. "I hope our luck doesn't change. It's been good so far."

"Not with that colt it won't," George said. "Not with him."

But while they awaited the racing of the second heat, it seemed to George as well as to Tom that their luck had changed—for the worse. The bad news came in a letter from Dr. Morton which the race secretary handed to them. Tom and George read it together.

Dear George,

I've decided that it'll be best for Jimmy if we move him to a Pittsburgh hospital. I can't understand why his condition hasn't improved more than it has during the last few months, and I want to have him where I can watch him more closely and have all the facilities for any treatment that may be necessary. It may be that complications have set in, and I'll certainly keep in touch with you.

I'd like to caution you about something. I know you've been sending Jimmy clippings from magazines of the various fairs at which you've raced. It does Jimmy a lot of good, I know, to see Bonfire's name listed as the winner in these race results. But I must warn you to note carefully what is printed on the back of any clippings you send in the future.

A month or so ago, Jimmy read on the back of one you'd sent that Miss Elsie Topper had left the Ohio fairs and was racing her black filly, Princess Guy, at Maywood Park, the night raceway just outside of Chicago.

I don't have to tell you how Jimmy feels about the night raceways. He bellowed for days that Miss Elsie had betrayed him, and I had all I could do to quiet him down. So please be more careful in the future.

> *Sincerely,*
> *Henry Morton, M.D.*

They finished reading the letter together, and Tom said, "I guess I did it."

"Maybe I sent it," George returned gravely. "I don't know. I'm worried about him, Tom."

"Do you think we should go back, George?"

"No, I don't, Tom. We can do more good for him here. He'll worry more than ever now with hospital bills to pay."

"Jimmy should've realized we were disappointed in Miss Elsie's going to the raceways, too," Tom said.

"He probably did," George said, rising from his chair. "But that didn't help any. Let's get Bonfire ready. You and him have got work to do." Then he stopped and turned to Tom. "Jimmy oughta quit knockin' himself out worrying about other people. It's Miss Elsie's life an' she can go an' race nights if she wants to." Shaking his bald head, George walked into Bonfire's stall.

Tom followed George into the stall and pulled off the colt's blanket. "I just got to thinking about that clipping of our winning the race at the Port Royal Fair. The one you're going to send Jimmy."

George removed his hands from Bonfire to take out his wallet. The clipping was there; a complete page of race summaries. He unfolded it and turned it over to read the back.

A full-page advertisment met their eyes, an advertisement showing a man wearing a white shirt. The headline read: "ANNOUNCING THE SILVER KNIGHT SHIRT." The advertising copy beneath it went on to say: "The Phillip Cox Company takes great pleasure in naming its newest shirt creation after SILVER KNIGHT, the top two-year-old colt of the year. And like SILVER KNIGHT our new shirt is outstanding in every way! It has the same racy lines . . . the same smoothness and beauty! And don't forget it's designed by amateur sportsman Phillip Cox, who knows what makes a champion! He's done it with the great colt, SILVER KNIGHT . . . and he's done it with this new, startling, racy SILVER KNIGHT SHIRT! You'll find them at all good clothing shops. See them today! Wear them to the races tomorrow!"

George's fist closed about the advertisement. "Things would have been just swell if I'd sent him that," he said bitterly.

Just as bitterly, Tom added, "Amateur sportsman, they call him. Some amateur!"

Fifteen minutes later Tom had to forget Jimmy Creech and Phillip Cox and raceways and shirts, for he drove Bonfire onto the track for the second heat of the race. The horses took their warm-up scores and then approached the mobile starting gate. Having failed to finish the first heat, Tom was now on the outside of the field. He decided to trail the others during the race until he was ready to make his bid.

The car began moving away and the starter said, "Now, Mr. Messenger, don't come too close this time or the same thing might happen to you."

But Tom had no intention taking Bonfire too close to the gate this time. Going down toward the starting line, the starter called to him repeatedly to bring his colt up with the others. But Tom kept Bonfire back a little and liked what he felt through the lines. The colt was going well; he didn't fear the gate; he just didn't want to touch it again. There was less dust from the car's tires in his outside position, and that helped a lot, too.

"GO!"

The cries of the drivers rose with the sweep of the gate from their path; whips cracked hard against sulky shafts, and all fought to reach the turn first. All but Tom; he let them go and dropped Bonfire behind them.

The pace the leaders were setting was very fast, and Bonfire snorted eagerly when Tom let him out a little more to keep up with the field. All the horses kept their positions going around the track and entering the homestretch for the first time; they came down toward the grandstand in a closely packed group.

"Here they come, ladies and gentlemen," the announcer called to the crowd. "It's a beautiful race! Did you ever see anything like it? They're all tucked in, waiting to make their moves. It's Tim S. on top, followed by Sun Chief, then Hollydale . . ."

Tom had Bonfire close but a little to the right of the last horse. The colt was fresh and eager to be let out; he knew the signal would come soon now. As they passed the announcer's booth, Tom heard him call out, "They went the half in one o five, very good time!"

He had figured the time to be about that; he had never taken Bonfire so fast a first half-mile before. Yet the colt wasn't even breathing hard; the gradual work they'd done building stamina and endurance along with speed was now paying off. With the sprint to come, Bonfire would do 2:10 or better with no trouble at all.

Rounding the first turn again, Tom touched the lines and Bonfire moved away from the rail. Tom took him a little wide coming off the turn, for this was where he'd make his bid. Yet as he gave Bonfire the signal the colt had been waiting for, Tom saw that the other drivers were going to make their bids going down the backstretch, too. They all started driving hard and fanning out across the track in their efforts to get ahead of one another going down the long stretch.

But Tom let Bonfire go, knowing that there would be holes between the drivers and he'd get through someway. He felt the quick surge of Bonfire's amazing sprint; his seat was almost pulled from beneath him with the colt's drive; and the lines, as always, were jerked forward when Bonfire leaned into them with every ounce of power in his body.

Tom leaned forward with the lines to lessen their pull on his shoulders. He looked to Bonfire's side to see if the way ahead was clear. But there was no hole, for the horses ahead were racing abreast and the line extended across the track. Tom drew back a little on the lines to check Bonfire's speed.

Suddenly the lines broke and Tom's head and shoulders snapped back with the power of an unleashed spring. He went back over the sulky seat and only his desperate hands finding the edges of the seat saved him from falling off. He pulled himself up and threw the broken lines in his hands clear of the sulky wheels.

Bonfire was racing at full speed, the last signal Tom had given him. With all his blazing swiftness he was bearing down on the horses ahead, and there was no opening! Tom called to him, but Bonfire's ears were pitched forward and he heard nothing but the racing hoofs ahead of him.

Nothing would stop Bonfire. He would run the others down in his attempt to get by! The danger to all was only too evident to Tom. There was only one thing he could do to stop the racing colt.

Quickly he removed his feet from the stirrups and placed them on the shafts of the sulky on either side of Bonfire. Leaning forward, he grabbed the colt's tail and drew himself up until his hands were on the sweated, moving hindquarters. For a fraction of a second he hesitated, then he saw the horses ahead and knew Bonfire would be on top of them in a second—or at the most two!

His hands moved farther across Bonfire's back as his feet went up the shafts. He straddled the colt, then flung himself forward to reach Bonfire's head and bridle.

It took only a touch from Tom for the colt to lessen his speed. Yet it wasn't any too soon, for when Tom had him under control Bonfire's head was above the rear wheels of two racing sulkies. To have gone any farther would have meant a bad accident. He brought the colt to a stop while the field drew rapidly away from them.

Back at the stables, George said, "Your luck's still good, Tom, or you never coulda done what you did." Then he added confidently, "We'll make up for losin' this race at Reading."

Tom hoped so, for Jimmy Creech needed money desperately now. And racing the colt was the only way to get it. He pulled Bonfire's head down close to him.

Reading Fair and Princess Guy

18

At Reading, it was like coming home for Tom. It was the fair he knew best, and a warm, homey feeling glowed within him while he walked the tree-lined avenues. In the same barns and buildings were the same sleek brown-and-white Herefords, the black-and-white Holsteins, the short-necked coal-black Angus steers—all mooing or bellowing as they had done at previous fairs. And there were the goats and the pigs, the chickens and the roosters, the giant Percheron horses—all groomed glistening clean.

All was the same, yet each year people came with the same amount of anticipation and eagerness. Never were they disappointed and they looked upon everything as though this was their very first fair. It had been that way at each and every fair Tom had attended during this long season. He knew it would never change.

From the long outdoor restaurants not far from the high grandstand came the smells of roast beef and pork and sauerkraut—Pennsylvania Dutch cooking at its best. The men in front of the restaurants pleaded with people walking by to "Get your tickets for the races, then come in and enjoy the best hot roast beef and mashed potatoes you've ever eaten!

"This is the place to meet your friends, folks. Come in, sit down and rest. See that lady leaving? She just told me she's full right up to the ears! She never tasted such good pork and sauerkraut. That's what we like to hear, folks! And that's what you'll be saying, too! It's cool and clean inside. So come along. Join us!"

And there were the calls of the barkers of other concessions. Tom listened to them all.

"Thirsty? Step right up here for some of our old-fashioned root beer made the way you like it! Hungry? Try our hot franks!"

"Guess your age within two years, lady . . . or you get your pick of any of these valuable prizes!"

"Hey! Hey! Hey! BINGO. We're ready to start the next game, folks. Hurry! Hurry! Hurry! You may be the big winner this game. Come in and try your luck!"

The fairs get right inside of you, Tom thought, *just as Jimmy and George said they did.* Turning to the track, he saw the horses working out. And far on the other side was the fair's midway with its red trucks and spinning Ferris wheels making a vivid-colored background for the bare racing strip of the track's backstretch.

And, of course, Uncle Wilmer and Aunt Emma were there, making the Reading Fair seem even more like home.

They had come early this morning, the day of George's and Tom's arrival with the colt. They planned to come to the fair every day, Uncle Wilmer had told Tom, and "to hang" with the money it would cost them. This year was

extra-special to them. Besides, just to look at that colt standing in his stall was worth every cent of admission to the fair.

And when Tom had worked Bonfire, Uncle Wilmer said,
"Just watchin' him is something nobody could set no price
on! He's a real 'goer,' that colt is!"

That night, Tom and George went back to the farm with
Uncle Wilmer and Aunt Emma. When they went over the
bumpy road leading to the farm, Tom stuck his head out the
window of the car, watching for the Queen in the pasture.

It was dark and he couldn't see her; but she neighed repeatedly at the sound of the car. When Uncle Wilmer
stopped at the gate, Tom ran to the pasture fence and whistled. From far down in the pasture came the sound of hoofs
and he knew the Queen was on her way to him.

"You men stay with the mare," Aunt Emma said. "I just
need to warm things up on the stove. I got everything
ready."

Tom heard the Queen jump over the small stream that
cut the center of the pasture; then she was coming up the
slight slope leading up from the stream. Tom heard her
grunt as she plunged over the crest of the embankment; then
he saw her, the white blaze that split her dark face standing
out in the darkness. He ran forward to meet her, and George
and Uncle Wilmer left him alone with the Queen.

An hour later they sat down to another of Aunt Emma's
sumptuous meals, and ate hungrily and long. When it was
over and the dishes were done, Aunt Emma left the men
alone. "You'll be talkin' horses," she said. "And I've seen
enough of them for one day."

Uncle Wilmer scratched the top of his egg-shaped head.
"You heard any more about Jimmy?" he asked.

Tom shook his head, then said, "Not since he went to the hospital."

"The doc said he'd let us know as soon as they found out anything," George added. "I'm afraid he's really sick this time, Wilmer."

"I believe it," Uncle Wilmer said soberly.

They were quiet a long while, then Uncle Wilmer asked, "Why are you waitin' until Friday to race the colt? Why you doin' that if you need money to pay Jimmy's hospital bills?"

"It's a classified race—the only one we can get Bonfire in," George shouted.

"How much money will he win?" Uncle Wilmer asked.

"Three hundred and twenty-five dollars, *if* he wins," George replied.

"He'll win, all right," Uncle Wilmer said. "Ain't so much money, though, when y'got hospital bills."

"We know that," Tom said.

Uncle Wilmer turned to the boy, looked at him for a while, then rose to go to the corner cupboard; on top of a pile of copies of *Hoof Beats* was a list of activities at the Reading Fair, and he brought this back to the table.

"Why don't you put the colt in this race for two-year-olds on Wednesday? That's a good purse, all right, eighteen hundred dollars." Uncle Wilmer stopped talking to figure to himself, then added, "That'd be nine hundred dollars, when you won it. That kind of money would be a big help to Jimmy, all right."

"It would," George agreed. "But that race is a Futurity."

"Heh?" Uncle Wilmer cupped his ear.

Tom was closer to him, so he said, "George says that two-year-old race on Wednesday is a Futurity. That means every colt racing in it was nominated for the race even before he was foaled. The owners nominated the foal that was to come of their mares. Jimmy didn't do that."

"And it cost money to nominate the foal," George added, shouting. "Then you have to keep your colt eligible for the Futurity by paying more payments right along until he becomes a two-year-old and goes in the race. Jimmy didn't have that kind of money!"

Uncle Wilmer nodded his head understandingly. "Too bad," he said. "The colt would win, all right. There's only one top colt in that race he'd have to beat, from what I read." Reaching for the local newspaper, he drew it toward him and adjusted his glasses. "Yep, here it is," he added. "The colt I meant is a filly. Princess Guy, they call her. Says here that she's owned and driven by Miss Elsie Topper." He looked up from the newspaper. "That must be the Princess Guy I been reading so much about in *Hoof Beats*." Turning to the paper once more, he nodded. "Yep, it must be, all right, because it says here Princess Guy raced at Ohio fairs and the Maywood Park Raceway in Chicago an' never was beaten. She has a record of two o four which makes her the favorite, easy."

At the surprising news of Miss Elsie's coming to Reading, Tom and George looked at each other in astonishment, but neither said a word.

Tuesday morning Tom was bringing Bonfire off the track from his early workout when he saw two large and very impressive horse vans come to a stop before the stables. The lettering on their sides told him they had come from Roosevelt Raceway, Westbury, Long Island, New York.

George said, "Here they come, up for some sun to race in the Futurity tomorrow."

As they removed Bonfire's harness and sponged his sweated body, they stole frequent glances at the colts and equipment being unloaded from the big vans. It was the first time this season they had encountered any raceway stables; having lived and raced with the Jimmy Creeches, they had forgotten the glittering, glistening polish of leather, brass and nickel of the money-backed stables.

Tom didn't recognize either of the two drivers. "I thought one of them might be Ray O'Neil," he told George, remembering the well-known raceway driver who had smashed Jimmy's sulky wheel at Reading two seasons before.

"Didn't you read where he's drivin' for the Phillip Cox Company now?" George asked, while running a dry cloth over the colt's body. "He's been giving Silver Knight all his records at Roosevelt Raceway. Got the colt down to two o four last week."

"I missed that," Tom said. He threw the cooling blanket over Bonfire. "I'll walk him, George," he said, leading the colt away.

Early that same afternoon, Miss Elsie's trailer drawn by her jeep came down the shed row. Tom and George rose from their canvas chairs before Bonfire's stall the moment they recognized her at the wheel. A groom was sitting beside her. Miss Elsie's arrival stirred activity and interest up and down the row, for in her trailer was one of the two top two-year-olds of the season and perhaps of all time.

Miss Elsie stopped before an empty stall, and when she heard Tom's call and saw him and George, she pushed her way through the crowd and came quickly toward them.

She had cut her hair shorter, but that was the only thing different about Miss Elsie. Her horn-rimmed glasses moved up and down as she wiggled her nose while she talked and smiled at them. Only when they told her that Jimmy was very sick and in the hospital did she make an attempt to draw her lips tightly over her prominent white teeth.

"I want to do anything I can for him," she said seriously. "You know that, Tom, and you, too, George."

"We know it, Miss Elsie . . . and thanks. But you know how Jimmy is," George replied.

"I know," she said. "He never took a favor from anyone in his life. His kind don't. But I want to help, if I can," she offered once more.

Then they talked about her black filly and Miss Elsie was all smiles again. "Princess Guy's *it,* just as I knew she was going to be," she said. "And she'll go faster than her record of two o four. I know she will."

"You shouldn't have no trouble in the Futurity," George said. "I hear there'll only be three other horses in it. Your filly scared all the others off—they knowin' how fast she is, I mean."

"I don't think she'll have any trouble, either," Miss Elsie said confidently. "No two-year-old can keep up with her . . . and that includes Silver Knight, too," she added quickly. "The Princess will take care of him Saturday night."

"At Roosevelt?" George asked quickly.

Miss Elsie nodded her short-cropped head. "In the Two-Year-Old Championship Race," she said. Then Miss Elsie left to help unload her black filly with the four white stockings.

George said, "She's excited about her filly, all right. But Princess Guy hasn't changed her any. She's still a mighty good woman . . . Miss Elsie always will be."

But Tom had turned to his colt. "Yet she never even asked about Bonfire," he said. "She never even asked."

George turned to him. "That's Miss Elsie," he said. "There's only one two-year-old in the world for her now, an' that's her filly. She can't see no other."

The next afternoon, Tom, George and Uncle Wilmer stood at the paddock rail watching the racing of the Futurity, and they learned why Miss Elsie was so proud of her black filly.

The program and the announcer called it a race, but it wasn't. The Two-Year-Old Futurity that day was an exhibition of extreme racing speed given by Princess Guy. Miss Elsie, identified as a woman in her orange-and-blue racing silks only because that fact was pointed out to the crowd by the announcer, drove the filly to win the first heat by ten lengths and the second by fifteen.

The spectators, expecting a closer race, didn't leave the stands disappointed, because after Princess Guy finished the second heat it was announced to them that the filly had set a new world championship record for two-year-olds of 2:03! Yet the majority of the people who witnessed this creation of a new world record, including George and Tom, were surprised at the sensational time. For the black filly strode so effortlessly, never obviously changing her stride or beat from start to finish, that they had had no idea she was traveling so fast. She had given everybody the impression she could have gone much faster with only a little more effort.

Walking back to the stables, George shook his head as

though still uncertain about the sheer speed of Princess Guy. "She's like a bird," he said, almost to himself. "She flies an' you don't even know it. She jus' steals over the ground like nothing I've ever seen. I saw her do it or I wouldn't believe it."

Uncle Wilmer mumbled something in reply to George, but Tom didn't say anything until they reached Bonfire's stall and sat down in the chairs. "Do you think she was going all out, George? She didn't seem to be at all."

"I got an idea she was," George returned. "I think Miss Elsie was lettin' her go all the way. But you'd never know it to watch the filly, like you say," he added. "That's the kind of a racer she is."

"When Bonfire goes all out you know it," Tom said.

"That's the kind of a racer he is," George replied. "They're different as day an' night. Put them together on a track and somethin' will happen. I don't know what."

They sat there for the rest of the afternoon, discussing the black filly and the blood bay colt and awaiting Aunt Emma's return from the pie contest. Tom and George were going to the farm again that evening.

And when Aunt Emma joined them it took just one look at her constant smile to know that her mincemeat pie had won first prize this year. She removed the blue ribbon from her handbag for just a moment so they could see it; then she put it away carefully once more.

Bonfire had been fed, watered and bedded down for the night, and they were in Uncle Wilmer's old car when the race secretary handed George a special delivery letter. After taking a look at the return address, George turned to Tom, sitting next to him. "It's from the doc," he said grimly.

With fumbling hands he opened the envelope and Tom leaned over to read the letter with him.

Dear George,

I thought it best to let you know immediately what we've found and what has to be done.

Jimmy's condition is serious. A very rare and severe complication has set in, that of perforation of the ulcer. By that I mean the ulcer has made a leak or hole right through the wall of Jimmy's stomach. The result is that food in the stomach leaks out into the belly cavity, causing shock and the most severe pain.

Surgery is absolutely necessary, because the leak must be closed. It is a difficult, delicate operation, since Jimmy's condition is poor. It calls for the services of a specialist, and I have already talked to one in Boston. He is flying here tonight and the operation will take place sometime tomorrow morning.

I'll let you know the outcome. Try not to worry, for Jimmy is in the best of hands and a successful operation will mean that he'll be a well man again. The surgeon plans to remove the ulcer entirely, if possible, as well as close the stomach leak.

Remember, too, that Jimmy is my very good friend as well as yours—and I'll do everything possible for him.

Sincerely,
Henry Morton, M.D.

When they finished reading, they said nothing and passed the letter on to Aunt Emma and Uncle Wilmer.

"Then the operation was performed this morning," Tom said in a low voice. George said nothing, and kept his eyes away from Tom.

Uncle Wilmer waited silently behind the wheel. After a

long while, Aunt Emma broke the silence. "Take us home, Wilmer," she said. "A hot meal will help."

But at the farm they only toyed with the chicken and dumplings, and made no attempt to eat Aunt Emma's mincemeat pie. She didn't urge them and finally cleared the table and washed the dishes herself; then she left them alone.

Uncle Wilmer turned on the radio softly, thinking it would help.

Tom said, "Jimmy's a fighter, George. He'll be all right."

"I hope so, Tom."

"And Dr. Morton said the surgeon would remove the ulcer when he closed the leak in his stomach," Tom said. "He'll be a well man again, George. Just like he was before all this happened."

George nodded, but said nothing.

"Should we go home?"

"What good would it do, Tom? He's got the best care there is." George turned to the boy for the first time in a long while. "We need money more than ever now . . . lots of it to pay the surgeon. Fees for good men like him come high, and Jimmy deserves the best there is."

Tom nodded soberly.

"And knowin' Jimmy," George went on, "I know he'll get well fast if we can give him money to pay his bills."

"But how, George?" Tom asked desperately. "Even if we win with the colt Friday—"

"It only means a few hundred dollars, all right," Uncle Wilmer finished for him.

Tom turned to his uncle. He appreciated his being there, but he hoped he wouldn't ask any questions. He didn't feel like shouting tonight, just so his uncle could hear.

"There has to be a way we can do it," George said. "There's just got to. . . ."

And then they heard the singing commercial on the radio.

> *Heigh-ho! Come join us here.*
> *To Westbury, Westbury,*
> *That's where you cheer*
> *The horses, the horses,*
> *a-racing each night*
> *Beneath the stars, under the lights.*

The singing stopped and the announcer said, "Yes, folks, the races at Roosevelt Raceway, Westbury, Long Island, are a treat for the whole family! It's a night beneath the stars, watching America's fastest horses. It's the big event of the country fair brought to the city, folks. So come one, come all to Roosevelt Raceway tonight. Post time for the first race is at eight-forty. And we're only forty minutes from Pennsylvania Station in New York City. So hop on a train tonight and join us! But if you can't come tonight, folks, be sure to come Saturday night. That's the night of the Two-Year-Old Championship Race! The foremost colts in the country, including Silver Knight and Princess Guy, who today shattered the world's record at the Reading Fair, will be racing for that *big* purse of ten thousand dollars. So make a date now to join us at Roosevelt Raceway Saturday night."

When the announcer finished, George turned to Uncle Wilmer. "How far is it to New York City from here?" he asked quietly.

"Never been there. But I reckon it's under a hundred miles."

Tom saw the light in George's eyes. "George—"

But George was on his feet and walking toward the issues of *Hoof Beats* piled on top of the corner cupboard. Taking the most recent issue, he thumbed through it until he found what he wanted; then he took his seat again, reading the magazine.

The kitchen clock ticked noisily while Tom waited for George to finish reading.

Finally George spoke, and his voice was so low it seemed as though he were talking only for his own benefit. "Entries are accepted up until noon the day before the race. That's Friday. Today's Wednesday. Entry fee is five hundred dollars. One dash. Winner to take seventy-five percent of purse. That's seven thousand five hundred dollars." He stopped muttering to remove from his pocket the small book in which he kept their account of money on hand. "I've got three hundred dollars which I've been goin' to send Jimmy. Two hundred more would do it. I got to get it."

"I got two hundred dollars, all right."

It was Uncle Wilmer who had spoken. Tom turned to him in amazement, not only because of his uncle's astounding offer of two hundred dollars but also because George's voice had been just above a whisper and his head had been buried in the magazine; Uncle Wilmer *couldn't* have read his lips!

"George, you hear me?" Uncle Wilmer shouted. "I got two hundred dollars to race that colt against the best colts. He's no small-time colt! He's a champion! And I'm tired of readin' about this Silver Knight and that blamed filly Princess Guy! I want to see my colt beat 'em all!"

George was on his feet. "You'll lend it to us, Wilmer?

You'll give us a chance to help Jimmy with just this one race at the raceways without us ever tellin' him about it?"

"I been sayin' that, all right," Uncle Wilmer shouted. "I got it right now." And he strode across the room to the corner cupboard.

"Then you aren't deaf . . . stone deaf . . . at all," Tom said, when his uncle passed him.

"I ain't sayin' a thing about not bein' deaf!" Uncle Wilmer shouted. But he turned quickly in the direction of the porch when he heard the soft creaking of the outer door and knew his wife was on her way to the kitchen. "Heh, Tom?" he asked, cupping an ear. "What you say?"

George took the money from Uncle Wilmer, put it in his pocket, then turned to the boy. "Are you game, Tom, to try it . . . at night?"

The boy nodded, and George said, "Then we'll head for Roosevelt Raceway tomorrow."

"And I aim to be comin' along," Uncle Wilmer said. "I aim to see my money race, all right."

Luck of the Draw

19

Tom never asked George what he thought Jimmy might do if he ever learned of their taking Bonfire to Roosevelt Raceway. George had said they'd never tell Jimmy, and Tom let it go at that. This was George's show, and he'd made the decision to go to the Raceway; the rest was up to Tom and the colt. The job ahead of them would be the most difficult of their short racing careers.

They left the Reading Fair Thursday morning in Sadie with Uncle Wilmer sitting quietly between them. They trailed Miss Elsie and the two big vans from Roosevelt Raceway. Miss Elsie had taken the news of their going with no apparent surprise or concern. She was all business again. The only thing that mattered to her was getting her black filly to the raceway and winning the championship race. Whether or not she felt that Bonfire would provide any competition for her Princess Guy was not evident in her manner or face. She said only that Tom and George could follow her to Roosevelt Raceway, for she had made arrangements with the two raceway drivers at Reading to follow them, not knowing the way herself.

"It's four hours to New York," George said, when they left the fairgrounds behind, "and about another hour more to Roosevelt."

"We ought to be there by three o'clock then," Tom said.

And that was the extent of their conversation for hours and the many miles that passed beneath Sadie's smoothly worn tires. George had to push Sadie right along to keep up with the fast-rolling vans ahead.

Within two hours they left the farms and cultivated fields behind and moved speedily along a four-lane highway. The traffic became faster and heavier; they were still a long way from New York, but already they could feel the rapid beat of its city heart.

The country and fairs were behind them and Tom couldn't help feeling a deep sense of remorse stealing over him; the feeling heightened with every mile that brought them closer to the city and farther away from all he had grown to love so much. While he watched Miss Elsie's trailer and the speeding vans ahead, he very often thought of the leisurely, relaxed way he and George had driven through rolling countryside from one fair to the next.

He and George and Uncle Wilmer and Bonfire were going far afield, and he wondered what would be the outcome of this penetration of the city and raceway. He had all the confidence in the world in the speed of his colt, but he had learned also that a race wasn't always decided by speed alone. And night driving would be as foreign to him as to Bonfire.

Finally they were moving along narrow, traffic-congested

streets, threading their way toward the tall skyscrapers far in the distance.

"There's the Empire State Building," Tom said, pointing a finger toward the long, slender needle, much higher than any of the other buildings, that pierced the sky.

George only gripped the steering wheel more grimly and said nothing; neither did Uncle Wilmer, whose eyes never turned from the street ahead as he sat tense and straight.

Suddenly they were going down into a deep black hole of a tunnel; Uncle Wilmer unclasped his hands and put one on Tom's knee and the other on George's.

Tom muttered, "Holland Tunnel . . . we're going under the Hudson River."

The lights of the tunnel flashed by in quick succession; the wheels and motors of cars and trucks increased to a deafening, shattering roar that blasted their ears. When they emerged from the tunnel and were out in daylight once more, there was no relief, for spread before was the heavy traffic of downtown New York.

No one spoke after that, not even Tom.

Across narrow one-way streets and up crowded avenues they followed Miss Elsie and the vans ahead. And when that was over, they found themselves high on a bridge, crossing the East River to Long Island. Then came New York City suburbs and, after an hour more, cleared fields that skirted the highway; occasionally they saw a small truck farm.

The vans ahead slowed down and turned left off the highway. Not far away was the green-and-white-painted arched entrance of Roosevelt Raceway; beyond rose the mammoth grandstand, its many flags flying in the afternoon breeze.

George drove Sadie through the entrance behind the

others. *This was it!* Everything they had known was behind them, and George and Uncle Wilmer looked upon it all with new eyes, as did Tom.

They passed the gate to the track and saw the flashy green-and-white awnings of the paddock. Beyond was the racing strip, and within the racing oval was still another track; around it many horses were having a workout.

They left it all behind to go to the barns, and never in their lives had they seen so many stables and horses.

Only then did George speak. "There must be at least five hundred horses stabled here," he said in amazement.

They found more horses beyond the barns, for another track was there; this was being used, they saw, for slow jogging.

Still following Miss Elsie's trailer, they observed everything there was to see, but said nothing.

They did little that afternoon except to find their stable and to care for Bonfire. Yet they watched with keen, interested eyes everything that went on. They were among strangers here, and no one paid the slightest attention to them; not even Miss Elsie, who went about getting her filly ready for Saturday's race and ignoring those who wanted to talk to her about Princess Guy; she seemed not the slightest bit interested in the activity of the raceway. Miss Elsie could have been at another country fair for all the attention she paid to what went on about her. She was here for one reason alone and that absorbed her whole being.

While Tom and George had as much—and more—at stake as Miss Elsie, they couldn't ignore the raceway and its people. For here was the crux of Jimmy's illness; his resentment and bitterness toward the night raceways and their "killing of my sport"—as he put it—was now on trial before their eyes. So they watched everything that happened and every man there.

"It's a racin' *plant,*" George said, "just as they call it. It's big business an' streamlined all the way."

Tom nodded; but Uncle Wilmer only moved his canvas chair closer to Bonfire's head as though he needed the colt to protect him from all he saw.

Tom sat there and tried to stop himself from thinking too much about Jimmy Creech. "It's still too early to hear from the doctor," he told himself. "And no news now is good news."

Bonfire sneezed and Tom went to him. "Guess we'd better put the sheet on him. Getting cool with the sun going down," he told George.

He stayed with Bonfire awhile, fondling the colt and feeding him carrots. Two nights to go, he thought, tonight and tomorrow night; then we'll be on the *stage.*

That's the way Tom thought of Roosevelt Raceway at the end of his first day there. A giant, mammoth spectacle geared for modern racing. He and the others were backstage now getting ready for the big night show. In a way it was exciting. But he missed the noises of the fair, the friendly people who had always come to their stall knowing horses and wanting to talk about them. There were no spectators here now . . . just the performers.

What would the show be like tonight? What would his reactions be to it? Would he, like Jimmy, become embittered by this swift turn *his* sport had taken?

Night came and with it life poured into Roosevelt Raceway. Giant floodlights brightened the track and grounds as though it were daylight.

Tom and George closed the upper door of Bonfire's stall.

"Let him get his rest," George said. "It'll be better for him."

Uncle Wilmer refused to go to the track with them, so they left him behind with Bonfire, and made their way through the black mass of people streaming through the main entrance gate and overflowing the grandstand. They found they couldn't get near the rail without entering the grandstand gate, so grudgingly they went inside to stand in the packed area between the first tier of the stands and the rail.

As Tom looked at the track, he realized more than ever that this was *the stage.* He rose high on his tiptoes to see the racing strip over the heads of the jam-packed people between him and the rail.

The track lay smooth and untouched beneath the bright glare of the lights. The infield was green, seemingly too green to be real grass. The blackness of night was beyond the lighted backstretch; there were were no red trucks of a fair's midway, no spinning, gleaming Ferris wheels. And these, Tom found, he missed very much.

So modern, so brilliant—and yet, too, so artificial, this stage.

Turning to look behind him, he saw the thousands in the stands, afraid to move lest they lose their seats. Just to the right of the grandstand was the paddock, where the horses were taken fully an hour before the race. The gay, colorful awnings looked even more green and more white under the lights than they had during the day. Shaped like a horseshoe, the paddock was fenced off and forbidden territory to all spectators—to all except officials and the drivers of those horses which were to come out onto the track for the first race. Tom thought again of the friendly people at the fairs who would follow them from barn to track, always talking, always so close. They would resent very much a fence that kept them apart from the horses; and Tom found that he did, too.

George said, "More older drivers here than I thought there'd be, Tom. Listenin' to Jimmy, I thought they'd all be young squirts."

"More young guys, though," Tom said, "than the old boys." And he said it in defense of Jimmy Creech.

"Yeah," George admitted. "But that's good, Tom. We need young people like you and them."

"You mean you like *this*, George?"

And the way in which Tom said *this* caused George to turn quickly to him.

"No," he said thoughtfully, after a long silence. "It's not for me . . . not from what I've seen so far. But I don't want to condemn it 'cause it isn't for me, the way Jimmy does. Like I said once before, every person to his own likes. Our sport ain't always belonged to the fairs, you know. Before the fairs we used to block off roads in the center of town an' race every day. Guess you could call this a super blocked-off road." He paused, laughing at his own comparison.

"And although it isn't for me or Jimmy or maybe for you," George added sincerely, "it's good for our sport in a lot of ways. Raceways like this all 'round the country mean a lot more people are takin' to our sport, and in time they'll learn to love it the same as we do." George paused again, this time to think for a while before going on.

"When I think about it," he said, "what I'd like to see happen more than anything else is to get all these people out to the fairs to see what they're missing. If they enjoy the races here they'll like fair racing even more. They'll *feel* the difference themselves. And that, Tom, will be the best thing that ever happened to them and to our sport."

Tom said, "Then I guess you and Jimmy have a lot in common, George. You both want to get the people to the fairs, to get it back the way it was."

"Not quite," George replied. "Jimmy hates raceways like this an' wants to see an end to 'em. I don't. I say let the raceways give city folk a taste of our sport and get them interested. Then some way get them out to the fairs in the daytime to see the real thing . . . to *feel* it as they can't here."

Promptly at eight-forty, post time for the first race, there was a ringing of the paddock bell and the horses paraded onto the track. Roosevelt Raceway officials prided themselves on an efficient, to-the-minute prompt race program—and the reasons were apparent to Tom beginning with the ringing of the paddock bell.

There was no delay in the post parade. A red-coated marshal led the field past the grandstand and drivers and horses were introduced. There was no lagging by any driver and they kept a close single file. The announcer gave only the name of the horse and its driver, leaving the spectators to consult their programs for information as to color, breeding and owner; this, Tom realized, was super-efficiency aimed at getting the horses away fast in the first race. And he missed the leisurely, friendly voices of the fair announcers, acquainting the crowd with all information despite the fact that it appeared on the program.

The two warm-up scores were short and fast; then the

parade filed behind the mobile starting gate awaiting them at the head of the stretch. Tom saw the flashy, long white four-door open limousine. This, too, was in keeping with spectacular Roosevelt Raceway!

The car moved, and behind its barrier the horses and drivers came down for the start. Gleaming coats of horses and the colorful silks of their drivers flashed beneath the lights. When they swept across the starting line, the lights in the grandstand dimmed. The brilliantly lighted track was now the center of attention. The show was on!

Tom watched closely as each driver fought hard to reach the turn first. He saw them move into it and come around, some tucked in close to the rail, others already making their bids for the lead. His eyes never left the tightly packed group all through the race as he watched the strategy of the drivers. They passed the stands the first time around still close together, still fighting for positions . . . and they continued that way all around the track again, coming down the home-stretch in a hard-driving finish that called for a photograph to decide the winner.

When it was over, Tom knew that the strategy used here was no different from that at the fairs. Maybe the raceway drivers cut their turns a little closer and took more of a risk getting through narrow openings, but otherwise there was no difference. Strategy that won races at fairs would win them here.

The lights went on throughout the grandstand, and George said, "One dash an' it's over for them. No more heats . . . nothin'. Just pick up their purse money and look forward to another race."

"You can't make any mistakes in a dash," Tom said.

"No," George agreed. "You get no chance to get back at
'em in the next heat like you do at the fairs." He paused to
look at the horses still on the track, their drivers awaiting
the results of the photo finish. "That old boy was right up
with the young fellers," he said.

The picture was developed and the results of the first race
were announced to the crowd.

"The old fellow didn't win it," Tom said afterward.

"No . . . they pushed him back," George replied. "These
young fellows make up for their lack of experience by takin'
more chances. You'll have to watch 'em, Tom, on Saturday."

Suddenly the announcer said to the packed throng, "Your
attention, please." A hush settled over the stands, and he
went on: "We would like to call your attention again to the
feature race on Saturday night's program. It's the Two-Year-
Old American Championship Race! Ten of the nation's top
two-year-olds will meet in one dash for a ten-thousand-dollar
purse. The field includes Silver Knight, Phillip Cox's outstanding gray colt, heralded by many who have seen him
race this season here at Roosevelt as the wonder colt of the
decade. Matching strides with Silver Knight will be Princess
Guy, the black filly which Miss Elsie Topper drove to a new
world's record of two o three at the Reading Fair this week.
Rest assured, ladies and gentlemen, that the meeting of Silver Knight and Princess Guy Saturday night will result in
still a lower world record mark for two-year-olds!

"You won't want to miss this race! So make your seat res-
ervations before leaving the raceway tonight!"

When the announcer had finished, Tom turned to
George. "No mention of the other colts in the race . . . or
Bonfire," he said a little bitterly.

"Bonfire's record of two nineteen at the Port Royal Fair don't mean much to 'em," George returned. "Not when they're talkin' about two o three record colts."

"But . . ."

"Sure, I know, Tom. We ain't let Bonfire out. But we will Saturday night."

Nodding, Tom turned to look toward the paddock where the horses were coming promptly onto the track for the second race. He couldn't see much over the heads of the people in front of him, so finally he turned again to George. "The announcer said there'd be ten horses in the race Saturday night. That's a big field, George."

"Too big," his friend answered. "The track has room only for nine horses across it. It means whoever draws the number ten position will have to follow the others, racing behind the pole horse."

"That won't be good," Tom said thoughtfully.

"No, it won't. Not in a fast field like that one's going to be. You got to try to get out first with Bonfire, Tom. That way you can let him go . . . an' you won't have to worry about the drivin' of those guys behind you. Get Bonfire out front and keep him there. He'll stay there."

"I know he will . . . *if* I can get him out."

"Number ten position will be the only one to stop you from gettin' him out, Tom . . . and the chances are only one in ten that you'll draw that spot."

"I hope our luck holds, George—for all of us and for Jimmy."

"The luck of the draw," George muttered. "Tomorrow at noon we'll know."

The next day, exactly at twelve o'clock, Bonfire was entered in the Two-Year-Old Championship Race. George turned over the five-hundred-dollar entrance fee to the race secretary, then stepped back in the office to make room for the other people who were entering their colts. He rejoined Tom and Uncle Wilmer in a far corner of the room, and waited with them for the entries to be finished and the draw for positions to begin.

Miss Elsie was there, but she only nodded to them and did not speak. Phillip Cox entered Silver Knight, then joined his driver, Ray O'Neil. Cox gazed several times at Tom and George, as though trying to remember where he had seen them. Finally his glances ceased, and Tom knew that Coronet was too far removed from this Raceway and Cox's fight with Jimmy Creech too long ago for the wealthy sportsman to remember either. Not at this moment, anyway.

Neither did the slender, long-legged Ray O'Neil remember them from the Reading Fair two seasons before, when he had offered Jimmy Creech a new wheel for the one broken during the race. Frank Lunceford was in the room, too. It was Lunceford who had hooked sulky wheels with Jimmy at the Bedford Fair, the crash which had sent Jimmy to the hospital. George looked at the chubby, heavy-set man for a long while, expecting Lunceford to remember him because together they had gone to the hospital with Jimmy. But Lunceford didn't recognize him, either.

There were other young drivers in the room, and like Ray O'Neil and Frank Lunceford they were well known on every raceway track throughout the country. They had been through the drawings for position in championship races before, yet their faces and voices made it evident to Tom that they were as tense as he was. Like him, they knew that the luck of the draw would play an important part in the Two-Year-Old Championship.

The entries for the race closed, and, just as the announcer had told the crowd the night before, there were ten starters. Now would come the draw for positions.

The positions were to be assigned by lot. The race secretary put the name of each horse on a slip of paper, then deposited it in an upturned hat on his desk; his assistant stood beside him, shaking a box which was closed except for a very small opening. Tom heard the rattling of the balls inside the box. He knew there were ten balls, numbered one to ten.

"Please," he mumbled to himself, "any number but ten."

Uncle Wilmer turned to him with keen, eager eyes. "You'll win with Bonfire even from ten, all right," he said.

Tom managed a grim smile. No longer did they have to raise their voices for Uncle Wilmer to hear them; deafness was just a convenience, a way for him to escape Aunt Emma's wrath.

After shaking the hat with the slips of paper in it, the race secretary placed the hat on a shelf behind him. He couldn't see inside the hat now; no one could.

"Ready, Bill?" the secretary asked his assistant. "Let's go, then."

No one in the room moved or talked when the race secretary drew one slip of paper from the hat and simultaneously his assistant shook out a numbered ball from the covered box.

"Victory Boy," the secretary said, "number five position."

Tom turned to Frank Lunceford, driver of Victory Boy, and saw the smile on the man's round, chubby face.

"That's okay," Lunceford said, turning and leaving the room.

"Raider," the secretary continued, drawing another slip of paper and reading it. He picked up the next ball that had been shaken from the box. "Number nine," he added.

Another man left the room.

"Silver Knight," the secretary said. Every face in the room turned quickly to Phillip Cox and Ray O'Neil, standing together, then all gazes shifted quickly to the ball on the desk. "Number two position," the secretary added.

Phillip Cox uttered a sharp yell, then left the room with his arm across Ray O'Neil's shoulders. Silver Knight had one of the best positions in the race; Phillip Cox's luck was holding good.

Tom looked at Miss Elsie and saw that she was very worried. She was moving uneasily about the room now, and her glasses shifted up and down as she wiggled her large nose.

The race secretary was drawing faster now. "Volomite's Comet . . . number four position."

Smiling, another man left the room.

"Princess Guy," the secretary said next.

Miss Elsie stopped pacing, and her face was tight and drawn as she waited for the secretary to pick up the numbered ball.

"Number one . . . the pole position for Princess Guy."

Miss Elsie's large teeth seemed to fill the room when she smiled, then she left quickly.

Tom started shifting uneasily while the secretary called off more positions with no mention of Bonfire. The number seven position went next, then numbers six and eight. There were only two more positions left to be drawn—number three and number ten!

George and Uncle Wilmer moved a little away from Tom in their uneasiness. Across the room stood the only other representatives of a horse in the race, the driver and the owner of Chief Express. They too moved about nervously, then stood still as the race secretary reached for the hat.

"Please, please," Tom mumbled to himself, "not ten. Give us a chance, give us *three*."

"Chief Express," the secretary said, then he reached for the moving ball.

All eyes watched it come to a stop. And they saw the number even before the secretary read it off.

Number three!

The men at the other end of the room yelled together and rushed for the door, leaving Tom, George and Uncle Wilmer alone with the secretary.

"Y'might as well pull it out of the hat anyway," George grimly told the race secretary.

But already Tom had started for the door.

Before reaching it, he heard the secretary say, "Bonfire."

Then came the sound of the rolling ball, the very last ball in the box, on the desk. "Number ten position."

Opening the door, he heard the footsteps of George and Uncle Wilmer behind him.

"It's too bad," the race secretary called after them. "But it's the luck of the draw."

The Two-Year-Old Championship

20

Bonfire had been in his paddock stall for more than an hour, waiting for the championship race to be called. He wore his light racing harness but not his bridle, and he was not yet hitched to his sulky. Behind him, standing upright against the wall, were the long shafts of the sulky, ready to be lowered and hooked to him.

He wore Jimmy's old white blanket with the red borders over his harness; for the September night was unusually cool and the sky overcast. There were no stars, and only the galaxy of floodlights shattered the darkness. Bonfire blinked in their brilliant glare and uneasily nuzzled Tom's hand.

The boy stayed with him every minute, turning only occasionally to glance up the line at the other two-year-olds stabled according to their positions in the race. In the number 1 paddock stall was Princess Guy, and Miss Elsie never moved from her filly's side. In the next stall was the gray colt, Silver Knight, and standing before him were Phillip Cox and his driver, Ray O'Neil. They kept glancing at the

black filly in the next stall, but never looked at any other
colt in the race. Silver Knight was muzzled just now to prevent him from nipping anyone; his meanness was well
known. He wore a brilliant red-and-white blanket across
which was lettered, "Cox Clothing Company."

George said, "You never said what you think of him."
And he nodded toward Silver Knight's stall.

Uncle Wilmer moved closer to hear what Tom had to say
about the gray colt.

"He's too coarse for me," the boy said, keeping his eyes on
Silver Knight. "I've watched him work. But he's rugged and
can go. He lacks the finish, though. I like to see them clean
like Miss Elsie's filly and our colt. His legs are good boned
and shaped well, but his feet will give him trouble one of
these days. They're too large and flat."

George and Uncle Wilmer nodded in agreement.

"That's jus' what I would have said about him," Uncle
Wilmer said impressively. "A horse is only as good as his
feet . . . an' his are too large and flat, all right."

George said, "I hear Cox was offered seventy-five thousand
dollars for him just tonight, an' he turned it down."

"He's not for me." Tom said, turning back and running
his hands beneath Bonfire's blanket. "Even if I had that kind
of money."

They had nothing to do but wait for the call, so they
stood restlessly and a little sheepishly amidst the strange sur-
roundings. The paddock was empty of men except for
owners, drivers and track officials. They could see the milling
mass of humanity on the other side of the high wire fence
which separated the paddock from the grandstand. Track
guards filed up and down alongside the fence, an extra pre-

caution to keep spectators away from the horses. No, it wasn't at all the same as at the fairs. And in the grandstand, and standing in front of it right up to the rail, were more people than any of them ever had seen in one group before. The great number of people was overwhelming, even a little frightening.

Tom turned away from them to think of Jimmy, to wonder again why they still had heard no word from Dr. Morton. He knew George was worried, too, but neither of them had mentioned it to the other. Tom knew that he shouldn't be thinking about Jimmy just now—not with so much ahead of him and Bonfire.

Ever since the drawing for positions, Tom had discussed with George and Uncle Wilmer the only race strategy he could use from his number ten position. Yet now he turned to them again and spoke of it. He wanted to make certain of what he had to do.

"I'll keep him close behind Miss Elsie," he said. "Right from the start I'll go along with her and her filly . . ."

"She'll get you out in front of the others, if you keep Bonfire breathin' down her neck," George said. "Her filly's got the speed to get her out in front. You jus' follow close behind an' go out with her."

"An' once you're clear of the others," Uncle Wilmer added, "you can pull out from the rail an' go around her and that black filly. Bonfire can do it, all right," he said confidently, turning to the colt to run his hand down the red-braided forelock.

It was then they heard the paddock marshal shout, "Hook 'em up, boys. We're going out in a few minutes."

Tom swallowed hard. The *show* was about to begin! And

now each stall was the scene of much activity.

George and Uncle Wilmer went quickly to either side of the colt and, reaching the sulky, pulled down the shafts. Without removing Bonfire's blanket, they hitched the sulky to the harness.

Tom talked softly to his colt while he put on the light racing bridle and adjusted the head number 10. He was still a little nervous and his uneasiness communicated itself to Bonfire, for the colt began tossing his head. Tom ran his hand beneath the heavy black mane, rubbing the silken coat. "We're on, Bonfire," he said. "We're going out."

The clear call of the bugle sounded above the noise of the crowd, silencing the stands. Blankets were whipped off the two-year-olds and they stood naked and eager beneath the bright lights. The black filly with the four white stockings left her stall with Miss Elsie holding the lines and walking behind the sulky; the gray colt came next with Ray O'Neil holding the lines and Phillip Cox leading Silver Knight to the paddock gate. Then the other colts followed, until it was Bonfire's turn to go.

George took him by the bridle, while Tom and Uncle Wilmer walked behind.

"You ain't got a thing to worry about," Uncle Wilmer told the boy. "You got all the colt there is, all right."

Tom said nothing.

"And you remember you're wearin' Jimmy's silks," Uncle Wilmer went on. "They seen more races than all these other silks put together. They'll give you all the luck you need, all right."

The red-coated marshal sat astride his horse, awaiting all racers to reach the track for the post parade. Impatiently he beckoned George to hurry up his colt. But George didn't take Bonfire out of his slow walk.

At the gate, a paddock guard stopped George and told Tom to get into the sulky seat.

"You an' Bonfire do all you can, Tom," George said. "We don't expect any more."

Tom drove Bonfire onto the track, and joined the post parade.

Ahead, all along the line, silks shrieked their colors beneath the brazen lights. To Tom's left was a black mass of people. He turned from them to watch the red hindquarters working smoothly between his outstretched legs, and to talk to his colt—to quiet him and himself.

The announcer's voice came over the public-address system.

"Ladies and gentlemen!" He waited until the crowd hushed. "The horses are now parading for the Two-Year-Old American Championship Race. Number one is the world's record holder, Princess Guy . . . a black filly by Mr. Guy out of Little Mary. . . ."

Tom looked in the direction of the announcer's booth, surprised that the raceway officials were taking a few extra minutes to give the background of each horse.

". . . Princess Guy set her record of two o three at the Reading Fair this week; she is being driven by her owner, Miss Elsie Topper of Coronet, Pennsylvania, the foremost woman driver in the country.

"Number two is Silver Knight, holder of this raceway's track record for two-year-olds of two o four. He is a gray colt, owned by the Phillip Cox Clothing Company of Pittsburgh, Pennsylvania, and is being driven by the leading driver of all night raceways, Ray O'Neil. Silver Knight is sired by Volomite and out of . . ."

But whatever the announcer had left to say about Silver Knight was drowned out by the cheering supporters of the gray colt.

Tom turned to them, and saw Phillip Cox rise to his feet from his box near the finish line. He waved his hand to those behind, accepting their cheers for his colt, then he sat down again.

Finally Bonfire passed the announcer's booth.

"Number ten, who will trail the field at the start, is Bonfire, a blood bay colt, sired by the Black and out of Volo Queen. Bonfire is owned by Jimmy Creech of Coronet, Pennsylvania, and is being driven by Tom Messenger."

That was all the announcer had to say, but it was enough to cause Phillip Cox to stand again, this time looking directly at Bonfire and Tom Messenger as they passed opposite his box. There was recognition in his eyes; now he well remembered Coronet and Jimmy Creech.

Ray O'Neil turned in his sulky seat, as did Frank Lunceford, to look behind at Bonfire and Tom. They too now remembered Jimmy Creech.

"The field will take two warm-up scores, then go behind the mobile starting gate," the announcer said.

Nervously, Tom turned Bonfire to go down the stretch for their first score. The colt snorted, then bolted. Quickly Tom's hands moved down the lines; there was a shortening of stride as Bonfire obeyed Tom's hands. Angry with himself, Tom settled back in his seat and never looked at the crowd again. This was no more than another fair race, despite the people, lights and glitter. What won at the fairs would win here. But he must give Bonfire his chance. He must make no mistake.

All the way down the stretch, Tom saw and heard only his colt. And when he stopped to turn him back again, he knew that he and Bonfire were ready together.

He was taking the colt past the paddock gate when he saw the commotion there. The guard was struggling with someone, who finally evaded his arms. It was George, and he was halfway to Tom when the guard caught up with him again. But George waved the yellow paper he held in his hand and shouted to Tom, *"Jimmy is all right! He's okay, Tom!"*

Tom only had time to wave his hand to indicate he had heard before the guard pulled George away from the track.

All the way back past the grandstand, Tom thought of Jimmy Creech. He'd be a well man now! He'd be himself again!

But the moment Tom turned Bonfire down the track for his second warm-up he forgot Jimmy Creech, forgot everything but the muscles sliding beneath the red coat in front of him.

Back at the mobile starting gate awaiting them at the head of the homestretch, Tom brought Bonfire alongside Princess Guy. He turned to Miss Elsie to smile at her, but the woman never looked at him. She continued her low humming to the black filly. Miss Elsie had word for no one now but Princess Guy. Neither did the gazes of the other drivers waver from their colts. They were ready for the race.

The white limousine was drawn up at the far side of the track, and the wings of its gate were closed, allowing the field to go by. When all had passed, the starter motioned his driver to pull out to the center of the track and to open the wings of the gate.

Tom took Bonfire a little farther back than the others, for

he was to follow them. Turning the colt around, he saw that the others were all in position and going toward the mobile gate. Nine horses stretched far across the track as they moved down to the barrier. Tom took Bonfire over to the rail, close behind Miss Elsie.

Slowly the limousine started moving and the horses followed the gate.

"Easy! Easy!" the starter called to the field. "Slow down! You're all coming too fast!"

And they were, Tom saw. All the horses in the line ahead were pushing their noses close to the gate. Each driver was anxious to get away. They were going to fight for the lead—all of them!

Bonfire sensed the eagerness of horses and drivers, and his pace quickened. Tom slowed him down; there was no place for them to go—not yet.

The limousine ahead moved a little faster, and Tom kept Bonfire's head close to the orange-and-blue silks Miss Elsie wore.

"Mr. Lunceford, keep your position!" the starter called.

Tom glanced at heavy-set, chubby-faced Frank Lunceford and knew that he was even more eager than the others to get his golden chestnut colt, Victory Boy, away first from his number 5 position. Lunceford had moved closer to the driver on his left, forcing the others to move more toward Miss Elsie and the rail. But Miss Elsie ignored the spinning wheels of Ray O'Neil's sulky on her right and didn't give way an inch; she was in a good spot, bringing her black filly down just a few short feet from the rail.

Tom knew that no one would beat Miss Elsie to the turn, for no horse in the fast-moving line could match Princess

Guy's speedy break—none except, perhaps, Silver Knight. The gray colt might stay with the filly. In a few seconds now he'd know.

Princess Guy and Silver Knight.

Tom was certain it was these two Bonfire would have to beat. So he forgot about Lunceford and the rest of the field. He'd go along with the black filly at the break and she'd lead him out in front. *Just follow Miss Elsie. Just follow Miss Elsie.*

Like a tremendous and powerful incoming wave, the line of horses increased their speed behind the fast-moving gate. The grandstand spectators rose to their feet at the rushing pound of hoofs. As a team the country's top two-year-olds swept beneath the lights of the starting line.

"GO!" shouted the starter.

To the shriek of the drivers, Tom let Bonfire go behind Miss Elsie. Strides quickened like unleashed springs and still in one line they went for the first turn. No colt gave way, and Tom knew from his vantage point behind that never would there be another fight like this for a first turn. Every driver in the field had decided to make a desperate bid to obtain the lead at the beginning of this race.

Tom's heart stilled during the fight for the turn. He could do nothing but keep Bonfire's nose close to Miss Elsie's back, hoping desperately that her black filly would reach the turn first . . . for he would then be directly behind her, and ready to make his move for the lead.

Suddenly there was a break in the long line across the track and the drivers drove their horses closer to the rail. Only Silver Knight and Frank Lunceford's chestnut colt came on to match strides with Princess Guy; the others moved over toward Tom.

Sweeping into the turn, Princess Guy, Silver Knight and Victory Boy strode as a team, stride for stride, wheel to wheel.

Tom kept his position directly behind Miss Elsie, but racing alongside Bonfire now were three other colts. And behind them came the third tier of the last three horses.

There was no slackening of stride by any colt in the race. They were making one constant bid, and Tom knew this speed was much too fast for so early in the race. But no driver slowed his colt. Spinning wheels were but inches away from one another. O'Neil and Lunceford were trying to force Miss Elsie closer to the rail to save themselves ground going around the turn. But she held firm. The drivers on Tom's right were forcing him, too. But he held his position right behind Miss Elsie.

Coming off the turn, they entered the backstretch. Princess Guy was moving effortlessly, her hoofs hardly touching the ground in her graceful flight. Tom knew she was flying, for Bonfire was moving faster than ever to keep up with her. Surely the filly would now pull away from the heavy-footed gray colt and the long-limbed chestnut who strode beside her! If the black filly would pull away just a short distance, he'd go along with her to come out from the rail when he was past the gray and chestnut colts, then make his bid with Bonfire to pass Princess Guy.

But it didn't happen that way at all. For down the backstretch Silver Knight and Victory Boy matched the filly's long, sweeping stride. No horse or driver gave way—not even those racing alongside Tom.

They went into the back turn in the very same positions and still fighting. Once more, spinning wheels glistened ever closer as drivers moved over on each other trying to save ground going around the turn. Miss Elsie held. Tom held.

And at this point in the race, Tom knew two things for certain. One was that he and Miss Elsie had an advantage in that they were close to the rail and taking the shortest route around the track. Two, something had to give soon, for no colts of this age could travel so fast for so long. The killing pace would tell on the colts very soon, and he wasn't even certain that Bonfire had the necessary reserve. Never before had he called upon the colt for a supreme effort; yet very shortly he would ask Bonfire and the colt would give his answer.

Frank Lunceford went for his whip, coming off the back turn. He made a last desperate effort to get around Silver Knight and Princess Guy. But Victory Boy failed utterly before the ever-quickening strides of the black filly and gray colt, and the golden chestnut began falling back as the field swept down the homestretch for the first time.

Racing by the standing, crazed people in the grandstand, Miss Elsie opened up her black filly another notch, and now she actually seemed to fly. But Silver Knight had more speed as well, and when Ray O'Neil called for it, the gray colt surged forward with Princess Guy.

Tom's hands moved on the lines as he too called for more speed. And at the same time he heard the drivers on his right calling to their colts—and some went for their whips.

Bonfire's muscles gleamed beneath his sweated body, and he responded quickly to Tom's call for more speed. Tom knew then that his colt had no equal. He could feel the power—reserve power—flooding the lines he held. And it was good, knowing there was more to come!

The blood bay colt went forward with Princess Guy and Silver Knight, leaving the others gradually behind.

As they swept past the judge's booth, Tom heard the announcer call to the crowd, "Time for the half, one minute flat!" Never had two-year-olds raced so fast.

Miss Elsie was taking Princess Guy along at a killing pace and only two were left of the field of ten to challenge her.

Once more they went into the first turn and Miss Elsie sought to kill off the ponderous gray colt racing alongside by again increasing the filly's speed. Princess Guy leveled out as though she had wings. Tom wondered how much more speed this black filly had. When would she reach her limit? He touched the lines again to keep Bonfire directly behind Miss Elsie.

But Miss Elsie did not kill off the big gray colt on the turn, for he too had more speed and surged forward with the filly. Tom saw Ray O'Neil glance back at him as they went into the backstretch. He hoped it meant that O'Neil was worried, that Silver Knight had reached his utmost speed. He wanted Silver Knight to fall back, then he'd take Bonfire ahead and on to challenge Princess Guy.

It was getting time to make his move, even if Silver Knight didn't fall back and he had to take Bonfire around the gray colt. Somewhere along this stretch he'd make his move. He got ready for it.

Bonfire's nose was still close to Miss Elsie's head, and Tom knew she realized it was the blood bay colt—for he'd been there since the start of the race. Suddenly Miss Elsie began moving away from Bonfire! Seemingly there had been no increase of length or rapidity in the black filly's strides. But Tom knew she was going faster or she wouldn't be pulling away! Miss Elsie was going all out!

Tom called upon Bonfire for more speed and again came the quick response from the powerful, splendid muscles in front of him. The blood bay colt pushed his nose close to Miss Elsie's head again. But then the break came—the one for which Tom had been waiting. Silver Knight started falling back, inches at first, then several feet. Just a little more room and Tom knew he'd be able to get Bonfire between Miss Elsie's sulky and the slowing Silver Knight.

The gray colt came back to race alongside Bonfire, and Ray O'Neil was sitting alongside Tom while Miss Elsie and her black filly raced alone in front. Tom waited for Silver Knight to drop back a little more, just a few more feet.

But the gray colt stopped losing ground. Stride for stride he raced Bonfire. Startled, Tom glanced at the man alongside him, then quickly he turned to Miss Elsie's back again. If Silver Knight wasn't going to drop any farther back, Miss Elsie *had* to move ahead. *Otherwise he and Bonfire were in a pocket!*

But Miss Elsie didn't increase the speed of her black filly. Frantically, Tom watched the backstretch poles sweep by, and then they were going into the last turn. *He had to get Bonfire out of this pocket!*

He let Bonfire push his head closer to Miss Elsie. She must feel his breath! She must know! *She did.* Miss Elsie knew Bonfire was directly behind her and in a pocket. She had glanced back once to see the gray colt and Ray O'Neil alongside the colt behind her. *And she knew that the colt was Bonfire.* She was afraid, not of Silver Knight but of the blood bay colt! She was going to keep him there all around the turn, down the homestretch—*right to the finish!*

He had to get Bonfire out. "But not now!" he cautioned

himself. "Wait until we come off this turn. The only thing I can do is to drop behind O'Neil and then come around him and go after Miss Elsie. It's all I can do. And there won't be much time."

Tom heard the yell of the crowd as they came off the turn. The homestretch was ahead of them! He touched the lines, but this time it was to ask his colt to slow down, to watch Silver Knight and Ray O'Neil slide by . . . and then to come around in a last desperate rush to catch them before the finish line. He didn't think there'd be time to catch Miss Elsie and her black filly. He had failed his colt, George, and Jimmy Creech.

He touched the lines again, but still there was no response from Bonfire. The blood bay colt wasn't going to slow down! He knew this was the stretch drive! Everything he had learned from them, his every instinct, told him that this was the homestretch. *Jimmy Creech had wanted a colt with gameness and the will to win.* Bonfire was fighting to be let out, and it would cost him the race

For only by slowing down could Tom get him out of this pocket. Bonfire was pushing his head over Miss Elsie's when it happened. The heavy-footed Silver Knight faltered for the first time, picked up stride, then half-stumbled.

Quickly Tom turned to him, knowing the hard, fast race had told on those large feet. Silver Knight picked up his stride again, then faltered once more. This time it cost him the ground between Miss Elsie and Bonfire.

Miss Elsie glanced behind at the faltering gray colt; then she saw Bonfire's head come between them and she went for her whip. The blood bay colt was coming through the "hole" with less than a hundred yards to go!

Tom's hands moved quickly as he called for every last bit of speed from Bonfire. He felt the colt gather himself just as he had for every sprint at the fairs—and this in spite of the long, hard race behind him. Tom felt himself picked up and hurled forward; the colt's tail cut his face like the sharp lash of a whip, yet Tom never felt the pain. He couldn't see ahead, but it didn't matter; he knew the track was clear. Above the finish line was the long string of lights. And many yards before he and Bonfire passed beneath their brilliance, they had swept by the beaten black filly, Princess Guy.

Those who saw Bonfire create a new world's record of 1:59 at Roosevelt Raceway that night described the blinding speed of this blood bay colt no differently from the farmers and the small-town folk of the fairs who had seen Bonfire.

"His sprint is something that sets you afire," they said. "You see him gather himself, then suddenly it happens and you find yourself being picked up and hurled along with him, even though you're away up in the grandstand. But it's hard to explain exactly what happens to him and to you, when he goes. You have to see him yourself."

Back at Coronet

21

Two months later, Tom and George helped Jimmy down the hospital steps. They helped him even though he kept insisting that he was all right and had never felt better in all his life.

Tom knew that in all probability Jimmy was telling the truth, because for the first time in many, many long months he saw the tiny pinpoints of brown in Jimmy's hazel eyes. And when Jimmy's eyes were clear it meant that he was feeling very well. Still, he was weak from his many weeks in bed, and it was best that he take it very slow and easy for a while, just as Dr. Morton had told him to do.

There was a good chance, too, that Jimmy would follow Dr. Morton's instructions, for the pains he had experienced before the operation were of the severest kind. Jimmy hadn't mentioned them, but Dr. Morton had told Tom and George of Jimmy's terrible ordeal. He had gone on to say that the ulcer had been removed completely when the Boston surgeon closed the stomach leak. There was no reason now why

Jimmy shouldn't be in perfect health.

Reaching the bottom of the steps, George asked, "You warm enough, Jimmy?" The fall day was exceptionally cool and the mid-afternoon sun was hidden behind clouds.

Jimmy pulled the muffler about his neck. "Sure, I'm warm enough," he said a little defiantly. "No need to treat me like an invalid, George. I'm okay now, I tell you."

"I know that," George said, smiling. "It's just that it's cool for me, too."

They got in the car and drove through the streets of Pittsburgh. Jimmy sat between them in the front seat and was silent a long while, then he said, "The doc said Mrs. Davis wanted to stay on at my house. So I told him she could." He turned to George, adding quickly, "Not as a nurse . . . I don't need a nurse. She's goin' to do my cooking. She's a pretty good cook." Then to Tom, "Not as good as your Aunt Emma . . . but good for our town." He paused again, then continued as though more explanation of Mrs. Davis's presence in his bachelor home was necessary. "She needs a good home, the doc said, and she likes Coronet. She's pretty old, you know."

"Y'mean she's not like us *kids?*" George asked without taking his eyes from the road.

Jimmy laughed loudly then. "Yeah," he said, "that's it."

Tom felt Jimmy's hand on his knee, and he laughed with him. This was the old Jimmy Creech. Things were going to be . . .

"She just wants room and board," Jimmy said. "No money." And when he mentioned the word *money* he turned to George. "We got enough left to last us through the winter?"

Taking a deep breath, Tom turned away to look out the car window. Once again, it was coming. George had paid all the bills out of their winnings, and had shown the receipted bills to Jimmy. But even though the amounts shown on the statements were less than they had actually paid the Boston surgeon and the hospital, they were large enough to make Jimmy wonder how they'd ever done it racing *at the fairs.*

George said, "We'll get through the winter all right. You don't need to worry none, Jimmy. Like I been tellin' you, I'm still the treasurer of this outfit."

Jimmy sat back in the car seat, and although he was silent Tom knew he was still thinking about money. Finally Jimmy turned to him.

"I don't know how you an' Bonfire did it, Tom," he said sincerely.

"He's a champ . . ." Tom started to say, then quickly added, "I mean, he just didn't have any competition at the fairs."

"But, still I don't see how you did it," Jimmy insisted. "I never made so much money as you two did in any one season as long as I been racin'."

"Purses were bigger," George said, coming to Tom's assistance.

Jimmy was silent after that. But Tom shifted uneasily in his seat. He and George were just getting into this thing deeper and deeper by not telling Jimmy about Roosevelt Raceway. George wanted to wait until Jimmy was fully recovered. Yet how were they going to continue keeping this from Jimmy? How? When newspapers and national magazines, as well as all racing publications, still carried stories about the "phenomenally fast" blood bay colt owned by

Jimmy Creech of Coronet, Pennsylvania. When not a single day passed that many visitors, including photographers and sportswriters, did not come to see Bonfire!

They couldn't leave their colt alone for a moment. Even today they had hired a man to look after Bonfire while they came for Jimmy.

George had said Jimmy wouldn't visit the stables for a number of weeks, and they'd make certain he never saw a newspaper or a magazine that carried a story or an article on Bonfire's winning the Two-Year-Old Championship Race at Roosevelt Raceway.

Could they keep news of that importance from Jimmy Creech? Tom wondered and doubted it, now that Jimmy was out of the hospital. And he didn't want to think what would happen when Jimmy found out.

"We got enough left, George, to get us goin' next season?" Jimmy asked.

George nodded. "Leave that all to me," he said.

Enough money left? Tom fidgeted, even though Jimmy was silent again. To Jimmy's account in the bank they had deposited three thousand dollars. All that money even after they had paid every bill and bought all new racing equipment for the coming season!

And that wasn't all.

Tom's hand went to the letter from Uncle Wilmer that he carried in his pocket. The letter which read in part: "All kinds of folks have been a-coming here to the farm to see the Queen, just because she's the dam of Bonfire. They come from all over—Amityville, Earlville, Boyertown, Reading and some from Philadelphia and New York. I figured I could keep 'em away so I could get some work done around here by putting up a sign on the road telling everybody it costs a dollar to see the mare. But it didn't keep 'em away like I thought it would. Nope, more came even. And now I got more money than I can get in the corner cupboard bowl. You ask Jimmy what I should do about all this money. I figure most of it belongs to him—but I oughta get maybe ten percent of it for thinkin' this idea up."

In addition to all this, there was the wealthy man from New York City, who had arrived at Coronet one day the previous week, offering a hundred thousand dollars for the blood bay colt. When Tom and George had flatly refused this fabulous price for Bonfire, the story made the headlines of every newspaper sports section in the country.

Suddenly Jimmy turned to Tom, and the boy found it difficult to take his eyes from the window to look at him.

"You know what I'm goin' to do next season, Tom?"

"No, Jimmy. What?"

Jimmy slapped Tom's knee again. "I'm not one to be dumb enough to break up a winnin' combination like you an' Bonfire. The doc said I could go to the fairs, all right, but thought it best for me if I let you do all the race drivin'. I told him all about you an' the colt, Tom. So I'm goin' to do jus' that. I'm goin' to teach you all I can an' just watch you and Bonfire go. That's goin' to be just as good as anything I could ever ask for. And that's the way it's goin' to be."

"You mean it, Jimmy?" Tom asked excitedly. "You're going to let me drive him all the time?"

"Why, sure I mean it. I don't say anything unless I mean it."

"Tom and the colt are a winnin' combination, all right," George said.

Jimmy turned to him, noddingly wisely. "I knew that all along," he said. He was silent for a few minutes, then spoke again. "What'd Miss Elsie do with that black filly of hers?"

George replied more quickly than Tom thought he would.

"A race record of two o three at the Reading Fair," George said.

"No!" Jimmy half-shouted. "Then she broke the world's record for two-year-olds!"

"Yes, she *did,*" George answered quietly.

"Then the filly was the one Miss Elsie's been waitin' for," Jimmy said thoughtfully.

Tom was looking out the window again, hoping Jimmy would stop there. Everything George had said so far was the truth. Princess Guy *had* broken the world's record at the Reading Fair. It was after that that she had been beaten by Bonfire in a *new* world's record of 1:59. Yes, Princess Guy was the one that Miss Elsie had been waiting for. But Jimmy hadn't heard her say, "It's too bad for me, Tom, that your colt came along the same year. Princess Guy is still the one I'd wanted. She's faster than Mr. Guy, and that's all I could ask. It's no disgrace for her to be beaten by Bonfire . . . it's *his* year. But maybe next season will be *ours,*" she'd added hopefully.

"What race record did you give Bonfire at the fairs, Tom?" When the boy didn't seem to hear him, Jimmy repeated his question.

"He won in two nineteen . . . *at the fairs,*" Tom said.

"Port Royal Fair," George added quickly.

"You shoulda let him out more," Jimmy said. "He can go a lot faster than that . . . maybe even give the black filly some sort of a race. But she sure must have gone!" Jimmy added, shaking his head. "Just imagine *any* two-year-old going in two o three!"

Jimmy was silent after that, and Tom and George didn't speak either, for they had no wish to keep Jimmy on the subject of records.

They were well out of Pittsburgh and only a few miles from the town of Coronet when they came to the road leading across the fields to the stables.

"Turn here, George," Jimmy said. "I just want to take a peek at him."

Tom stopped breathing, while George's knuckles on the steering wheel turned white.

"Mrs. Davis probably has supper all ready for you," George said. "Besides, the doc said—"

"Mrs. Davis is workin' for me, and she'll wait," Jimmy interrupted, a little angry. "An' Doc Morton said for me to take it easy, nothin' more. He didn't say I couldn't take a look at my colt!"

Still, George did not slow the car to make the turn. "It's too late," he said. "I got to get home . . . so has Tom."

"Who's going to feed and bed down the colt then?" Jimmy asked, and he was more angry now. "You got to take care of him, haven't you? Well, I'll just go along with you *now*."

Tom saw the reddening of Jimmy's face. "Sure," he said, "you might just as well go along with us, then you can stay home and relax knowing everything is okay with Bonfire." Tom turned to meet George's surprised look. "It's late and Miss Elsie or the *others* won't be around to bother Jimmy."

"No one's goin' to bother me, Tom," Jimmy half-shouted. "You two treat me like y'would a baby!"

George was slowing the car, then he made the turn. No one spoke after that until they were within sight of the long gray sheds.

"Boy, it's good to see them again," Jimmy said, smiling. "That sight is better for me than any medicine in the world."

Tom's eyes were on the sheds, too. He hoped desperately that all the visitors to Bonfire's stall had gone. It was after five o'clock; they should be gone. If they had, things might work out all right. If they hadn't . . . well, he wouldn't think about that.

They approached the road that ran down between the sheds. Tom saw no cars at the far end, not even Miss Elsie's jeep. So she'd gone home for the day. George, too, was watching closely for any sign of visitors.

Then they turned into the row, and down at the end in front of their shed were the parked cars! But now there was no turning back.

Jimmy saw the cars, and then the people leaving Bonfire's shed.

"What are all those people doin' here?" He was surprised, but not excited. He just wanted to know.

"They must have come to see Princess Guy," George said quickly without turning to Jimmy.

Jimmy's gaze went to Miss Elsie's shed which they were passing. "Why aren't they there, then?"

"Miss Elsie's gone home, so I guess we're just getting the overflow," George returned. "After all, we got a good-looking colt, Jimmy."

Tom didn't know how George could think so fast, for he wasn't able to think at all.

George stopped the car a good distance from their shed. "What you stoppin' here for?" Jimmy asked.

Opening the door on his side, George said, "I thought I'd go first and get rid of those people. You an' Tom wait here."

"No, I don't," Jimmy shouted, moving behind George. "I don't stay anywhere I don't want to stay. And now I want to see that colt. I'm coming along." He was excited now; he didn't like the way he was being pushed around.

Tom could only follow him. He saw Jimmy walk beside George a moment, then his pace increased until Jimmy was half-running. George started to run after him, but finally gave up and came to a halt.

"What'll we do, George?"

"Pray . . . just pray." George tried to grin, and failed.

"Most of the visitors are out of the shed," Tom said. "Maybe Jimmy won't talk to anyone. He'll just take a look at the colt and come out again."

"Maybe," was all George said.

"But he'll see the new sulky and the training cart," Tom said miserably. "I left them near the door."

"And all the new harness and the wheels," George added quietly. "An' he can't miss those new blankets. Bonfire's wearin' one."

"And the hot-water heater," Tom said. "And the new pails and brushes and cloths and sponges."

George nodded. "Yeah, he can't miss any of the stuff."

"But he knows we need all of it," Tom said hopefully. "We'll tell him we had some money—a little money—left over."

"He knows how much that equipment costs," George said. "I can see him figuring it all up right now, just as though I was standin' right beside him."

"Then all he'll know is that we made more money than we've let on," Tom said quickly. "He won't know about Roosevelt Raceway. He won't know unless . . ." He stopped and his brow furrowed. "George! Where's that big trophy we got when Bonfire won the championship? Where'd you put it last?"

"That's what I been rememberin'," George said in a low voice. "I took it out of the trunk yesterday and put it up on the tack-room table. I jus' thought I'd look at it again."

"And it's still there?"

Soberly, George nodded.

"Maybe he won't go into the tack room. Maybe he won't," Tom said.

"We'll know any second now," George replied. "All we got to do is listen." But even as he said it, George started walking toward the shed, and Tom followed.

They were almost at the door when the bellow came. And the shrillness and fury of it caused them and the visitors who were on their way to parked cars to stop short. Then George and Tom were moving again, and when they reached the shed door, the last of the visitors came running out. George went inside and Tom followed, closing the door behind him.

Jimmy Creech stood at the other end of the shed, bellowing fiercely. He was holding the tall gold-plated trophy in his hands, reading the inscription on it. When he had finished he looked up and saw them; then the trophy came sailing through the air as he hurled it at their feet. It rolled past them, striking with a sharp ring against the door.

Bonfire shrilled at the sound of it, then moved uneasily back and forth in his stall. Quickly Tom went to him, going inside the stall to quiet the colt. He ran his hand up and down Bonfire's head while Jimmy Creech continued raging without making his words understandable.

George didn't move from the door. He waited for Jimmy to quiet down, but many minutes passed before Jimmy's angry bellows stopped; then Tom heard his footsteps coming toward them. He held Bonfire's head closer, wondering whether he was doing this to comfort the colt or himself.

Still trembling with rage, Jimmy stopped before the stall. He looked at Tom and the colt a long while before turning to George, who remained at the door. Yet he said nothing until he turned back to Tom again. *"Why?"* he asked hoarsely.

Tom said nothing, and Jimmy turned to George.

"Why did you do this to me, George? Why did you do this?" The fury had left his face and voice. He was bewildered, confused. Jimmy Creech couldn't understand why his friends, his best friends, had despoiled his colt by allowing him to race at Roosevelt Raceway.

"Why did you do this to me?" he asked again, his eyes searching their very souls as he turned from one to the other.

Tom waited for George to answer Jimmy, but George said nothing. The minutes passed and just as Tom thought he couldn't stand the silence any longer, George moved away from the door and came to a stop before Jimmy. His voice was low and calm when he said, "We needed the money, Jimmy. It's a simple as that."

"But I told you never . . ."

"I know what you told us," George replied in the same low voice. "But it was different this time. I decided it. Tom had nothing to do about it."

"You, my best friend."

"And that's exactly why I did it," George said without pause. "Do you have any idea, Jimmy, what it cost to get that Boston surgeon . . . to get you the very best we wanted you to have? Not the two hundred bucks you saw on his bill. No, Jimmy, his fee was one thousand dollars!"

"I'd rather have died than for you to get the money *that* way," Jimmy said, and his voice rose a little.

"But you didn't die," George said quietly. "You're *here* . . . and that's the way we wanted it to be. And I wanted you to see this colt race, Jimmy. You've never in your life *seen* a colt like this one . . . let alone owned one. He's a world's champion, Jimmy. He beat the best there is. He did one fifty-nine, Jimmy. Are you thinkin' of that at all? Or are your mind and body filled with so much hatred for the raceways that you can't even see a colt like this any more? He's yours, Jimmy. You bred him. You own him. All your life you hoped this would happen to you . . . never dreamin' it would come. But it has, Jimmy . . . *and you're not even looking at him.*"

George turned to Bonfire when he had finished. But Jimmy didn't turn. For a while Tom didn't think he was going to look at his colt at all. And he knew full well that this was the critical moment. Either Jimmy would turn to his colt, or leave the shed and never bother any of them again.

Jimmy took a step forward, and Tom thought it was all over. But Jimmy stepped in the direction of the colt. And he looked at Bonfire a long while before saying, "Take that blanket off him, Tom, *so I can really see him.*"

George didn't say anything all the while Jimmy's eyes traveled over every inch of the blood bay colt. He didn't say anything until he felt Jimmy's hand on his arm; then, without taking his own eyes off Bonfire, George said in a voice that trembled just slightly, "I want the same as you do, Jimmy. Remember that." He stopped then to put a hand on the colt's nose.

"I want to get people to the fairs, the same as you do," George repeated. "I want them to see *our sport* in the daytime and at fairs, where it belongs. I want them to love it as we do . . . and once they come to the fairs they'll truly feel and love our sport. And they'll come now, Jimmy . . . they'll come to the fairs, if only to see our colt. He's a world champion . . . an' there are more records for him to break. They'll come to see him, all right."

For the first time, George took his eyes off Bonfire to look at Jimmy. "*We're* going to do that, Jimmy. You and the colt and Tom an' me are going to help get it back the way it was."

Bonfire pushed his head hard against Tom's chest, and the boy stroked him softly, knowing that everything was going to be all right, very much all right, from now on.

ABOUT THE AUTHOR

Walter Farley's love for horses began when he was a small boy living in Syracuse, New York, and continued as he grew up in New York City, where his family moved. Unlike most city children, he was able to fulfill this love through an uncle who was a professional horseman. Young Walter spent much of his time with this uncle, learning about the different kinds of horse training and the people associated with each.

Walter Farley began to write his first book, *The Black Stallion,* while he was a student at Brooklyn's Erasmus Hall High School and Mercersburg Academy in Pennsylvania. He finished it and had it published while he was still an undergraduate at Columbia University.

The appearance of *The Black Stallion* brought such an enthusiastic response from young readers that Mr. Farley went on to write more stories about the Black, and about other horses as well. He now has twenty-five books to his credit, including his first dog story, *The Great Dane Thor,* and his story of America's greatest thoroughbred, *Man O' War.* His books have been enormously successful in this country, and have also been published in fourteen foreign countries.

When not traveling, Walter Farley and his wife, Rosemary, divide their time between a farm in Pennsylvania and a beach house in Florida.